To Colin

CW00507334

THE SEAL OF
HENRY STUART

with best wishes.

John S

2ⁿᵈ July 1999

The Seal of Henry Stuart

JOHN SEATON

HAMILTON CO. PUBLISHERS
LONDON

Paperback ISBN 1 901668 12 6

Publisher

HAMILTON & Co. Publishers
10 Stratton Street
Mayfair
London

CONTENTS

Illustrations by C. S. Creighton BEM.

CHAPTER 1
Starting the Game

Steven Manly sat at his desk, staring out of the small dirty, wet window, that was his only link to the outside world. He was not pleased with life at all, in fact he felt that life was passing him by, and all he had was a daily, and very boring routine, processing documents from one part of the country to another. He sighed to himself as the rain lashed the window with renewed vigour, '*what a pain it all is*' he thought, and was looking at his watch to see when the tea-break would be when he was interrupted by the office boy, Sandy, poking his head round the door excitedly.

"Mr. Manly, sir, a message has just come through on the 'tube', for you." He stepped into the room and placed a small metal container on the desk in front of Steve, with a flourish of triumph. Steve, having never received one of these in the two years he'd worked there, was intrigued as he read his name on the official address scroll. He unscrewed the top and withdrew a small brown envelope which bore an embossed portcullis on a red wax seal.

"Thank you, Sandy, you can go now." Sandy looked quite crest-fallen, gave a little wave of his bony arms and lurched out of the office, tripping over his feet in his haste. Steve watched him go with a smile on his face, '*what a lad*' he thought, '*always poking his nose into other peoples' business on a real need-to-know basis.*'

He looked down at the envelope and gently prized the red wax seal off the flap. He'd never received a message from the 'tube' before and he had always thought that this method of office communication was an old fashioned way for the 'hierarchy', as the top management were known, to contact their staff. He withdrew a small buff coloured piece of paper which had one typed line on it. 'Report to Room 516 at 14.00 hrs.' His forehead creased into a puzzled frown as he tried to think where Room 516 was, because as far as he knew, the office numbers only went up to 469. The rambling brick building he worked in, was a converted hotel, containing only four floors, yet Room 516 would indicate that there was a fifth floor. He folded the paper and slipped it into the top pocket of his jacket, leaving the metal tube in his out-tray for Sandy to collect. He walked across the office to his friend, Fred, who was an old-timer in the building, who had his head down, working frantically to keep up with the quota of work he was expected to do. Fred looked up like a startled rabbit. "Go away Steve, I'm too far behind for idle chatter," he swept the one or two hairs he had left out of his eyes, with an exaggerated wave of his hand. Steven took no notice and carried on with his question regardless of this rebuke.

"Now, my old mate, calm down, I only want to know where Room 516 is, OK?" He placed his hand on Fred's shoulder.

"Never heard of it, so bugger off before she comes in". Fred returned to his paper work with renewed vigour.

"My father used to say, that a person who swears has lost command of the English Language" rebuked Steve at the back of Fred's head.

"Arseholes" came the swift reply. "Now sod off."

2

"Thanks for nothing pal, don't come running to me when you break a leg". Steve left the room smiling to himself, then turned and said, "See you in the snooker room about four, and be prepared for a good thrashing." He ducked out of the way as a rubber was thrown in his direction. He went on his way smiling to himself at Fred's reaction.

'*Right*,' he thought '*I'll have to go to Gloria for advice.*' Gloria was his section leader with whom he had struck up more than friendship over the last year. She was a very ambitious woman, married to a barrister who always seemed to be away on business, which suited Steve just fine. She was also very attractive, well built, and tended to wear clothes that were really unsuitable for office work, proudly showing off her splendid bosom, under a variety of very tight sweaters. This caused much comment among her male colleagues, as to what they would like to do with her, if they were given the chance. Steve had had that chance many times, and knew she could see them all off if she wanted to. '*What a woman,*' he thought to himself as he approached her door. He knocked and walked into the perfumed garden of all their dreams.

Gloria looked up at him and sat back, bosom heaving majestically as she saw who was entering her office saying "Hello my darling, what brings you here at this time of the day and what a nice surprise, give me a kiss."

He leaned forward and kissed her on her cheek and stood back. "What's the matter with you?" she chided him. "Have you gone off me or something, come here," she pulled him down to her, and proceeded to kiss him ardently, pushing her tongue into his mouth passionately. He had just felt his manhood starting to react to this onslaught, when there was a knock at the door. They released each other and Steve stood back, covering his erection with a folder from her desk, as Sandy came in smiling at them both awkwardly.

"Yes, what is it Sandy?" an irate Gloria demanded, folding

her arms in such away as to uplift her bosom and increase her cleavage. Sandy was completely thrown by this, although he always looked forward to going into Mrs. Gee's office, for that very reason.

"I've forgotten why I've come here." The luckless Sandy blurted. "Sorry," he blushed, turned and went out fast.

"Poor boy" laughed Gloria at his retreating back. "Now, where were we, eh?"

"I've come to ask your advice on this note I've received from the 'tube' ... where on earth is Room 516?" He asked quickly, not wishing to be side-tracked at this time.

Gloria was slightly put out, but she took the piece of paper and gave it her attention, her eyes widening as she read it. She glanced up at him. "Well, you're highly honoured to get this sort of invitation. What have you been up to that I don't know about?" She looked at him, with a half smile on her face.

"Oh come on Gloria ... I haven't been up to anything, just tell me where I'm supposed to go". He reached forward and caressed her right breast and felt her nipple harden up straight away. She pushed his hand away, reluctantly, and handed the paper back to him with a sigh.

"All right," she confided. "You'll find this room by going to the fourth floor, go to the end of the corridor and into the lift control room. You will see a fire-escape door, go through that and there is an iron spiral staircase, go up that and at the very top you will find your Room 516". She leaned back and crossed her legs, showing a small flash of stocking-top, "And come and tell me all about it as soon as you can, my darling."

She suddenly reached forward and held his manhood, which by now had lost the urge. She laughed and squeezed gently looking up at Steve. "Tonight yes? He's away again for a few days." He nodded agreement and held her hand on his cock.

"Blast it darling ... I'll have to go now, to be on time, thanks for the information, darling, it all seems cloak and dagger stuff to me at the moment." He reluctantly removed her hand from his cock.

"It is," she murmured, "so don't joke about it and just be careful of what you say in there, just listen, now off you go." She pushed him away from her. "I've got work to do." She uncrossed her legs and sat up to her desk, he kissed her on the forehead and made his exit.

Steve went back to his office. '*Better make myself respectable*' he thought, straightening his tie and combing his hair, which was quite long and over his shirt collar now, much to his mother's disgust. He checked himself in the mirror. He was a good looking man, six feet tall, an athletic build, with dark brown eyes and a ready smile, which won him into the favours of all types of women, both the young and the older types. He enjoyed being with all of them, as he had a high regard for females and did not like to see, or read of, any violence against women. He also hated to hear his married workmates berating their wives, even if just joking. They annoyed him so much, having not even been engaged like so many of his friends were. He turned and bumped straight into Sandy, who was standing right behind him.

"Christ," he gasped, "what the hell are you doing, you daft sod?"

Sandy grimaced at this rebuke. "I only wanted to know if you wanted anything from the canteen."

"Go away, you nosey beggar, I know you are only trying to find out what the message was, so clear off."

Sandy scowled, turned on his heel and loped off, muttering to himself and waving his arms around in explanation.

Steven felt quite good now, and was feeling alert and quite sharp, mainly because he had not had a drink for a week, due to a stupid bet with his pal, Fred.

He locked his desk and proceeded to the lift-room on the

fourth floor, and found the iron stair-case.

'Well, how about that, I've been working here all this time and didn't know this stairway existed' he breathed to himself as he mounted the stairs. He was soon standing in front of a door, sporting a lionhead-style knocker and the number 516 set on a portcullis design. He squared his shoulders and vigorously knocked the lionhead.

"Come in," the command was issued in a gruff, abrupt manner. Steven entered and walked into a room full of cigar smoke and saw sitting behind a huge desk, a large bald, sweating man, who dwarfed the chair he was sitting in. He stood up and held a fat, gold-ringed hand to Steve, who was held in a grip of steel.

"Welcome to 516, Manly," the fat face beamed through the smoke. "Sit down and I'll brief you on what I'm looking for straight away. Don't like to beat around the bush y'know." Steve sank down into a red leather armchair and felt immediately at ease.

"Have a cigar," the fat hand pushed a box of Havanas towards him without waiting for a reply. Steve reached in and withdrew a large Monte Cristo, the biggest cigar he had ever seen."Here, let me snip it for you," the fat hand reached out again and deftly removed the tip, with a small gold snip he had on his watch chain, which looped across his ample waistcoat. He then tossed a small box of matches across the Steve, who noticed the portcullis sign printed on it.

"Always light cigar with a match, or the cedar-wood wrapper, if there is one, and never use a lighter." The voice emphasised the word, *'never.'* "Right, Manly, my name is Colonel Guntripp, and I am in charge of a Government department engaged in tracing subversive elements." The face was no longer smiling and was now being wiped with a large white handkerchief. "Needless to say" he paused, as if in thought, "this is Top Secret information that I am telling you, so you must not reveal any of our conversation to anybody, not even family ... yes?" He looked at Steve for agreement. Steve nodded, although his heart was now racing, as he realised what he was being asked to get involved with.

"I want you to read this." A document was pushed across the desk bearing the words, Official Secrets Acts, "and then if you would like to join us, sign it in the appropriate places and I will counter-sign it."

Steve slowly read the four pages, feeling the Colonel's eyes watching him intently. "Seems straight forward to me Colonel." He reached into his jacket pocket for his pen.

"No ... use this." A green-feathered quill pen was passed over to him with a pot of ink, on a gold stand. "It is one of my personal idiosyncrasies, but I like tradition." The explanation was added quietly. "Do you?" The question was asked as the Colonel rose up from his seat.

"Yes sir, I do," replied Steve as he dipped the quill into the ink-pot, "and I'm quite happy to sign this, and I will not repeat anything I am told by you, to anyone, although my mother will be difficult to handle as she always wants to know what I am doing." Steve signed the bottom of each page, re-dipping into the green ink for each signature and rolling a blotter over each time.

The Colonel, who had by now walked slowly round him, reached over and took the signed pages with a flourish. "I don't care what you have to tell your mother, Manly, just bear in mind that her life might be in danger should anyone want to get at you, through her, or indeed, any women in your life, girlfriends, wives and best mates, all of them might be in danger if they had an inkling of what you are going to do for me and the Country." The Colonel added briskly, "So bear that in mind at all times." He walked back to his seat, expelling a large volume of smoke as he did so. "I will now sign under your signature to make your appointment official."

"What appointment, sir?" queried Steve, who was feeling quite out of his depth by now, at the speed of events.

"Well, you cannot do this level of work as a clerical assistant, Manly, it would not do at all. You will need your own office, to maintain confidentiality at all times, plus you need the rank of higher executive officer to give you access to all the micro-fiches you will require," explained the Colonel as he pushed the documents into his black brief-case, with a gold crest portcullis on it. "I will contact your immediate superiors and get all the arrangements re your office and position confirmed, which should be in about a week or so, then we can get you started properly." The Colonel stubbed out his cigar as if to end the conversation.

Steve was a little perplexed at this and asked the question on his mind, "What am I supposed to do, sir?"

"Good God, Manly, I totally forgot to tell you that," the Colonel laughed at his own mistake. "Each week," he went on,"you will receive a line or two about people we are interested in. It may be from a conversation overheard in a bar, or from a phone-tap, and my field officers will give as much information as possible on the target person. Sometimes it will be only a nick-name or whatever, with an approximate age and accent and we want to find out where they live so we can intercept their mail and put a tap on their telephones, but whatever it is, we need you to use your initiative in giving us possible trace addresses. All straight forward stuff and ...," he touched his finger to his nose conspiratorially, "you will, in due course, be asked to join us in London, if you are up to the standard we require."

"Thank you Colonel, for giving me this chance, I will not let you down."

Steve stood up and offered his hand, which was immediately crushed in a vice, with the gold rings digging into his hand.

"See you don't, Manly, and I look forward to seeing you in London in the very near future, and get your hair cut, because it is far too long." The Colonel dismissed Steve with a wave of his hand. "You go back the usual way as I have my own private entrance." He turned amidst another cloud of cigar smoke as Steve left Room 516 and closed the door behind him

Steve stopped in the corridor and realised that he had not taken one draw on his huge cigar, which he now did, gripping it firmly between his teeth. He exhaled slowly, whilst thinking of all that had transpired in the last thirty minutes. *'Cloak and dagger stuff,'* he thought, *'no wonder Gloria had told him not to joke about it. Just wait until she sees me in my own office and with a rank equal to hers.'* A thought suddenly came to him that maybe Gloria was in the organisation already and that's why she knew about Room 516. *'What a dark horse. He'd have to be careful what he said to her all right.'* He drew again on his cigar, and blew a large ring of smoke. *'Yes,'* he thought, *'I think I can get accustomed to this style of life, plus all the extra money I'll be getting, bloody marvellous.'* He made his way slowly back to his office, just in time for the tea break.

Fred was sitting with both feet up on his desk, munching a huge chocolate Wagon Wheel. "Well?" he enquired, spitting crumbs out down his shirt. "Blast," he looked down and brushed them off briskly. "Come on then, tell me where Room 516 is."

"I got it wrong." Steve was doing his best to be non-committal and put on a bored expression. "It was Room 416 I wanted, not 516 ... and before you ask," Steve carried on, "it was an assessment panel, who said my work was showing promise, and that if I kept it up I would be in line for promotion." He paused, hoping that was enough to satisfy Fred for the time being.

"Since when did an assessment panel give out bloody big cigars then?" Fred pointed to the cigar in Steve's hand.

"This is a Christmas cigar I kept in case of a celebration." Steve blustered, turning red with stress.

"You can tell that to Gloria, she's like a cat on hot bricks.

She keeps popping in here every few minutes looking for you, so you'd better get your arse over to her room now, than we can all have some peace." Fred settled down with his racing paper, muttering, "Cigars, bollocks!"

"Righty ho! Off I go, wish me luck, eh?" He did not wait to hear any riposte from Fred as his mind was on how to relate what had transpired in Room 516. He wondered just how much she knew already ... *'well, he'd soon find out.'* He knocked on her door and poked his head round to find, to his relief that she was not there. He scribbled a quick note with the time on it, 15.00 hrs., then gratefully withdrew to a safe haven, namely the snooker-room, where the females were loath to go as it was too smoky and airless. He entered to find a small crowd in there already, and all the conversation ceased as heads turned towards him. He nodded to them all and chalked his name on the playing board then went and sat down to finish his cigar and read a paper. The men resumed playing and all was peaceful until Fred entered, and as soon as he saw Steve he blurted, "You jammy bugger. I've just heard you're getting your own office with promotion to higher executive officer, bloody Christmas cigar my arse."

Steve was astounded that this had become common knowledge so quickly and felt distinctly uncomfortable as Fred carried on like a fishwife. "Now we know why you've been knocking off Gloria, that's how you've got promotion. You lucky bastard, and if her husband finds out, he'll knock you off, he's a big bugger. I've seen him," Fred chortled, looking round to make sure everyone had heard him. The smiling faces were all nodding agreement and murmuring assent to this statement.

"That's a nice way to congratulate me, you old fart." Steve had recovered his composure by now, quickly covering himself by making light of the situation. Fred, unwittingly, had given him a way out of his predicament. Steve, making use of this, carried on talking, "I reckon you are just jealous of my obvious natural talent, so how about playing me for a fiver then, because I might be leaving you all in the near future to go South." He started to rub the blue chalk on the cue tip.

"Right, you're on." Fred slapped a fiver on the green baize. Steve covered it with another. "I'll break."

He settled down for the first shot when Sandy walked in with a silly grin on his face, tube in hand.

"Got another message, Mr. Manly." He looked at the table, "Are you losing already?" He sniggered and had to beat a hasty retreat, as a cue was lifted to threaten him.

"Messages from Heaven already." Fred leaned over and swept the two fivers from the table and put them in his pocket gleefully. "You lose by default."

"Hang on," Steve protested. "What do you mean, default?"

"Because when you've been here as long as I have, one knows that the 'tube' messages have always got to be dealt with straight away, so off you go" Fred chided him.

Steve stared at him for a moment then opened the message and read the contents. Fred was right, it contained two lines of information and ended with 'Message timed at 16.15 hrs. return a.s.a.p.' He stuffed the note in his pocket

"OK my friend you win, easy come, easy go." Steve turned and left.

Fred turned to the other players. "Well, I don't think he'll be with us much longer, I reckon he's got the 'Whitehall' seal of approval, so now we'll all have a chance with Gloria." Enthusiastic nods of approval greeted this remark, although they all knew they were simply dreaming on regardless.

Steve proceeded to the basement file-room, a journey he was to undertake many times in the next few months ...

He read the paper: MALE. WHITE. AGED 22 APPROX. First name 'Bob'. Surname believed to be COWLE. Accent. Scottish.

"Hello, Mr. Manly, can I help you?" Sandy appeared from behind the filing cabinets.

"What the bloody hell are you doing down here?" grated an irate Steve. "You seem to get everywhere."

"I've been transferred, sir. Don't know why though." He looked crest-fallen for a moment. Then ... "How can I help you, sir?" he blurted, waving his bony arms around.

"You can go and get me the micro-fiches for ..." Steve paused, thinking to himself, "for 1950 to 1955, OK?"

Sandy beamed. "Right away, sir. I'll set number 3 machine up at the same time. Do you know what letter of the alphabet you require?"

"Get me the 'C' files and ...," Steve wanted to assert his new found authority. "I want it set on number 8 machine, because it is in a more secluded area. If that's okay with you, of course?" Steve countered sarcastically.

"That machine has gone for service, sir," Sandy smirked happily, "so I'll set number 3 up, I'll have it set in a couple of minutes." He left a bemused Steve, contemplating how to win one over Sandy.

Machine 3 was soon set up by the very efficient Sandy and Steve settled down to scroll the 4 quarters of each year, from 1950 to 1955 under 'C' section. *'Bob'* he thought, *'would most like be short for Robert so check for COWLE. R.'* Half an hour went by before he gave up on that idea. Next he then checked for any COWLE with two initials in case Robert was a middle name, still no luck. Steve sat back scowling to himself. First bloody trace to do and he was stuck. He got up and shouted across the room to Sandy to fetch him all section '50-55. He returned to the machine and resumed scrolling from the beginning.

Suddenly, in the second quarter of 1950 he noticed COWLE entered as a mother's maiden name to McIAN R. He felt a surge of excitement. Could there be a connection here? He wrote the information down quickly and switched off the machine.

"Sandy, you can return the micros now."

"Yes sir," came the instant reply from behind a cupboard and Sandy picked up the micros in a flurry of activity.

"What's the rush?" Steve asked him.

"It's nearly five o'clock, sir, time to go home," came the muffled reply from Sandy as he disappeared out of the room.

'*Damn*,' thought Steve, '*I'd better get a move on with this*.' He left the machine room and proceeded to the main document registry area of all Births, Deaths and Marriages. He located the possible trace Birth entry and presented the information to a very annoyed clerk, who was putting his coat on in anticipation of getting away on time to go to an evening horse-race meeting due to start at 6.30 p.m. "You've picked a fine time haven't you?" he scowled as he spoke to Steve. "Can't it wait?"

"Sorry Morris, just do this as favour to me," Steve begged. "There's a pint in it for you," he implored him, putting a comradely arm around Morris's shoulders. "I'd do the same for you."

"OK," sighed Morris, slipping his coat off resignedly, "I'll be as quick as I can." He went into the dark recesses of his custodial world while Steve remembered he had a cigar to re-light. Morris was back within 5 minutes with the Birth Certificate in his hand. "There you are," he held the document out to Steve, "that's cost you a pint, I hope it is worth it to you," he added struggling to put his coat on again.

"You're a real pal, see you in the Wheatsheaf tonight, after the races, okay?" Morris nodded assent, and left Steve reading the Birth Certificate bearing the name of McIAN, Robert D.O.B. April 17th 19560

Father's Name:	McIAN Neil
Address:	29 Ringwood Road, Liverpool 7
Occupation:	Master Mariner
Mother's maiden name:	COWLE Maude

Steve was now 99% sure that this Robert McIan was the trace suspect, aged 24 and was using his mother's maiden name, for whatever reason now. He reached into his pocket and got the small container out, placed the certificate in it, with small piece of paper, on which he wrote the time - 17.10 hrs. He returned to his office and inserted the canister into the 'tube' and pressed the button with the portcullis on it and up it went with a quiet 'whoosh'.

Steve sat back and drew on his cigar, feeling well pleased with himself. He gave himself a few quiet minutes to calm down, then reached for his coat and hat, looking at the clock, which showed 17.20 hrs. He knew he would be in trouble with his mother now, because he would be home late and she would have his meal on the table, ready for him.

Four days went by and Steve had heard nothing from the Colonel, but at least it was Friday, which meant pay-day and the prospect of a good drinking session with all his mates down at the Wheatsheaf. Sandy popped his head round the door. "You're wanted by Mrs. Gees straight away ... I don't think you're in trouble though." He sniggered at his own little joke and withdrew before a reply was offered.

Steve locked his desk and strolled along to Gloria's office wondering what he was in for, because she had not made an effort to see him since their last Monday meeting. He knocked on the door tentatively.

"Enter," her voice commanded. Steve did as he was told. "Sit down Steve." He noted the sharpness in her voice. "I did think you would have been in touch with me ... before now," she stared hard at him, her eyes blazing mad. "I know you left me a pathetic note last Monday, by way of explanation, but really," she sounded exasperated, "I am most annoyed with you and now ... this ..."

Gloria indicated a letter on her desk. "Go on, read it." Steve picked it up, noticing the portcullis trade mark on the letter-head and read: "To all Department Heads: Please note that Mr. Steve Manly has been promoted to Higher Executive Officer from to-day, Friday the 14th June 1974 and will be

occupying his own office, on the fourth floor, Room 469."
Steve felt a warm glow of happiness wash over him as he read
on, "Mr. Manly will also be assigned a pool car, the M.G. TD.
Reg. No. HKG 812." The letter was signed: Colonel Harold
Guntripp C.B. O.B.E.

Steve threw the letter down on the desk and punched the
air. "Yes!" he shouted and planted a kiss on the astonished lips
of a sulky Gloria. "Aren't you happy for me, darling?" He
started to calm down as he saw that this news was not a happy
moment for the pouting Gloria. "What's the matter with you?
Aren't you happy for me?" He tried to hold her hand, but she
pulled away sharply.

"I do not understand what has happened about you, for you
to be up-graded to my standard when you haven't been here
five minutes, and I know you have not sat before a promotion
board." She was twisting her rings round furiously as she
spoke. "So you can only have by-passed the system on merit,
but what merit, I ask? Being good in bed?" She was, Steve
saw, very upset and all he could do was shrug his shoulders
saying, "Well, it beats me how I've got promotion, just luck I
guess."

"Get out of my sight, you make me sick, your sort," she
snorted at him.

"What sort's that then?" asked a very surprised Steve.

"The Silver Spoon sort, that's what," retorted Gloria, her
pretty face contorted in a sneer.

"You are rather jealous, I think," he replied as it dawned
on him the reason for this anger. She was upset at the power
and position he had just acquired. "I'm off now, if you have
nothing further to say," he added.

"Here's your stupid birthday card." She threw it across her
desk, in a fit of pique. "You might as well have it because I've
already written on it," she grumbled at him.

"Thanks very much for the thought." He picked the card
up and put it in his jacket pocket. "Cheers". He turned and left

the room leaving Gloria filing her nails furiously.

Steve's first thought was to get away from her as quickly as possible, leaving her to come to terms with his new promotion. He decided to go and have a look at his new office. He strode out with vigour to the lift and up to the fourth floor. He walked to the end of the corridor, to the last room on the floor, which was just by the metal stairway he had ascended only last Monday. He opened the door and was delighted to see he had been given a huge leather inlaid desk and matching red-leather, wing-backed chair. He sat down in it and was spinning round, like a school kid, when a voice said, "Welcome to our circle, Manly." The Colonel was standing in the doorway, beaming. Steve jumped out of the chair, highly embarrassed at being caught like this.

"I've just been told of my promotion, plus it is my birthday as well, sir," Steve blurted out.

"Take it easy, Manly, we know it's your birthday, that's why I'm here ... to take you for a drink and discuss things, if you are doing nothing else, that is?" The colonel added taking out a couple of large cigars.

He offered Steve one. "Come on," he said, "we'll go to 'Sam's muck middin' near Dale Street, we can relax there without being interrupted by anyone, let's go."

Steve struggled to keep up with him. They used the lift and went down to the basement car park. The Colonel strode towards a dark blue Rolls-Royce, whose driver sprang into action, running round to open the doors.

"Good Evening Colonel," the driver began, "where to Sir?" Steve noticed that, although the driver was smart, he had a small bulge in his jacket, under his arm. Steve had only seen this kind of thing at the pictures and he realised he was looking at the bulge of a gun-holster.

"Sam's Club, Henry, if you please."

"Certainly, Colonel." Henry settled them into the luxury of real leather. Steve was impressed, this was his first time in a

'Royce' and he felt like a million dollars as he settled back to enjoy the ride.

"Have a drink, the sun's gone down over the yard-arm." The Colonel pulled the door down of a small cocktail cabinet, full of bottles. "What's your poison?"

"Scotch on the rocks ... please." Steve hoped that was the right request.

"I'm going to have a pink gin, always do at this time of the day, keeps me from getting malaria". The Colonel laughed at his wit and just held on to glass and bottle as the car went round a corner. "Whoops a daisy," he grinned, pouring the most generous whisky Steve had ever been given, then threw a lump of ice in. "Where's the soda, Henry?"

"There is none sir, sorry I forgot," apologised Henry.

"I don't want soda Colonel, just ice," Steve added.

Steve settled back clutching his drink and watching the Colonel managing, somehow, to hold his gin and light a cigar at the same time.

"Now, Manly," the Colonel had got himself organised now and was surrounded by a pall of blue smoke. "I thought I would not see you until you came to London ... but," he added, "the possible trace you gave us on Monday was spot on. We went to that address you gave us where the parents lived, but they had moved and ..,." he laughed, "they left a forwarding address, wonderful. We put a tap on their telephone straight away and ... ," he enthused happily, "our target, Bob Cowle, rang his parents that same night. Talk about luck." He drew on his cigar as Steve did likewise, in order to maintain the camaraderie that was being offered.

"We managed to trace where he lives and now we have him tapped and mail interception under way. Looks like we've stumbled on a 'cell', thanks to you." A large mouthful of gin ended this wave of information.

"Well," responded a delighted Steve, "I'm only too glad my hunch turned out right." He leant nearer the Colonel so that the driver, could not hear. "But ...," he hesitated, "what do you mean by 'cell'?"

Another cloud of smoke erupted from the Colonel's mouth, after which he had a large gulp of gin and he continued. "Firstly, Manly, you don't have to whisper in front of Henry, he and I go back quite a few years, we were in Aden in '67 and he saved my life in Oman, when we were in the British Army Training Team during Operation Jaguar in '71, mind you," he grinned widely, "I've gone to seed since then." He patted his stomach, cigar ash falling over his waistcoat. This he brushed off with the other hand which held his drink. This then spilt down him. "Blast it." He gulped down what was left and drew on his cigar again.

Steve leaned forward, "Sorry Henry, I'd no idea."

"That's all right, sir, don't worry about it." The reply came over Henry's broad shoulder as he swung the car into the club car-park, pulled up swiftly and raced round to the Colonel's side and opened the car door for him.

Steve noticed for the first time that Henry's eyes were never still. He was taking note of all that was around them and was very alert, even watching a lady pushing a pram past and only relaxing when a baby's cry came from within the confines of the pram.

The Colonel guided him through the lobby into a recess which had two armchairs and a small table. Henry sat across by the main lobby where he had a good view of all people coming in and out.

Two drinks arrived and were placed quietly down in front of them. "Your usual Colonel." The waiter smiled at him.

"Thank you Jose, put the bottle just here," he indicated his right and Jose placed the ice-bucket down carefully, giving the bottle of champagne a twist, to settle it down.

CHAPTER 2
Standing By

"You asked me what a 'cell' was," the Colonel paused, "well, that refers to a small number of people who are dedicated to the downfall of Democracy ... to inflict a Dictatorship on the United Kingdom, by any means at their disposal." His face was very serious now. "And it's my work, with fellow officers, to stop them by using any means at our disposal ... follow?"

Steve nodded in agreement and drew heavily on his cigar, his nerve ends were jangling around like live wires. "Who do you think they are, Colonel?" he asked reaching for his drink.

"Communists, Russian bastards who would murder their own grandmothers for a case of vodka." He spoke quite vehemently, sitting upright with tension. "That's why we need men like you, to help gather the intelligence we require on these damn commies, so we can slap them down before they get a hold on our Country." The Colonel was at his most commanding as he carried on, "I want you to come to London ... not straight away though, but in about a month, we'll give you a lot more traces to do in the meantime ...," he paused a moment, "will you join me?"

"I will be honoured to, sir, thank you for the trust you have put in me, I won't let you down, you just give me the word, thanks for a terrific birthday present."

Steve rose and lifted his glass in celebration to the Colonel, who, now smiling, lifted his in return. Steve would recall this moment, with bitterness, three months later.

"Have you seen today's Times?" The question came through another cloud of smoke. Steve shook his head, feeling slightly embarrassed, as that was not a paper he ever read.

"You'll have to start y'know," came the admonishment to him, "because a couple of lines at the bottom of the page reveals that Wilson, our good P.M. is going on another official visit to Moscow. I don't mind telling you, Manly, he's got us worried, he told the Commons yesterday he was going, no date set yet though." He settled down in the big armchair lost in thought, chewing the cigar-end to a soggy stump.

Jose re-filled their glasses and studied the bottle, then looked enquiringly at the Colonel.

"Right, let's have another." The Colonel answered the look and Jose went off beaming, for more Black Label. Steve was not used to all this 'posh' drinking, as he was a real ale man himself, plus the cigar was having its effect on him. He was trying to talk sense, but the words were coming out in a jumble, the last thing he remembered was having his arm round Henry's neck, laughing like an hyena, thinking the world was lovely ... ... so lovely ... Through the mist of pain, Steve heard a woman's voice talking to him in sharp, short sentences ... ...

"Fine thing, to have your old mother finding you stretched out in the flower-bed declaring you wanted a wee-wee ... you," she tried to find the words "you a grown man, talking like that, what was wrong with you?"

Steve tried to reply, but his mouth as not functioning at all. "And don't give me that you were drunk," she railed on, "I reckon you must have eaten something that's disagreed with you." She had brought him a cup of tea and as Steve struggled to sit up his head went into orbit. He sipped the tea and wondered if there was a bucket nearby, as he doubted that he could make the toilet.

"I had too much to drink with my new boss, down at 'Sam's muck middin' in Liverpool ... sorry if I've been a nuisance."

"Too much to drink," his mother intoned. "One sniff of the barmaid's apron would be enough for you." She straightened the bed-clothes. "You can tell me all about your new boss over breakfast ... bacon and egg do?" She stepped back, as a multi-coloured stream of vomit covered the bedclothes.

Steve heard her talking as she left the room, "You can clean that up yourself. It's a good job your father isn't here, I just do not know what he would say if he could see you now."

Steve lay back and waited to die and was promptly sick over the dog's head which had come to investigate the noise. "Sorry Buster," thought Steve as Buster ran out of the bedroom in a state of shock and Steve vaguely remembered hearing his mother's scream in the distance.

He woke the next day, Sunday, to the sound of church bells ringing away, reminding him he was still alive ... just.

He got up and stripped the bed, which was untouched by his mother as she had threatened. He opened the window to let fresh air in, as Buster cautiously nosed his way into his bedroom. Steven tousled the dog's head. "Sorry for the little accident but your poor dad was ill." Buster looked up and smiled, tongue hanging out, tail wagging hard.

"I'll take you for walkies after breakfast," he promised to a now delirious dog, "calm down or I'll be in trouble again." He stroked Buster gently and guided him out of the room. "Let's go and see how long I have to wear sack-cloth and ashes." He walked into the kitchen where his mother was but she pretended not to hear him and carried on tuning her little radio.

"Hi mum," Steve said as brightly as he could.

"Don't you 'mum' me," was the terse reply. "I just don't

know what to make of you," she paused as she found the 'Archers' on Radio 4, she turned to face him. "You come home ill and expect me to look after you, no wonder you never meet any nice girls, 'Sam's muck middin' indeed." She turned the sound up on the radio as Steve vaguely tried to protest his innocence.

"What's more you treat this house like a hotel, and I'm not having it, do you hear? Now leave me in peace I want to listen to this." She took the radio through to the lounge with Buster in tow, as if on an invisible lead.

"I'm going to work in London, in September, anyway," Steve retorted defensively to her retreating back.

"Good, the sooner the better," the lounge door was slammed shut with a vengeance. Steve stared at the door for a moment, then he realised he did not need to make any excuse now for leaving his mother, as she had just told him to go, in no uncertain terms. He went and got his golf clubs and drove to his Golf Club, for his usual Sunday game.

He liked his golf and had managed to get his handicap down to scratch, by playing at least four times a week, much to his then, girl-friend's, annoyance. He smiled to himself as he remembered the fateful day she had given him an ultimatum. "Either the golf goes, or I do," she raged at him one Sunday night six months ago. He'd chosen golf, which had made her very upset.

All his mother said was, "When you make your bed you must lie in it."

"What a load of rubbish mothers talk," Steve thought as he entered the Artisan Hut of the Royal Sandgrounder Club.

"Hi, Steve," came the cheerful shout from a Plus-Four, rotund figure with matching tam-o-shanter, "how's life treating you these days?"

"Couldn't be better Philip. I've just been promoted, with oodles more money, my own office and MG TD," he paused. "I may even become a full member of the Sandgrounder one day."

"Very nice for some people, eh? But well done you, we'll have to have a drink on it, but hang on old boy, how will this affect your golf? I thought you wanted to get a Tour Card and go Professional?" queried a concerned Philip.

"I've still got time to do that Phil. I was only 23 last Friday, y'know," Steve reminded him, giving Phil a dig in his ribs, playfully.

"What's the new job then?" The question hit Steve like a bolt from the blue. He hesitated, thinking quickly. "I'm being transferred for a couple of years, by my Department, to London, but I'll still be doing the same old routine job, only under more pressure I believe."

"Well a change is as good as a rest, they say," Philip remarked. "Let's go and play golf ... £20 yes?"

Four hours later in the hut bar, Philip gave Steve £20 "There you are, you lucky sod."

Steve taking the money said, "Isn't it funny, Phil the more I practise the luckier I seem to get. Never mind, do you want a pint?"

"No thanks pal, but if I don't go home now my wife will be giving my dinner to the cat. Thanks all the same. Will you be able to play Wednesday evening?" Steve nodded.

"Okay, see you then, around 5 p.m. Cheerio."

Philip left, at speed, to beat the cat's dinner time. He had lost this race a couple of times and the cat had received an up-lifting experience each time but out of sight of his wife.

Steve made his way home, quite happy, as his game could not have been better. Two under par gross 71.

His mother was sitting having tea in the lounge. He took a deep breath and entered. "Hello mum," he bent and kissed her forehead, "hope you've had a nice day."

"Humph, if you call being by myself all day, nice." She sipped her tea slowly, then carried on, "Of course I understand that your golf and your so-called friends come before me." She leaned forward and put her cup down, "So when exactly do you leave me then?"

"I've been given promotion at work and I will have to work in London, for about two years, I think." Steve kept any trace of excitement out of his voice as he tried hard to sound matter of fact.

"What about your precious golf?" was the sarcastic reply.

"I've no idea what will happen about that, mother. I think my golf will have to wait until I've sorted my life out," he said. "I'm more worried about you being on your own, because I don't know when I will be given time off to come home to see you," he added quickly, seeing his mother ready to launch off at him again.

"It's simple son," his mother retorted, "you get on a train at Euston, easy isn't it? Anyway, I really am glad you have got promotion, your father would have been very proud of you." She seemed to be relaxed now much to his relief, as this was his main problem solved if she accepted his move.

Steve went out of the room leaving his mother to listen to her radio programme and made his way to the garage to clean his golf clubs and have time to think quietly.

"There's a woman on the 'phone for you. I think she's not well," his mother said disapprovingly, standing back for Steve to get past her. "She didn't give her name," she added with a knowing look.

Steve picked the 'phone up, turning his head away from his mother's direction. "Hello, Steve here."

"Oh, Stevie, darling, I'm so sorry to have been cross with you on Friday," he heard Gloria's voice breaking slightly and a little slurred. '*She's been drinking*' he thought. '*I wonder where she is, Christ, I hope she isn't 'phoning from home.*' Panic set in.

"It's just that I miss you so much." She started sobbing. "I don't think I can bear the thought of you working in London. I want us to be together."

His mother decided to dust the picture rail nearby, Steve faced away from her.

"Well, it's nice to hear from you again," he said, hoping his mother would go away. "It has been a long time since we last met," he was desperately trying to keep calm.

"I suppose your nosey mother's there? ... Silly cow," Gloria sniffed, "can't she let you have any privacy at all?"

"Yes, that's right," he agreed hoping Gloria understood.

"We can meet next week to discuss those papers okay?" He smiled at his mother as he spoke.

"Sod you," Gloria snapped and slammed the receiver down much to Steve's relief.

"Who was she?" his mother asked putting her duster away.

"A Section Leader from work with a problem," he replied.

"A drink problem, by the sound of her," his mother said.

"Is she a girl friend I don't know about, and if so, why wouldn't she give me her name? Is she married?"

Steve laughed nervously. "Don't be silly, mother. She isn't a girl friend of mine and her name is Mrs. Gees, so there's nothing for you to worry bout okay? She's a work colleague." He grinned at his mother to reassure her.

"Don't kid me," she said, "I'm your mother, remember? I know when you are telling lies, but," she went on, "if you do not wish to tell me, then I'll think you are getting involved with a married woman. ... Don't deny it," she added as Steve started to protest his innocence. "Just don't get caught, I do not wish to have an irate husband coming round here looking for you, thank you very much." His mother swept out of the hallway, pushing him to one side contemptuously. Steve watched her go feeling quite tired now. He looked at his watch and saw he still had time for a pint, down at the Wheatsheaf.

"Hello Steve," said Walter as Steve walked into the crowded bar, "what's it to be then?" Walter was poised holding a tankard up to the beer pumps. His stubble beard and semi-bald head made him look like a Greek peasant. His striped shirt sleeves were rolled up and he was wearing a black waist-coat.

"You look like you should be working in a Taverna, matey," Steve laughed. "Make it pint of Guinness and a small Cointreau chaser," he added pulling his wallet out.

"Certainly sir," Walter replied with a mock salute and clicking his heels to attention. "Ve haf vays of makin's ze dinkie doos, for ya, ya?" He laughed at his own attempt to speak with a German accent.

"Zis is verry gut offen ya," Undt how muchen issen dat?" he enquired. Now aware that two people at a nearby table were looking at them in a strange way.

"All zer Marks in undt vallet, mein herr, undt makes it snappy, osser vise yar issen a dead ducken, tuit suite." They both fell about at this verbal garbage and failed to notice the two people walking up to the bar.

"We have been listening to you both making fun of us because we are Germans and we wish to see the Manager and complain, because you have been very rude," the rather irate man stated, his buxom wife nodding in agreement but clutching onto her husband tightly.

"Look here," Steve explained, "Walter and I always talk stupid when we meet, you've got to laugh eh?"

"You English are so silly. Come along little liebling. Let's leave this awful place ... tch!" and they both waddled out into the night, shaking their heads in bewilderment.

"Another lot of satisfied customers," Walter exclaimed waving them bye-bye behind their backs. "What brings you here on a Sunday night anyway?" asked Walter enquiringly.

"I've just had an argument with my lady friend and upset my mother to boot, so I thought I'd come and see you, you old twister," replied Steve as he pocketed his change. "I just wanted to tell you that I will be going to work in London shortly, I've been promoted ... I'm up-graded."

"Just think, though," remarked Walter, "if you turned your golf into an earner, you would make a lot more money and have a nice time travelling round the world." He wiped a cloth over the bar and emptied a couple of ashtrays.

"I agree with you Walter, but I need to get away now, to get away from my mother, I mean ... I can never take any girl friend home with mother sticking her oar in, and I can't have one stay over-night, there'd be hell to pay."

Steve finished his pint and chaser and pushed the glasses forward for a re-fill. "I simply cannot afford the cost of backing myself for a couple of years, although I have tried to find a sponsor ... does the Wheatsheaf fancy sponsoring me then?"

Walter laughed aloud, "Don't be silly, my boss is saving up for a Rolls-Royce, so you've no chance Steve." He carried on polishing glasses and holding them up to the light to check for marks. He carried on, "Did you hear who won the US Open today, at Winged Foot? ... No! ... Well it was Hale Irwin."

Steve perked up, "What was his total?"

"There you are, I wrote all the scores down for you, I've just taken golf up myself now, due to you, I went round in 124 yesterday." He made a pretend golf swing behind the bar, causing Dot, his assistant, to duck, protesting about the danger he was to her. Everyone at the bar joined in with laughter and loud debate.

"Cheerio, Walter, see you Dot." Steve gestured farewell.

"Not if I see you first," came the swift reply from a grinning Walter, his arm wrapped round a happy Dot.

The following day Steve arrived at work, going straight to his new office and slipped past Gloria's office as fast as he could, without running. He got to 469 unlocked the door and breathed a sigh of relief as he shut the door behind him. There was a knock at the door. Steve's heart missed a beat. "Yes ... come in." He was suddenly tense.

"Hello sir." Sandy's head poked round the door. "Did you

have a nice week-end sir? I went bowling myself, got four strike-outs." He beamed at Steve and held out another 'tube' message for him, which Steve snatched from him.

"Get me a cup of tea, now," he commanded sharply, snatching the 'tube' off Sandy he went to his desk and started to open it.

Sandy beamed and deflated Steve with, "You have your own tea-maker plus everything you want, in the wall cupboard, sir." He walked across the room and opened a huge floor to ceiling cupboard which was a mini-kitchen and also a min-bar. "There you are sir, I'll fill your kettle and then I must go to see Mrs. Gees," he smirked, "'cos she wants to know when you come in." He headed for the door, falling over the waste-paper basket.

"You tell her," Steve pretended to read the message out of the 'tube', "that I've been called away to a very urgent meeting and that I will be in touch later."

"Okay, will do, but she has to see you urgently, she said."

Sandy went on his way happy, thinking only of his bowling.

Steve read his message which was timed at 08.00 hrs. He had received information about a woman, who was to his amazement, a lady wrestler, the paper read:

Female. White. Aged about 19 yrs. First name CAROL.

Surname. McIAN. Accent Scottish.

Wrestles under the name: GODZILLA

Steve smiled to himself, this would be easy, as she must obviously be a sister to the first trace he did last week and who ever was sending this had not collated the two together. He could not believe that anyone would make the basic error, in his opinion, of not connecting the two 'targets' with each other. He locked his office and went to see Sandy, forgetting to switch his kettle off.

The basement file room was very busy and it took Sandy a while to sort a machine out for Steve. He soon found his 'target' and went with the information to Morris, who was having a crafty cigarette.

Morris looked up. "Where did you get to on Friday night?" he complained. "I went to the Wheatsheaf, as we agreed, to have a pint with you and you never turned up," he said accusingly, taking a drag on his roll-up. "Well?"

"Sorry Morris," Steve felt embarrassed, "I was suddenly waylaid by someone." He remembered, with a shudder, of what happened to him that night, with Colonel Guntripp.

"So you got your birthday treat off Gloria then?" Morris's face cracked into a grin. "Good for you, you lucky swine, I wish I had birthday's like that," he enthused.

Steve jumped at the chance to cover his Friday night by agreeing with Morris that he'd had a wonderful time with Gloria and added, "I could hardly walk on Saturday," which made Morris rock with laughter. "Can you do this one for me, Morris?" Steve handed the paper to him.

Morris returned after a few minutes, with the required copy and handed it, without comment, to Steve.

Steve went back to his office and found it full of steam and a burnt-out kettle. He opened his window to let the air clear then he duly dispatched the Birth Certificate in the 'tube' and sat back with a very satisfied feeling of a job well done. He would change the burnt kettle for someone else's later. He smiled as the thought hit him. A knock at the door jolted him into action.

"Are you in sir?" Sandy's voice asked plaintively.

"Come in," Steve said, hiding the kettle out of sight.

"Coo ...! Don't it feel clammy in here?" Sandy's eyes were looking round like a hawk for the cause of this.

"Never mind that, what do you want?" Steve asked briskly.

"I've brought you the keys to your car, they have put it in Bay 'A'." Sandy sounded very impressed with this position. "It's a lovely maroon colour and it is full of petrol. Here's your pass for the petrol pumps. Do I get a ride in it?" He asked hopefully.

"No." Steve took the keys, "Now sod off and get some work done." Sandy's head dropped as he slowly exited.

Steve put the pass in his wallet, next to the photo he had of Gloria, which reminded him to call in on her office.

He knocked on her door half hoping there would be no reply, but his hopes were dashed as he was told to enter.

Gloria sat looking straight at him. She had a hint of tired eyes and she looked at her watch. "Glad you could fit me in," she started ... then her face softened. "Sorry for ringing you at home yesterday, I had too much to drink, but don't worry," she added, "that nerd of a husband of mine had to go to Cardiff Sunday morning and I was missing you so much, I couldn't stop myself from ringing you. What on earth did your mother think?" she asked in a whisper. She held her hands out towards him, puckering her red lips. He went across to her and joined hands, dropping a quick kiss on her very shiny lips.

"Don't worry darling, no harm done. I couldn't see you earlier but," Steve pulled his car keys out, "look I've got the car now and I wondered if you fancied a spin in it, at lunchtime?"

Gloria pulled him down onto her knee and gave him a long, hard kiss until they were both breathless. She broke away and kissed his cheeks softly, looking into his eyes with a tender expression, the he kissed the tip of her nose.

"That sounds wonderful to me. I've never done it in an MG before." She laughed excitedly at the thought.

"I doubt very much whether it is possible in that small car," countered Steve, caressing her breast as he talked.

"We'll give it a damn good try," Gloria laughed putting her hand down between his legs and felt the response she hoped for. Gently squeezing her erect manhood until Steve had to pull her hand away before he got damp trousers.

He got off her knee but couldn't resist slipping his hand inside her blouse and under her bra until he was able to roll her lovely erect nipple between his fingers. Then it was Gloria's turn to push him away before she got too wet.

"See you at lunchtime then." Steve adjusted himself and kissing her on the forehead, departed a happy man.

Gloria watched him go as she adjusted her clothes and so did Sandy, who had watched the whole scene through a fanlight from the office next door. He climbed down off the chair he'd used and went off to the Gents to try to dry the wet patch he had acquired on his trousers by standing under the hand airdryer. He scuttled along the passages to the Gents at high speed taking no heed of people calling him. This had been the most exciting day in his life.

Steve got back to his office, completely unaware of all the happiness he and Gloria had inadvertently given Sandy. There was a message waiting in the 'tube' tray which just said they had received the information he'd sent earlier.

He had thirty minutes to kill until lunch so he retrieved the kettle and went to the drivers' rest room where good luck went his way. No one was in so he quickly swapped kettles and returned to his office, only grinning when he was safely out of sight. "My need is greater than theirs."

He filled it up and found there was no plug on it. '*Bastards*,' he thought, '*you can't trust anyone nowadays*.' He stuck a note on it for the cleaners to find a new plug, while back in the drivers' rest room, a hunt was on for whoever had burnt their kettle.

He met Gloria in Bay A at 12.30 p.m. and he helped her into the car, noting the nice flash of leg as she tried to keep modest at the same time, because they were being watched by curious office workers, as they walked past.

Once they left the built-up area Steve pulled over into the first lay-by much to Gloria's concern.

"Not here Steve, it's far too public," she protested.

"Don't be a silly girl," replied Steve, "I want to put the hood down and feel the wind and sun on us." He got out and folded the hood down. "Right, let's go," he leaned across and they kissed lightly, enjoying being together.

Gloria undid her coat and tuned her face to the sun letting her hair hang loose. She caressed the gear stick lovingly. "What a nice car you've got," she purred quietly.

"You're a real prick-teaser," he laughed, taking her hand off the gear stick and kissing it warmly.

He drove to a nature reserve set amongst pine trees, with squirrels running around. He switched off and got out, then held the car door for Gloria to get out.

"Ooo ... quite the gentleman eh?" she exclaimed as she stood up. "What now? I'm not dressed for walking you know."

"I have in the back, a blanket ... or should have, for picnics. I told the drivers to put one in for me, let's see now if they have managed to do that little job?" He leant over the driver's seat and saw a large tartan blanket lying on top of a wicker hamper. He removed the blanket. "I didn't order this," he informed Gloria as he opened the lid, which revealed a chilled bottle of Chablis, plus smoked salmon slices, lemon wedges and a small amount of brown bread and butter in cellophane. Wrapped in some serviettes were a knife and a corkscrew.

"Well this beats me", remarked Steve as Gloria hugged him tightly in excitement, ... "Oh, hang on," he unfurled one of the serviettes, "I thought so ... look," he showed Gloria a corner of the serviette. "A portcullis. I can guess who organised this little lot and look here there's two glasses ... how could they know I would not be alone?" He was feeling very wary of this intrusion.

"Oh never mind, darling let's enjoy it, who cares who put it in the car. It's obviously for you, so come on." She grabbed the blanket and raced ahead of him to select a nice secluded area, not without difficulty as she had high heels on. She stopped and kicked both shoes off and stuffing them in her coat pocket ran on, giggling like a schoolgirl.

"Come on slowcoach," she teased Steve as he sank into the sand under the weight of the hamper.

He joined her just as she threw the blanket on the ground, smoothing it out as best she could. He put the hamper down and got the glasses out and the corkscrew as Gloria took her coat off, folded it neatly and bent over to place it as a head-rest.

The sight of her bottom, with her briefs and suspenders outlined on her thighs, was too much for Steve and he leapt forward, grabbing her round her waist and pressed his ever-hardening cock against her skirt-covered bottom. She fell forward laughing, "You randy sod let's get ourselves organised first, at least." She pushed him off. "Get the wine open, because I do not think we will be going back to work today ... we are going to celebrate your promotion, like we should have done on Friday, except for my little show of jealousy. I intend to make that up to you so much, you won't want it again for a long time." She sat up smiling provocatively and leaned back on her hands. "Come on big boy, get the drinks poured," she said as the bottle popped open, "and I want the cork as a momento of our love for each other, you can slit it and put a coin in it for me."

"That's only for champagne isn't it?" he queried.

"I don't care, that's what I want ... pleeease," she implored him, "I'll do anything you want," and again the provocative smile was shone at him.

"Okay darling, here's to us," and their glasses were touched together with a little ting and the heat of the sun beamed down on them as the chilled wine went down, like the drink of the Gods was made to do.

She leaned across and kissed him and to his surprise she had wine in her mouth which she blew into his mouth at the same time as the kiss. He sucked every drop greedily from her mouth as she pushed her tongue into his as far as she could. They broke off for air, gasping and laughing together.

33

"That was bloody marvellous, darling. Where the heck did you learn that trick from?" Steve nibbled her ear lovingly.

"I just thought you'd like it," she replied, stroking him on his arm. "Didn't you like it?" She suddenly sounded alarmed at the thought.

"Of course I did, it was just a surprise to me that's all. Anyway it's your turn now." He filled his mouth with wine for Gloria and gave her a wine kiss in return, which she drank as hungrily as he had hers, until she had to stop for air.

"Wonderful," she murmured, lying back holding her glass aloft, "Isn't life lovely?" Her eyes were sparkling more than Steve had ever seen them before and the pupils of her eyes seemed to be twice their normal size, making her look warm and inviting and full of love.

Steve propped himself up on one arm and put his glass down to free his hand, then slowly stroked his hand up her blouse, playing with the buttons on the way. He could see that she had a pretty bra on, with lace edging, that seemed to push her breasts together, making a lovely cleavage. He caressed her breasts slowly, feeling her nipples starting to get hard. He carefully undid each button, starting from the top one until all visible buttons were undone then he slowly pulled her blouse aside, revealing her lovely body.

He leaned forward and kissed her, on both cups of her bra, then licked his tongue over the hidden nipples as Gloria started to gasp with pleasure. He slipped a bra-strap off her right shoulder and slowly eased it down, until her nipple was almost showing.

He lifted his head and kissed her passionately and he felt her respond by pressing her stomach hard against him. He kissed her all the way down her chin and neck, then down to the soft curve of her heaving breast. He grasped her bra-strap with his teeth and eased it down until her erect nipple sprang out, tickling his nose as it did so. He kept pulling the strap until all her breast was showing, then started to kiss her, gently and slowly, round and round her nipple until his mouth was directly over her nipple, then flicked his tongue out and caressed and teased her lovely, hard, pink nipple.

He closed his lips around her nipple and licked it against his teeth, as Gloria pulled her other strap down with a flourish. He switched his attention to this other whilst still manipulating the first one with his hand. He pushed both breasts together and then got both nipples in his mouth at the same time. He sucked hard, Gloria was really squirming now, pushing herself harder against him. He stroked a hand down her stomach, massaging her at the same time until she suddenly broke free and whispered to him that she must take her skirt off to stop it getting creased. She undid her zip, with Steve's help and wriggled out of it and carefully put it to one side, then lay on her back, her breasts as smooth as satin.

Steve saw she had matching white silk underwear on and lovely stockings that made her legs shimmer in the sun. He stroked her legs up and down then pushed his hand gently between her legs. Gloria made a low groaning moan and her legs opened wide for Steve to caress more. He rubbed his fingers down over the crutch of her briefs and was amazed to feel how wet she was. He slid a finger under her briefs and felt the warm, moist, love spot waiting for him. He worked his finger round on her clitoris, making Gloria moan even louder. Loud enough for Steve to remember that they were in the open and hadn't looked for people for a while.

He looked around briefly. "Don't stop," she begged, rubbing his finger hard against her clitoris and suddenly she gave a big gasp as she shuddered to a climax, clamping his hand hard between her legs. She lay back with a big sigh. "Sorry, Steve I couldn't wait, you were lovely to me, you gorgeous man," and she pulled his hand from between her legs and kissed his wet fingers, lovingly.

Steve started to undo his trousers to let his rampant erection out into the sun when Gloria asked 'had he brought some protection with him'. The look on his face told her the answer ... no.

"Hell," he breathed heavily, "I haven't, because I didn't know we would be together at lunchtime." He lay back, angry with himself for not having any protection with him, his erection starting to subside. Gloria turned on her side.

"Come on," she cradled his deflating penis. "We can't have this, I won't be that selfish ... wait a second." She turned on her back and slipped her briefs off, then wrapped them round his penis. She started to slide them up and down, slowly at first, then increasing her grip, getting faster until Steve groaned in ecstasy and she felt her briefs go wet in her hand.

"There," she whispered, "that's better isn't it darling?" She tossed her briefs into the open hamper.

Steve lying back contentedly nodded agreement. "But you have no knickers to wear home, darling, what will you do?"

"I shall go straight into the bath because if that nerd," she spat the word, "is home, he'll be working on his precious papers for some court case, or other."

She sat up and Steve watched her as she put her bra back on, then she leaned over and retrieved her skirt.

She borrowed a handkerchief from Steve and dried herself then they both dressed quietly, but happily.

He put the returned handkerchief in his pocket although Gloria said she hoped his mother wouldn't find it and that he should throw it away, now.

"That's going under my pillow, so mind your own business," he teased her. They had another long, hard kiss before gathering up everything and returning to the car, as happy as two lovers should be. Steve drove her to the end of her road. "Bye bye Mrs. Gees." He waved cheerily to her.

"Thanks for the lift, Mr. Manly," she replied cheekily and walked slowly to her house, forcing herself not to look back, in case the 'nerd' happened to have come home.

Steve drove straight to the Royal Sandgrounder, to play

nine holes, relaxed and happy with life, completely unaware that all their afternoon activity had been relayed to a receiver in Room 516 via a small radio transmitter set in the handle of the wicker hamper.

The receiver operator relayed this to Colonel Guntripp who was in London.

"Fine," he grunted, "he isn't talking about his new job to his lady friend ... that's a good sign." The last remark was to congratulate himself on a good choice of new operative.

The following weeks set a routine for Steve, receiving three 'tube' messages a day. There was one trace that was quite difficult, with the name of Petrak. He eventually traced the family in Russia, by using the political Box 500, the only Russian trace he had been asked to follow.

He was now buying The Times, as he felt this would enhance his image, despite Fred's derogatory remarks to the contrary.

Steve enjoyed his new found status and made sure he had a clean, ironed shirt on each day, courtesy of his mother, who was being very supportive of him now. She even went for a ride in his MG which she enjoyed. Relaying all the details of her ride to all her friends at the Bridge Club, the same day, singing her son's praises to them, proud of his achievements.

CHAPTER 3
London Commands

Thursday 27th was his first monthly pay cheque since his promotion, and Steve had only that on his mind when he was disturbed by his 'phone. He slung his paper down, which he had only that minute picked up and barked, "Yes?"

"Hello Manly," the Colonel's voice answered quietly, "Have you read today's Times yet?"

"No sir ... I've only just received my copy," Steve lied.

"Well, I want you to look at the photograph on the front page, reference Heathrow and then read the article about royal flights being diverted to Northolt ... okay?" The 'phone went dead.

Steve did as he was asked and read about a combined security clamp-down by armed soldiers and police after intelligence reports had given warning of a possible terrorist attack by Arab guerrillas. Mr. Yitshak Rabin, Israel's new Prime Minister, was expected to arrive at the weekend. Two flights carrying the Queen and Mr. Wilson were turned from the airport yesterday to Northolt.

Steve read that more than 150 troops from the Blues and Royals plus the 2nd Battalion, the Grenadier Guards, had arrived in convoy during the afternoon armed with submachine guns and self-loading rifles and patrolled around the main overseas terminals. The police set up road blocks and were searching cars, while the troops patrolled the perimeter road in Ferret cars.

The operation was the most intense military and police measures ever mounted in England and in addition to the troops it involved a large number of armed police.

The soldiers had come from their base at Victoria Barracks, Windsor, where they had been alerted at the last minute. Top-level discussions had been held between the Army, the police and government officials, earlier in the week.

Steve finished reading all this and sat back wondering what to make of this, as it all seemed a straight forward anti-terrorist operation to him.

He did not hear any more until 4.30 p.m. Just as he was enjoying looking at his new pay-slip the 'phone rang.

"What did you make of that article then?" The Colonel sounded as if he was keeping his voice down. Then Steve realised that he must have been drinking.

"Well Colonel, sir, I do not see anything to be worried about, in fact," he added, " the terrorists should be the worried ones. What am I supposed to think?" Steve asked perplexed at the whole situation.

"Never mind Manly," the Colonel sounded quite stern, "just bear that article in mind and when you come to London we'll discuss it further ... see you." The 'phone went dead.

Steve had no further contact with the Colonel for a few weeks, but kept doing the 'traces' daily, striking up quite a rapport with Morris in Birth Register, sharing the horse-racing tips and discussing Gary Player winning The Open from Peter Oosterhuis, on Sunday the 14th.

Steve now made sure that he read the Times first thing every morning without fail, noting all bombing events by the IRA and reading about the world news because he felt a need to keep an eye on the state of affairs everywhere.

He went to see his friend Philip at the golf club.

"Hello stranger," Philip said as they shook hands. "What will it be ... bitter?" Steve nodded. "Two pints of bitter Laurence, in straight glasses. I've been waiting for you to turn up so that we can enter the Captain's Prize."

"Sorry Phil ... it's my new work," Steve apologised to him.

"Well, there's just two entries open, I'll go and put our names down ... that is unless your girl-friend is lying on your pyjama-cord again?" Steve smiled remembering last night when his elbow and knees were rubbed sore by the friction of Gloria's polyester sheets.

"Well, are you on or not?"

"Yes, I am, here's a fiver go and enter us."

Philips waddled off in his plus-fours, whistling happily.

"There's a vacancy here now for a Pro'," Laurence said.

"What's happened to the new Pro' ... he's only been here six months?" Steve sounded amazed.

"Caught in bed with the Captain's wife."

"Did no one warn him about her?" Steve asked.

"Nope," replied a smiling Laurence, "but he went down with flags flying."

"Why?" asked Steve seeing Laurence trying not to smile.

"His twenty-one year old daughter was in bed with them as well." Laurence and Steve were still laughing when Philip returned.

"I see he's told you then," he observed dryly.

"It could have been worse," Steve said drying his eyes.

"How could it be worse, he's lost a good job," Philip replied.

"It could have been me," Steve started laughing again.

"You haven't?" Philip said aghast at this impropriety.

"I went to his daughter's eighteenth birthday three years ago and finished up in bed with her," Steve explained merrily. "Her father had got absolutely legless and her mother was so angry with him that when she found us in bed together ... listen to this," Steve urged a willing audience, "she simply stripped off and joined us in bed."

"You lucky devil," Laurence wheezed trying to get his breath back, "no wonder you kept quiet about that, you'd have been black-balled and no mistake. Here, have a drink on me," and the weekend went into a blur from then on.

"What do you make of this?" Fred was sitting in Steve's office reading his Times on Monday morning.

"Think of what?" Steve queried taking the paper off Fred.

"The article about private armies standing by to take over the Country. Sounds bloody silly to me," Fred commented dryly. Steve quickly read the article trying not to show how interested he was in it.

He read how various groups of people were banding together because of their concern about the immediate future of Britain to lend a hand in the event of what is described as 'a breakdown of law and order.'

General Sir Walter Walker, who had retired two years earlier as Commander in Chief, Allied Forces Northern Europe, advocated the eventual setting up of regional volunteer forces in England similar to the old 'B' specials in Northern Ireland. He said 'loosely knit' groups are already in existence and the best organised was a group called the Unison Committee for Action. They were financed and are involved in many parts of the country. Action Group, formed from the National Association of Ratepayers claiming six million members was to make its main aim to search for a new national leader.

Colonel David Stirling, founder of the Special Air Service had said 'there are many people in Britain now who think some kind of crunch is coming. Moving into the installations owned by the Government is a very delicate business and that this is one reason for the secrecy surrounding those people who have already made positive plans.'

Steve put the paper down and said to Fred, "I agree with you, for once, it's all a load of bollocks, take no notice if it ... it's just scare mongering," he added.

"Would you join an organisation that wanted to overthrow our Government?" Fred quizzed him looking Steve straight in the eye.

"Not my scene at all I'm afraid. I'll stick to just playing golf," Steve asserted. "Now, hoppit I've got work to do, see you lunch-time okay?" Steve said light-heartedly, to keep Fred from asking further questions. Fred agreed and hauled himself out of the armchair, groaning with the effort. "Don't ever get old Steve, it's bloody awful." He limped off, loosening his joints on the way. Steve watched go fondly, he liked Fred because he spoke his mind to anyone, mainly because he had given up years ago on any thought of promotion.

The 'phone rang. "Hello Steve, fancy coming round for dinner?" Gloria sounded really happy. "The 'nerd' has flown to Madrid this afternoon for a few days, so we'll have my house all to ourselves so don't tell me you're busy," she implored him.

"Sounds good to me," Steve jumped at the chance. "What time do you want me round?"

"Make it about seven, you wonderful man." She blew a kiss down the 'phone and hung up. He felt marvellous and made a note to get a bottle of wine and some flowers to take her.

The 'phone went again, Steve snatched it up. "Yes darling?" he asked, assuming Gloria was ringing back.

"Hello Manly," the Colonel's voice replied, "who's darling then when she's at home?" he laughed.

"Sorry Colonel, my mistake," he spluttered back. "What can I do for you?"

"The article in the Times about private groups, have you read it?" he barked commandingly.

"Yes sir, is there any truth in it?" queried Steve.

"Bear it in mind when I see you in London, that's all." Once again the 'phone went dead.

Steve sat back and started to wonder about what he was getting into by going to London. It seemed to be a world of politics that he had no experience of. In fact, he did not even belong to any political party. He looked at his watch and decided it was time for lunch when Sandy knocked and entered carrying a black leather brief-case. He explained, "This arrived in a special delivery, they think it's for you, sir." He passed the case to Steve. The gold embossed portcullis had the initials FO underneath it and attached to the handle, with tape, were a couple of keys to fit the brass locks at either end.

Steve was delighted to receive this as it made him feel that he had already been accepted by London.

"Thanks Sandy, it's a great brief-case, eh?"

"Yes sir," Sandy nodded his head. "I wish I had a case like that, my mum would be ever so pleased," he said wistfully as he departed to inform everyone about it.

Steve unlocked the case, noting that it had a code-lock set inside the first opening. He opened this second lock as it was not engaged and found a piece of paper with all the instructions on how to programme the code-lock with his own code. A warning was also written that once set, any attempt to open the case using a wrong code would result in a small explosive going off which could disable the person trying to get it open and then activate a chemical in the case to destroy the contents.

'*God*' he thought '*they really mean business with this. I only hope it never goes off by mistake.*' He shuddered at the thought as he read the setting instructions carefully. On the instructions it said 'do not use numbers easily associated with you, such as your 'phone number or house number, birthday date etc. as these are the first numbers that an unauthorised person will try.'

Steve, who had immediately thought of his telephone number as a code felt a little bit subdued to think he would have been an easy prey to an expert code-breaker and tried to think of an unforgettable code, as his very life could depend on it.

He put the case to one side to give it some thought and went for lunch and a game of snooker with Fred.

"Are you on the 'case' then professor?" Fred said, grinning at his own little joke.

"I gather you have seen Sandy then, the little wassock," Steve replied picking up his snooker cue. "If he comes in here I'll blue his bloody end for him."

"He doesn't mean any harm," Fred replied, "he just cannot keep his mouth shut, that's all."

"He'll open it once too often," Steve growled, "then pow, he gets it." Steven gesticulated with his cue, violently.

"How is the new car going?" Fred changed the subject

"It goes very well," Steve answered, "but when it rains and the hood is down it's a bit of a sod to get it up quickly."

"That's because it's a poseur's car, it's for pulling birds you randy sod," Fred laughed and carried on talking to the whole room now. "I bet you have not had a bloke in it yet have you?" He asked as all the men waited for the reply, grinning to each other knowingly.

"Well no, not yet," came the embarrassed reply. "I'm too busy."

"We all know you're too busy." Laughter went all round the room as Fred leant over and broke off the frame. "Mind you," he carried on, "everyone else who qualifies for a car gets a Ford Consul, but you get an MG, strange, isn't it?"

"Bollocks," was all Steve could reply at this observation.

He told Gloria what had been said that evening as they rested after a strenuous bout of love-making.

"It is unusual," she agreed. "I think that you are being

44

marked out for something very special." She rolled over and straddled him then started riding him like a horse.

"And now I'm going to give you something special," she purred and started playing with her own nipples, groaning softly, as Steve amazed himself by rising to the occasion yet again, for the fourth time that night.

Afterwards, she said, "I've asked for a transfer to London, what do you think of that?" she asked a completely knackered, sweating Steve.

"What does your husband think?"he replied guardedly.

"I don't care," she retorted, "it's my career, I can do what I like ... he follows his own career anyway."

She got up and went to the bathroom. "So what do you think of my idea darling?" came the question again.

"Not one of your best in my opinion," replied Steve carefully. "I will be back in a couple of years and I reckon we should wait ... don't you?" he cajoled her.

"I reckon," she put her head round the bathroom door, "I reckon they want you in their 'team' ... yes?" She looked long and hard at him. "So you want to keep me in the dark for my own safety. That's it isn't it?" she implored him.

Steve was stumped by the honesty of Gloria's approach and could only remain speechless, which gave Gloria her answer.

She left the bathroom and came over to him, sitting down on the rumpled sheets and put her arms round him.

"You don't have to worry about me, darling. I'll be a good girl and be the dutiful wife, until you come back." She ran her fingers through his hair. "Make sure you do come back, I don't want to read about you being a dead hero in the papers, okay?" Steve kissed her and gave her all the assurance he could that all would be well for them.

"When do you go?" she asked with tears in her eyes.

"About two weeks now, I think," he answered nuzzling her ears. "You're some woman, you've knackered me." He laughed and she tried to smile through the tears as they settled down side by side, she wrapping her legs round him as if she was never going to let him go. They went to sleep merged as one person, in a cocoon of love and tenderness.

Again the weeks went by, with Steve doing all the traces he was asked to do. His office had been redecorated even more luxuriously than before, with a large settee installed and when Steve asked why he was shown it was a bed-settee and that Head Office had ordered it. "Just sign here, sir," was the request. Steve complied but without understanding.

Steve soon found out why, when he received a 'tube' message to standby for an important request coming in from a field-agent, somewhere in Europe, in the next few hours.

He sent a message to his mother that he would not be home that night, via Sandy, on his bike. He waited until midnight then thought he had better get some sleep so he folded down the bed. He found the bedding, all neatly put away in the recesses of the hollow bed-head, plus a large fluffy dressing gown and a toilet bag containing soap and toothbrush and razor.

He trotted off down the dimly lit corridor to the toilet. His mind completely on the work he was doing he literally walked into the night security officer, with his dog, doing their security clocking round. The resulting reaction was all over in a couple of seconds, with Steve nursing his leg once the officer had un-clamped the dog.

"Bloody hell man," Steve gasped. "Hasn't anyone told you I was staying for the night?" He held his leg tightly as he spoke to the red-faced officer.

"No sir, not a word," the officer replied, "and nothing was put in my hand-over report when I came on duty, sorry sir."

He apologised while having to restrain his dog from finishing Steve off, its eyes glaring yellow and mouth pulled back in a snarl.

"Just hang on to that bugger. I'll see the Head of Security to-morrow. It's not your fault officer." Steve had calmed down a little by now. "So don't worry, you were only doing your job and if I had been an intruder I would have had no chance against you and," Steve nodded, "him."

"Thank you sir, I'll enter it up in the duty log ... will you be staying any more nights?" he enquired dutifully.

"Believe me officer I will personally make sure security knows when I stay again. I assure you ... good night." Steve limped off towards the toilets.

"Do you want me to get the first-aid box for that leg wound?"

"No I'll be all right ... good night again."

The officer turned, pulling a reluctant dog round with him. "Come on boy, you deserve a treat now for guarding me," he ruffled his dog's ears fondly. "I've got a nice boiled sheep's head for you," he added and off they went, as one.

Steve cleaned his leg and went back to his office just as his 'phone went.

"Hello Manly here," he advised whoever had rung him.

"British speaking," answered a male voice, "listen hard 'cos I've got to keep on the move. The information is that the Scottish Laird is here in Villajoyosa with the Swedish connection ... now have you got that Manly?" He paused then went on with an afterthought. "That's not your real name is it?" came the terse question.

"Yes, why?" asked a perplexed Steve.

"You are obviously not in the 'proper 'team yet. That must be why I was asked to use you. Oh well, fair enough." The voice seemed to question and answer himself to his own satisfaction, then the 'phone went dead.

Steve looked at his watch and timed the message received at 01.30 hrs. but what did he do now with this information he asked himself. Not knowing the answer, he decided to pour

47

himself a night-cap out of his mini-bar.

Three large night-caps later he slept like a log, waking only to the startled cry of the early morning cleaner who had come into do his room not knowing anyone was there.

Steve struggled to focus on her as she backed out of the room, apologising profusely for disturbing him and shut the door behind her. He heard a gabble of excited female voices discussing her shocking find.

The real shock to Steve was the fact that a cleaner could come and go in his room, whenever they had to clean. *'Who gave them a key,'* he wondered to himself, having assumed he was the only one with access.

He lay back thinking about this intrusion and realised that since he had had his own office, it had been cleaned every day and he simply did not realise the significance of this, mainly that his office was not secure or secret. This was an education to him and taught him a lesson about the pitfalls of security connected with his new job.

He went to shower and shave before the day staff came on duty and quickly got dressed. He stored his bed away, which was just as well because the 'phone went.

"Morning Steve," he heard the Colonel say, "anything to report yet?" in his usual brisk manner.

Steve was slightly thrown by the fact that this was the first time the Colonel had called him by his first name.

"Yes sir," he consulted his notes. "At 01.30 this morning person calling himself 'British' rang and said the Scottish Laird was in ...," he peered at his scribble, "in a place called Villajoyosa with the Swedish connection and that was all he said ... apart from the fact I answered with my own name, which seemed to upset him sir."

"Right Steve, well done and don't worry about your code name. We will give you a name when you come to London." Then before Steve could ask when, "Where the hell is this place Villajoyosa? Find out Steve, I'll call you back as soon as

I've read my paper."

A knock at the door revealed that Fred had arrived with the paper. He limped in and started to put the kettle on. He looked at Steve and said in an astonished voice, "Where the hell have you been?"

"What do you mean?" replied an anxious Steve.

"You are still in the same clothes as yesterday and ...," he grinned ,"the women here will certainly notice that fact and put two and two together and make five. What's doing?" he asked. "You can tell me, I'm your friend. In fact, I reckon I'm you're only friend, matey." Fred poured the water into the coffee percolator as he spoke.

"I have been here all night working and that's a fact," Steve said as he saw Fred's face break into a big smile.

"Yes, I believe you, thousands wouldn't," replied Fred cheerfully sinking into the settee with a groan of relief.

"I had to send Sandy to tell mother I was working all night," Steve explained grimly, taking his coffee over to the armchair. Fred sensed that things were as explained. "So they've got you now then?" and settled to read Steve's paper without needing an answer.

They drank their coffee in silence until Fred put the paper down and asked, "If you've been here all night you must be bloody hungry ... I'll tell you what, I will go to the canteen and get you a 'toasted bacon' does that sound all right to you?"

"You are a pal, Fred. I must admit that I'm a bit hungry, but," he stopped Fred in his tracks at the door, "you don't know where a place called Villajoyosa is do you?"

"I do sir," Sandy's voice came from outside the door causing Fred to pull up short with a gasp. "Christ." He saw who it was and went on his way muttering about youth and all the drawbacks associated with them.

"Come in Sandy, my dear friend," said Steve with exaggerated charm, "tell me where it is and I'll get Fred to buy you a brandy." He gushed on the suspicious Sandy.

"Your mum's dead narked with you sir. I gave her the message like you said, but I think she did not believe me." He was smirking now and enjoying telling the tale.

"Never mind that," Steve snapped, "where the hell is this place?" He showed the word to Sandy.

"It's on the Costa Blanca, near Alicante," he stopped then. "It's in Spain," he said, airing his knowledge further.

"I know Alicante is in Spain, thank you very much ... oh have a coffee for the information and thank you for your help with my mother," Steve said gratefully.

Sandy poured himself a coffee and sat down for the first time, in the lovely armchairs, glad to be a part of whatever Mr. Manly was doing. Steve read his paper until interrupted by the 'phone. "Yes? Manly here," Steve said.

"Steve," the Colonel was back in touch.

"Excuse me sir," he turned to Sandy, who was just thinking he would be getting more information than ever. "Out you go Sandy, this is private," and poor Sandy had to haul himself reluctantly out of the chair, but left the office a lot happier now that he felt he was a part of 'it'.

"Sorry Colonel I had someone in the room," he apologised, then followed with, "I've found out where the place is now." Steve felt all important now, but the Colonel said, "So have I. It's in Spain, but never mind that, read today's paper re Lord Longford and the private armies. I want you to remember all these articles for after you've come back from Spain." The 'phone clicked dead.

Steve stared at the receiver in his hand. *'What did he mean when I come back from Spain'*, he wondered to himself.

"Here you are pal, don't say I never do anything for you," Fred walked in bearing two toastie bacons. "Oh yes, and I called into the post-room and there was a letter for you." He looked at the envelope, "It's from a travel firm. You going away then?" he queried. "You dark horse, you kept that to yourself, who you going with, you sly bastard?" Fred was in his element now. "It wouldn't be a certain married lady would it?" he chortled passing the envelope.

"Bollocks," retorted Steve throwing the letter un-opened on his desk, "give me a toastie I'm famished now," and they sat and ate in silence until Fred gave a grunt and said that he had better do some work before he was told off by his department manager.

The envelope was snatched up by Steve as soon as Fred left the room. He opened it carefully and extracted a return ticket to Valencia, for the following day, leaving from Northolt Airport at 10.00 hrs. arriving 14.00 hrs.

To say he was amazed was an under-statement. *'What on earth was he supposed to do out in Spain'* he asked himself. The 'tube' rattled into life. Steve opened the shuttle, now nervous of what he would find, but all it contained was one line to say he would be picked up at home at 05.00 hrs. tomorrow, Friday and taken to Northolt, plus an I.D. card and permit for a person called Matthew York.

The picture on the I.D. was of himself and a small note was attached telling him to sign his new signature at the bottom of the card and on the permit, in his new name.

'Bloody marvellous,' he thought to himself, *'my passport has my proper name on it and it is out of date, so how the blazes do they get round that?'*

He locked his office with a wry grin on his face, as it seemed so pointless to lock it now, still rules were rules. He walked into the office reception area to sign out when the Commissionaire saw him and held out a brown envelope. "Just arrived, Mr. Manly, by special courier ... good job I caught you before you left."

Steve thanked him and hurried down the steps and went round the corner to bay A for his car, opening the envelope as he did so and to his astonishment he was looking at a British Passport, which when he opened it revealed his picture alongside of the name of Matthew York.

Occupation stated as 'comedian'.

Steven was really astounded at the speed at which the events of the last 24 hours had taken place. He drove home with his mind in a whirl to a frosty reception from his rather irate mother.

"So," she folded her arms like a fish-wife going to do battle with an errant neighbour, "so you've managed to come home then. Hungry are we? or just need some clean clothes?" Her lips were tight and grim.

"Oh come on mother," Steve protested, "I'm a grown man now, not a little boy. I can come and go as I want without asking your permission, y'know." He tailed his remarks off as he saw his mother's face start to crumble, not used to Steve retaliating like this. He carried on now with his news of going away to Spain, for an unknown period of time tomorrow, early in the morning. He would, of course, leave her his room rent as usual.

"Who are you going with?" was the first question when she had got over the shock of him going away.

"No-one mother, I've decided to have a break for a few days," Steve lied, hoping that she would let it lie.

"It's that woman isn't it, you're just like your father, men!" she declared reaching for her beloved cigarettes.

"Men! You're all the same. Now I will get your suitcase packed, I will not let it be said that I do not look after my own son." With that she left, leaving a trail of smoke in her wake.

The suitcase his mother produced was bulging with clothes. He thanked her and took it to his room and off-loaded half of it, not wishing to hurt her feelings when she was trying so hard to look after him.

He set his alarm for 04.00 hrs. and told his mother not to get up as he was leaving at 5.00 a.m. The alarm seemed to go off as soon as he fell asleep or so it seemed and as he switched his bedside light on, Buster came racing in, followed by

Steve's mother carrying a full breakfast tray.

"No son of mine goes away without a proper breakfast," she said as Steve tried to protest and at the same time tried to protect his breakfast from the exuberant Buster who had launched himself onto the bed in anticipation of food.

"Stop it you daft dog." Steve tried to control Buster. "Thanks mother, you should not have bothered, but thank you anyway, much appreciated." He ate this mini-feast quickly. The doorbell went at 4.55 a.m. precisely and when he opened the door he found that his driver was Henry, the Colonel's chauffeur.

"Hello sir, where are your bags?" Henry said with a smile. "Long time no see," he ventured as Steve's mother came to see who was taking her son away.

"Oh, I know you," she said asserting herself on the conversation, "you brought my son home when he was ill and I do not want the same thing again, do you hear me young man?"

"Yes, ma'am, I hear you," Henry replied with a straight face, "I'll make sure he is not ill again."

"You do that," she snapped at Henry.

"Mother, I've got to go, the money is on my dressing-table, or was." Steve saw Buster running out of his dressing-room with a mouthful of £5.00 notes.

"You bad dog, come here," his mother commanded running after the crazy Buster who was having a ripping time.

"Come on Henry, let's go while the going is good." He closed the front door as quietly as he could.

Henry loaded the bags into the Rolls Royce and Steve's journey to Spain and the unknown had started.

CHAPTER 4
Spanish British

Steve had no sooner sat in the car when Henry passed him some cassette tapes saying, "Those are for you, Mr. York, to learn about your background before we get to the airport."

There were two tapes and he settled down to listen to this person's life who he was to become. '*Damn*' he suddenly remembered he had not said good-bye to Gloria in his rush to leave the office.

"Henry I want you to do me a favour and let Mrs. Gees at my office know that I'll be away for a few days." Steve was happy he had remembered to do this.

"What office is that Mr. York?" Henry replied in a murmur.

"What do you mean 'what office?'" Steve paused, "my office where I work, of course." But by now he had suddenly felt that all was not going to be that simple.

"Play your tapes Mr. York," Henry advised, then said quietly, "It's in your best interests to forget who you were when I picked you up. You," he advised Steve, "are now a Mr. Matthew York, so I advise you to play those tapes and learn them well, they could save your life." He pushed a switch and a small light came on over Steve's head. At the same time a screen silently slid up, closing off access to Henry.

Four hours later they were at Northolt and had gone through identification procedures with no problem, as Steve now knew who he was supposed to be, an extrovert comedian, going to do 'gigs' at night clubs in Benidorm.

The 'tapes' even gave a selection of jokes for him to learn should he be asked to tell one whilst in company.

A map of Benidorm and general map of the Costa Blanca were also included. He searched the Index for Villajoyosa and found that this village was some considerable way from the resort of Benidorm. He would need a car at the very least if, indeed, he had to go there. He had no instructions yet and could only give a guess as to his work details.

The flight, in an old RAF Britannia, was uneventful and he used the time reading his new passport and memorising the dates of flights to different countries that were shown in it, in case customs had a query for him.

There were only five other people on the plane, three of whom were in uniform and two civilians. One of the civilians was chatting to his companion in a loud voice and Steve realised he was a Londoner and was going out to Spain as a courier. They took off at 10.05 a.m. *'not bad'* thought Steve *'for timing'*.

The courier stopped talking for the take-off and lit a small cigar as soon as the 'No Smoking' sign went out.

He looked across the aisle at Steve and holding the cigar up said, "Soon get more of these in Spain, dead cheap over there isn't it?" he queried looking for Steve to agree.

"I don't know," admitted Steve, "this is my first time."

"You'll soon get used to it ... this is my ninth time," he added proudly, patting the official case handcuffed to his wrist. "Damn awkward going to the toilet with this on." He laughed at the scene he was portraying to Steve. "Still I only have it until we land then, bingo, buy some Duty Frees then straight back to Blighty." He turned back to his companion, leaving Steve to wonder about what was in the black case that had to be sent in such a manner.

They landed smoothly and the plane taxied over to the cargo bays, set well away from the passenger terminal.

Two plain clothes security men came aboard and inspected all their documents closely. The uniform personnel were allowed off straight away. The two couriers were already known to them and there was a bit of banter between them before they both left down the stairway at the cabin door.

Steve passed his documents to the officers and while they were reading them he idly watched through the porthole as the two couriers walked over to a large black limousine parked next to the plane.

Suddenly a small grey car raced round from the other side of the plane and sped past the two men, leaving the man who had been talking to Steve laying on the tarmac. He was clutching his leg in pain, still attached to his case.

Steve looked at the two officers standing in the aisle next to him and saw that they were not taking any notice of this at all. He looked out again and saw the grey car had stopped and the woman driver had got out. She was having a very agitated conversation with the injured courier on the ground. She stomped angrily back to her car and drove off, faster than before.

Two men had got out of the limousine while this was going on and stood there watching intently, until she had gone.

One man leaned down to the courier on the tarmac and appeared to unlock the case off his wrist, then they, with the other man, climbed back into their car and drove off leaving him still lying there, holding his leg.

Steve looked back to the security men questioningly, but to them nothing seemed to have happened at all.

"You are English comedian Señor?" one asked with a frown.

"Where are you staying Señor York and for how long?" asked the other, passing his passport back to him.

"I am staying at the Hotel Corrida, in Villajoyosa," Steve was glad he'd read that at least, "for about three days, so I hope it's a good hotel," he added trying to lighten them up a little.

They made no answer and went off down the aisle and started talking to one of the pilots at the top of the gangway.

Steve looked down through the porthole again and saw that ambulance had picked up the courier and was driving off at speed.

"What really happened there?" he asked a bored flight attendant as he left the plane. He was told that the woman was a pilot who was late for her flight and was taking g a short cut, but the silly Englishman simply did not move out of her way quick enough and now he was being taken to hospital. The attendant shrugged a 'so what' attitude.

Steve was relieved to hear this as he had thought there was a more sinister reason than a straight forward accident. He made a mental note to stay alert himself.

He had no trouble going through Valencia Airport until he sat in a taxi and asked to go to Villajoyosa. The driver shook his head from side to side, gesticulating wildly, which left Steve in no doubt that the driver did not wish to go as far as Villajoyosa that day, or any other day.

Steve climbed out and retrieved his one case while being soundly cursed in Spanish.

"Señor York?" a voice came from behind him. Steve turned and saw a small, dark man, sporting a couple of days' growth of beard holding a placard with 'Yorc' written on it.

"Yes, that's me." Steve held his hand out and was immediately grabbed by a rather grubby hand, with dirty broken fingernails and a gold ring on each finger.

"Señor York." He smiled and Steve smelt the ascetic fumes on his breath that told him the man had been drinking.

"Ah Señor, my name is Jaime and I," he pointed to his

chest proudly, "am your driver for as long as you require." He beamed. "Come, we go." He swept Steve's case up and headed across the road to the car-park opposite with Steve following along thankful this had been organised.

"Where to Señor?"

"Hotel Corrida in Villajoyosa, please," replied Steve.

The wild drive to the hotel was one that Steve would always remember, and it was a very thankful Steve who arrived at the Hotel Corrida, in one piece.

"You are a very fast driver Jaime," Steve joked ,"are you as fast when you're sober?" He enquired of a puzzled Jaime who looked totally lost by this facetious remark.

"Never mind, Jaime, just joking," Steve said grimly.

"Ha! ha! English joke, very funny," Jaime laughed out of politeness at the crazy English joke. He got out of the car and helped to get Steve's case out.

"When will you want Jaime to come again Señor?" he asked Steve happily, completely unaware of the terror ride he had just inflicted on his passenger.

"Wait here until I check in, there might be a message waiting for me, okay?"

Steve turned and walked towards the hotel reception, noticing for the first time how warm it was and that he was walking through a small avenue of palm trees and pretty flowers with little fountains of water in front of small water-falls tinkling through the lovely green foliage.

Jaime watched him go with detached amusement. 'Crazy English' he thought and took his old tobacco tin out of his pocket and started to make a roll-up cigarette.

The reception was nice and cool in contrast to the heat outside with a large silent fan lazily sweeping the air above his head. Steve put his case down at the deserted reception desk and glanced at the clock on the wall noting with surprise that it was 6.00 p.m. He looked at his watch which showed 5.00 p.m. He realised that he had not adjusted to Spanish time and he was altering his watch when the receptionist returned in a flurry of papers, which she flung down to one side and turned to Steve with a large smile revealing the most perfect set of pearly-white teeth.

"Good evening sir, can I help you?" she said in perfect English, brushing a straggle of grey hair off her forehead.

"Yes, I believe you have a booking for me, Matthew York."

"Let me see, she studied her booking chart, running her well-manicured fingers down the list. "Ah, yes! Here you are sir, room 69. It's a single en-suite for three nights." She paused reading closely. "I see we have already been paid for your full board, plus an allowance for the bar drinks. How very nice sir," she remarked as she turned to get him the room key. "They must think highly of you sir," she added passing him his key. "Please ask if you want anything at all, I'm here most of the time ... oh I nearly forgot, Mr. British is waiting to see you. He's in the bar, shall I call him?" she asked making as if to leave the desk.

"No." he stopped her, "no thank you, I want to take my case to my room first, which way is it please? And may I say I think your English is perfect," he added making her blush a little.

"It should be," she replied, "because I am English," she explained smiling at him. "I came on holiday two years ago and stayed." She spread her arms out. "Because it is so nice," she explained, then went on, "your room is in the courtyard ... through those doors along there." She pointed to Steve's right. "It's nice and private, do you want your case carried?"

"No, I can manage all right," he assured her.

"Oh thank goodness, because there is only me at the moment." She laughed, relieved that she did not have to carry his case. "Dinner is at 8.30 ... silly me ... can you please sign the book. Me and my memory," she added pushing the book to him.

Steve signed the book, becoming aware of her scent for the first time as he did. He pushed the book back with fresh appraisal of her. She showed her sparkling teeth which were enhanced by the dark red of lipstick on her soft lips. She looked at the book then back at him with a frown. "Well it seems as though you have changed your name to ...," she looked down, "Steve Manly, Mr. York," she informed a horrified Steve, who could only mumble that he had just been reading a book on the plane, about a Steve Manly.

"I will cross it out, Mr. York and you can sign again, no harm done," she advised a very nervous Steve, who did as he was asked then made a quick exit to his room, feeling her eyes watching him go.

He entered his room and flung his case down in anger at his stupid mistake. *'What a wonderful start - blowing my cover on the first sodding day.'* He admonished himself and looked round his room. The room was cool and although she had said it was a single, the bed was larger than he expected and covered with a patchwork counterpane. There was a cane armchair and a pine writing desk in one corner. A palm plant which had grown tall enough to reach the ceiling was in the other corner.

He went into the bathroom disturbing a solitary lizard on the window-still which raced off in a green blur through the bars of the window. Steve pulled the shutters across and switched the light on. He picked up a large soft bath-towel and decided to have a quick shower before meeting British. He stripped off, then, needing to relieve himself he lifted the toilet seat, feeling the cold of the marble floor under his feet. He flushed the toilet and stepped back in alarm as the toilet rumbled and then exploded such a fierce jet of water into the bowl that it flowed over Steve's feet making him dance out of the way.

He caught sight of himself in the mirrored tiles. Naked and dancing like a lunatic. He stopped dancing and laughed at this ludicrous sight he was looking at. He started to pose in various positions, displaying his muscles like Mr. Universe.

He held his flaccid penis tenderly. *'Well little fella, I wonder if you are going to enjoy Spain.'* He pulled his foreskin back. *'You have to be kept squeaky clean at all times m'boy.'* He waggled his penis up and down as if it was agreeing with him. Steve stepped into the shower very cautiously, in case it was as fierce as the toilet.

It worked perfectly for him and he used the shower gel out of the complimentary pack he found by the marble wash-basin.

He towelled himself down vigorously and after applying a liberal amount of talcum powder walked into the bedroom. He realised straight away that someone had been in and turned the bed down while he had been in the shower, plus a small wrapped chocolate had been placed on his pillow.

He picked the chocolate up and saw that it had been actually made in one of Spain's oldest chocolate factories here in Villajoyosa. Steve was putting it down on the little table at the side of the bed when the 'phone rang.

"Hello," he answered warily, "York speaking."

"Eileen, the receptionist, Mr. York. I thought I'd better remind you that Mr. British is still in the bar," she advised him quietly, then added, "did you find your little night-cap I left on your pillow?" she enquired teasingly.

"Thank you for the reminder ... Eileen," Steve replied, "I did wonder who had turned the bed down."

"Well you were in the bathroom talking to someone called 'little fella' I believe, Mr. York. So you could not hear me knock." She was giggling now as she let him know what she had heard. "Don't forget if you want anything," she was now talking in a whisper, "you looked wonderful in the mirror."

Steve felt embarrassed with this revelation that she had seem him doing his muscle flexing routine. He felt his penis start to come to life at the exciting thought of her listening and watching him. He put the 'phone down without saying anything. For once he was at a total loss for words.

He got dressed as fast as he could, but thinking of Eileen at the same time. He reckoned she must be twice his age, in her mid-fifties, but he had to admit she had kept herself looking very smart, and well manicured.

He had decided to put on his brown suit, to be as smart as possible for his first meeting with a colleague. He strolled across the courtyard following the signs to the Matador bar.

He entered through a curtain of vines hanging from trellis work overhead. He stopped to survey the area, which was rather small, with alcoves set back, hidden behind vine covered arches.   He walked over to the deserted bar and looked at himself in the backing mirror of the bar.

"Never trust a man in a brown suit, Mr. York," came a voice hidden behind the vines of the alcove and held them back to observe a portly figure of a man in a floral shirt and matching shorts. He had stocky, hairy legs and he was wearing black leather sandals. His beard and long hair were bleached white and his skin was weathered dark brown.

Under his ample waist he had a leather pouch with the word 'British' burned into the leather. He stood up slowly and his piercing blue eyes met Steve's, without feeling, as he held his hand out to Steve.

"Glad to meet you British," Steve shook his hand warmly, glad to meet a friendly face. "Who says that about brown suits then?" he queried trying to break the cold stare.

"The City, of course." British sat down with a thump.

"Blast it," he exclaimed. "I really must lose some weight." He patted his stomach. "I went on a diet for two weeks once and all I lost was fourteen days." He laughed at his own joke. "There's a lot of money gone into this pot." He rubbed his stomach again and went on in explanation. "It's the City of London I'm talking about, it's a well-known saying there, so if you ever get involved working in the City, change your bloody suit." He leaned forward. "I won't charge you for that information this time." He sat back shaking in mirth at his dry wit.

"I am in your debt then," Steve said stiffly, feeling very uncomfortable now, wishing he had dressed casually.

"Don't take my remarks to heart," said British aware that Steve was not happy with his statement, " just thought I would put you right, no hard feelings eh?" He held his hand out to Steve again. "Life is too short."

Steve shook on it and then smiled. "Sorry British, I'm a bit on edge because I have never done this sort of work before and," he lowered his voice, "I cocked up in the register book as soon as I arrived."

"I know you did," British countered instantly, sitting back and finishing his drink.

"How did you know?" queried Steve in amazement.

"Simple," he paused, "Eileen told me, she's one of us, didn't you know? Anyway," he put his drink down and shouted round the corner, "Antonio, bring us dos coffees and dos le grande Cognacs, por favor."

"Si, señor," answered a voice from nowhere. "Pronto."

"Do you like my command of Spanish?" he asked Steve with a grin. "Not bad after three years living here eh?"

"I guess not," agreed Steve not knowing if British was joking or not.

"Right, let's get down to business ... first take your jacket off ... yes? Then roll your sleeves up and remove your tie." British looked Steve straight in the eyes as he talked, placing both hands on the table. "Then we both know neither of us is wired-up, okay?"

"Wired-up?"

"Christ! Haven't they trained you at all?" British sounded exasperated. "Wired-up means taping a record of our conversation," he informed a subdued Steve, who did what he was asked to do, putting his jacket over the back of the seat and having removed his tie, now sat opened-necked, with sleeves rolled up, facing British, "but one cannot be too careful in our job and I do not know you well enough yet Steve ... I mean Matthew." He corrected himself sharply with a tense grimace. "I must be getting old ... anyway you have been sent to take back information on a meeting of lefty loonies that's happening here, in Villajoyosa to-morrow morning. Why they sent me a untrained body beats me." He sighed resignedly. "But I must just carry out my orders on this issue, without question, so I hope you don't finish up dead, Matthew. These are 'heavy' people who would stop at nothing if their precious plans were found out. We believe that they are looking into taking over the British Government with a coup and place their own people in power."

He finished talking as Anonio came into view, carrying a tray of drinks, which he proceeded to serve with a flourish of professionalism and stood back to admire his artistry, producing a comb and sweeping his short, black, oiled hair back carefully. "All my own hair," he grinned and carried on with, "all my own teeth." He grinned even wider showing his teeth, "and ... I shower before and after ..." He paused for dramatic effect then turned and left them with an "adios amigos."

"What's he taking about?" asked a bemused Steve.

"He means he is a ladies' man, regular Don Juan," answered British, smiling at Steve's lack of knowledge.

"Now then where were we ... oh yes the meeting is to-morrow as I've said, so I will meet you by the station at 08.00 hrs. and remember to bring your gun ... oh bloody hell don't tell me," he looked hard at Steve, "no fucking gun?"

Steve shook his head. "I've never so much as fired one, sorry, British." He apologised, wishing like mad that he could be somewhere else. This was not what he was expecting at all, he thought, just to push paper around in a nice office environment that's what I'm here for.

"Right, at least you're honest with me, Matthew, so this is what we'll do. Meet me at 06.00 hrs. instead and I will bring you a gun and we will go and pop a few bullets on the beach. It's the least I can do, to give you a chance to defend yourself if we run into trouble, okay? ... By the way, what is your cover job?" He enquired drinking his brandy back in one swallow.

Steve followed suit and downed his brandy before he had enough courage to tell British his cover job.

"Well," he hesitated, fearing an adverse reaction, "I am a comedian, playing the clubs in Benidorm."

"Tell me a joke," British commanded grimly.

"Did you hear the one about the man that went fly-fishing and caught a five-pound blue-bottle," Steve snapped a joke instantly back at British who actually smiled at it and held his up in mock surrender.

"Enough matey, so long as you can pull one out on request if we are in company, that will be fine." British rose to make his exit and Steven reciprocated his question and asked what was his cover job out here.

"I'm a sand artiste."

"What's that, when it's at home?" queried Steve perplexed.

"I go on the beach and make models of ships, building or people, in the sand. It has been a great cover for me. I am accepted as an English eccentric by the locals, so no-one takes any notice of me or what I'm doing, good eh?" He turned to go telling Steve to remember his jacket, then disappeared through the vines.

"The bill, Señor." Antonio sprang round the corner waving the bar bill in Steve's face, but before he could answer, a voice said, "Take all Mr. York's bar bills over to the reception, please Antonio." Eileen smiled at Steve as she directed Antonio with a perfunctory wave of her hand.

"The restaurant is open now Mr. York," and she glided away leaving a trace of Chanel No. 5 in the air. Steve wondered what perfume she was using and he decided he'd find out from Antonio and buy her some as a present.

Antonio returned and came over to clear the coffee cups and brandy glasses away. "Señor ... I am told to make sure your are okay. Yes! and would you like another drink?" He paused, "on the house." He was positively beaming now.

"Yes I will Antonio, what do you recommend? I would rather eat here in the bar, if possible," Steve asked.

"Señor, I will bring you the best Champagne and," he advised, "some grilled sardines, speciality of the house."

"I'll go for that, por favor." Steve hesitated then asked, "Do you happen to know what perfume the señora wears?"

"Ah ... Señor," Antonio tapped the side of his nose slowly, "cuidado."

"Cuidado?"

"Si ... it means take care Señor York," Antonio carried on, "She is a strange one who keep to herself, even I," he pointed to himself, "have failed to have the pleasures with her, she is ...," he struggled for a description, "she is cold Ingles ice, but I know she wear the cinco French perfume." He smiled triumphantly remembering this.

"Cinco?"

"Si" Antonio held five fingers up. "Cinco."

Steve had seen some Chanel No. 5 in the display cabinet by the reception desk and knew the perfume he required now.

"Gracias Antonio," Steve said gratefully, "and bring two glasses," he indicated by pretending to drink, "with the champagne."

"Señor, the Señora will no sit with you, she is working." Antonio disappeared after his final remark, leaving Steve to sit and think about his situation. *'Hell! he'd only been in Spain a few hours and tomorrow he was going to be shown how to fire a gun on the beach and God knows what else.'*

He finished his snack of grilled sardines, drank the champagne and went off to bed, feeling nice and mellow, just as fellow diners seemed to be arriving to start their evening meal. He looked at his watch and saw it was 10.30 p.m. It seemed late to him to start an evening meal, he'd never eaten at the time himself.

He lay in bed, then suddenly thought he had better ring his mother to let her know he was all right. He read the list of International Numbers then picked the 'phone up and dialled home. There were two rings then his mother answered.

"Hello."

"Hi, mother it's me Steve. I've arrived in Spain and am in a very nice hotel. How are you?" he asked, knowing that she always found something to complain about.

"So you've found time to remember me, that's very good of you son. Where've you been until now, it's half-past nine," she admonished him and Steve felt her disapproving look even over the 'phone.

"They eat late out here mother," he tried to placate her. "In fact, I've just left the restaurant now to come and 'phone you," he lied, stretching out on the bed.

"Oh all right son." She sounded happier now. "I am glad you made the effort any way ... oh there was a message for you to 'phone that Sandy, at work when you can. He didn't say what it was about." She paused, "I have taken the hamper out of your car in case there was some food in it, but ...," she hesitated, "you'll never guess what I found."

Steve knew from her voice this was not going to be good news for him, but could not think what it could, so he answered, "No mother I don't know what you've found," but even as he said it, he realised what it was ... *'oh sod it.'*

"I don't mind telling you, Steve, it was a shock to find a pair of ... used knickers." Steve cringed from his mother's sanctimonious voice. "Do I know her?"

"There is no 'her' mother, I found them on the beach and thought I could clean the car with them, that's all," Steve was fumbling frantically for an excuse.

"I'll believe you, thousands wouldn't," she replied tartly. "I just hope you know what you're doing. I am going to watch the television now." She rang off abruptly.

Steve replaced the receiver calmly and now the drink was taking it's toll and he drifted off into a deep sleep.

His small travelling alarm clock seemed to go off as soon as he closed his eyes, but when he picked it up it showed that it was 5.00 a.m. He decided that it was a little too early to ring Sandy although the thought had crossed his mischievous mind. He showered and dressed then suddenly remembered he had not ordered any room service breakfast.

He decided that he would go to the restaurant in the hope of any food being left out for early starters. He quietly opened his room door and on the floor outside was a covered tray. He lifted to cover back and saw a small breakfast had been left for him of orange juice, bread, butter and marmalade.

He took it into his room and devoured it hungrily. As he picked up the serviette to wipe his fingers he saw the word 'cuidado' written in pencil on it, plus an x, making a kiss. *'Well, blow me'* he thought. *'She really is on the ball, I can't even remember to book breakfast, stupid bastard I am.'* He admonished himself yet again, at his lack of worldly experience.

He left the hotel in a good frame of mind, startling a little man watering the colourful plants in the sun.

"Buenos dias," Steve nodded to him, with a grin.

"Buenos dias, Señor." The man touched his flat cap.

Steve walked down the narrow streets, towards the beach, going through the old town, passing a huge Gothic church surrounded by very colourful houses.

He strolled along enjoying the early morning sun, happy the champagne had not given him a headache. He felt really fit and at peace with the world, when the calm was spoilt by the sound of a motor scooter being driven hard. He turned to where the noise was coming from and into view came British, who dwarfed the scooter as though it was a toy. He pulled up alongside of Steve, with wheels locked.

"Buenos dias, Matthew," he shouted through the smoke made by the tyres. "Get aboard pronto," he patted the pillion behind him.

Steve swung his leg over as he was told, thinking *'this is my first leg-over in Spain and it's on a scooter.'* He gave a crazy laugh, punched British on the shoulder and shouted, "Geronimo ... eeeh ... haa! Let's hit the road," and he did just that. As British opened the throttle Steve promptly fell off backwards, landing heavily on the dusty road. British stopped and looked back at him in dismay. "You are supposed to hang on to me, you daft sod, are you all right?" He was concerned he'd hurt his partner.

"Yeah," Steve answered, picking himself up and dusting down his clothes, "only my pride is hurt."

"Come on let's go then, and this time, bloody well hang on or we'll run out of time." Steve climbed warily astride and put his arms round British who opened the throttle once again. They set off followed by a trail of thick smoke as the little scooter pulled the extra weight.

They left the village and went towards Alicante for about 3 km then they turned off left and seemed to follow a small railway track for about 1 km until British drove them down a narrow path and onto a secluded beach which was surrounded by high cliffs.

"Here we are," he said dismounting, "the quietest beach in the area. We should not be disturbed here. That's why I got the scooter out ... can't get a car down here," he explained as Steve looked around at this beautiful scene with the sea lapping onto shingle, washing the pebbles backwards and forwards in a rhythmic pattern.

"Isn't it nice here?" he enthused to an uninterested British, who was busy untying a small bag that he been round his waist.

"I suppose so ... here ... this is the gun I've been told to issue to you." He handed Steve a dark green velvet bag tied at the neck with a drawstring. "It is clean, so if anyone runs a check on it, you won't be charged with any heinous crimes." He laughed at the thought, "And here is some ammunition, just a few clips to keep you going. When the time comes for you to go back to Blighty, pop it in the briefcase you were given ... yes?" He looked at Steve to agree but he was dumb-struck.

"Well ... I was given a briefcase, but I thought it was too dangerous to take on board a plane, with the special effects and all." His voice trailed off as he saw the look of disbelief in British's eyes.

British breathed deeply. "We fly from airfields the public do not use so that we are able to carry, within reason, what we want," he explained patiently. "But," he went on, seeing Steve looking like a wounded animal, "I know you have not been trained for anything, I don't know why, so I have to look after you." He paused to undo his own small bag and gently unfolded a cloth which revealed a menacing looking gun which he pushed into his belt at the back of his trousers.

Steve undid his bag and took out his gun. The name on the barrel was Smith and Wesson. Model 59. He pointed it playfully at British who nearly had a heart attack with fright. "For fuck's sake!" he shouted grabbing the gun out of Steve's hand. "Never point a gun at anyone ... ever, unless you're going to use the bloody thing, okay?"

"It's not loaded," replied a defensive Steve.

"I don't give a shit whether you think it's not loaded or loaded, I'm telling you, never, never point a gun, in fun at anyone," British raged at him out of sheer fright.

"Okay, keep your hair on, you've told me now. I won't do it again." Steve tried to placate the red-faced, heaving breathing British, who stood staring out to sea trying to calm down, by flexing his fingers until his knuckles cracked like snapping twigs. He stopped and turned, saying, "I am going to show you how to use a gun so listen and watch." For the next fifteen minutes British instructed Steve with basic firearms drill until he was happy Steve had understood what he'd been told.

Steve fired off a few rounds into a sand target from different distances and positions until British said, "That'll have to do. We have no more time left because it will take us about an hour to travel to the villa, so unload your gun now ... I don't want you behind me on the scooter with a loaded gun, thank you very much. It's not that I don't trust you," he paused, " 'cos I don't." He laughed at this little pun and kicked the sand target level. He knelt down recovering the spent bullets and slipped them into his leather pouch. "Can't be leaving bullets in the sand in case they're found, better to be safe eh?"

He kicked the bike into life and Steve climbed aboard and held onto British tightly. They returned to the main road, turned right and followed the coast road to Benidorm which they passed through in ten minutes.

"Where the hell are we going?" yelled Steve into British's ear because he had expected they were going to Benidorm.

"Moraira, matey, hang on," and they gathered speed, leaving the trail of smoke wafting aimlessly behind them.

CHAPTER 5
Rebel H.Q.

After riding for an hour, British stopped the scooter on a winding section of the road and pointed across the sunlit bay to a rocky headland.

"That's where the meeting is," he stated, wiping the dead flies off his coat, "in the old villa on the cliff top."

Steve looked up at the villa for a moment, thinking, then asked, "How do we get near enough to hear them, without being seen?"

"Good question, matey," came the answer, "bloody London think we are invisible. They think we can just walk in with our tape recorder, sit in a corner and record everything. Stupid buggers." British coughed and spit phlegm into the road. "But never fear, I have already been in the place, looking for casual gardening work and guess what?" he laughed, "they offered me the job, so I told them I would have to think about it ... that was about three weeks ago now." He added thoughtfully, then asked, "Can you climb?"

"A little bit ... I went to the Lake District a few times when I was a teenager and climbed in the Langdales," Steve answered, thankful he could do something at last.

"Well I'm relieved to hear that," replied British. "You've cheered me up no end, now I reckon we have a good chance of pulling this off," he declared happily, starting the scooter.

Steve started to eat an orange that they had picked from a small orange grove on the way.

"Chuck it away," British told him. "There's plenty more where that came from, so let's go."

Steve threw it into some bushes reluctantly and frightened a mangy, old, sleeping cat which took off like a rocket.

"I bet that's the first Spanish pussy you've seen, eh?" British teased him, as Steve re-mounted the pillion.

Steve simply grinned at this remark and countered with,"What would you have done if I couldn't climb up there?"

"Wait until you fell off, then bugger off back home, because I know an old saying ... 'he who fights and runs away, lives to fight another day' that's very true, so bear that motto in mind and you and I will get along just fine," British informed nodding like a wise old sage. They rode round the bay until British pulled off the road into a small plantation of trees.

"We'll leave the scooter here," British informed Steve, "and from now on we are on foot. Load your gun and do not take any personal belongings with you ... we will put everything under those rocks by the wall..." He paused, then said quietly, "Cut off any labels on your clothes ... here take my knife." British produced a well-oiled knife from a sheath he had strapped to his leg.

"Be careful," he warned Steve, "it's sharp enough to cut a fly's knackers off at twenty paces." Steve realised that the best way to do this was to simply strip off. He was soon standing naked in the warm sun, cutting the labels off his under-pants, shirt and trousers. British started to tell him the details of this mission as he did so.

"Right then Steve," he started, "this is the story so far. Up in that villa there is going to be a meeting between certain people on how to take over our government with a military coup and we," he paused ,"have been instructed to get as much information as possible and take it back to the Colonel ... yes?"

He looked at Steve for agreement, then went on. "The main man is a Lord Stuart McForson, a Scottish Laird from the Lowlands who thinks he should really be King Stuart the First of the United Kingdom. He is a very dangerous man and we believe he has a private army, plus powerful allies abroad who would love to step in and help him to achieve his aims, mainly communist based, do you understand?" he asked an attentive Steve.

Steve nodded and British carried on, "In the meeting there will also be a Martin Silverman, an American financier, who seems to be the main money raiser for this organisation since he lost his position as adviser to President Nixon when Nixon resigned a couple of weeks ago. Apparently he was chucked out by Nixon's replacement, Gerald Ford. He is extremely bitter about it. Then there is their weapon explosives armament expert, Gus Hall, who we don't know much about yet. We believe he buys the weapons they need ... we can't find out where their base of operations is yet, to store such weapons and do their training ... by the way," he explained further, "it was your information on a guy called Robert McIan, a couple of months back that put us on to this little lot." He congratulated an embarrassed Steve, "And his wrestling sister, Godzilla. I guess that's why the Colonel decided to give you a run in the field," he added, as Steve pulled his shirt on.

"There will also be a team of body-guards led by a Swede called Kai Svennsen. He's the best cold-blooded killer they employ. We know he was a para-trooper, then he became a mercenary in some of the African actions and he cut an ear off each person he killed, as proof, to receive his bounty payment ... not the sort of man to crack a joke with, Steve," advised British grimly.

"Cut peoples' ears off! Bloody hell, British," Steve gasped, "I hope I'm not on the losing side, that's all. My mother would be most upset," he said, trying to make light of what he had just been told, then asked, "can I ask you, why are you called, 'British'?"

"Because I used to work in a foundry making steel," British replied. "And because my name was Steele, my workmates nicknamed me 'British' after British Steel okay? Then when I joined the Army my nickname stuck with me."

"Hope you didn't mind me asking," replied Steve now fully dressed when suddenly he was jolted out of the relaxed state he was in by a man suddenly appearing out of nowhere startling him and British at the same time. Steve reached for his gun and British put a restraining hand his arm.

"Hold on Wyatt Earp," he joked, "he's one of us ... meet Aziz, the best knife thrower in the business."

Aziz was a small, swarthy but stockily built man, wearing a brown leather waistcoat and loose baggy Arab-style trousers. He wore a faded bandanna around his dark curly hair and was wearing a well-worn leather belt, that held four small knives at the front and, Steve saw, he had two large knives, in a double sheath at the back.

Aziz beamed at Steve. "Pleased to meet you, Señor, we kill all these pigs," he enthused, running his finger across his throat from ear to ear, "then we drink lots of brandy, yes? Get paid lots of money for Aziz to have many wives."

"Bollocks Aziz," replied British. "We are hoping to keep a low profile and not be discovered because we are out-numbered, you murderous little git," British said but showing a warmth in his voice.

"Anything you say boss ..." Aziz looked up at the fissured rocks. "It looks a bit loose to me so we had better climb one at a time, otherwise rock on head, hurty, hurty." He pretended to rub his head.

"Look at him, doesn't he look and sound a harmless, little sod, but I'd have him at my side in any arm-to-arm fighting, I assure you, Steve," British confided as Aziz started to scramble up the loose scree to the actual climb. They watched him until after about eighty feet, he stopped and waved to them to join him.

Steve made sure his gun was secure while British struck out up the scree with a small bag round his shoulders. It contained a tape recorder and, unknown to Steve, four stun hand-grenades. His gun was secure in his belt.

Steve joined the two of them on a narrow ledge, whispering together. British beckoned to him to be as quiet as he could be. "Talk only in whispers and sign language from now on," he whispered to Steve. "The buggers are only about a hundred and fifty feet above us now." He looked at his watch. "We have another hour before the meeting so we can take our time up here, okay?"

He turned and nodded to Aziz to carry on climbing. "We'll give you twenty minutes then we follow."

Aziz smiled and disappeared straight away, climbing straight up over their heads. They waited twenty minutes then British whispered, "Follow me in twenty minutes, unless you hear gunfire, in which case I expect you to piss off back to your hotel and with luck I'll see you there, okay? Take the scooter, I've left the key under the rocks with our effects," and then he was gone, leaving Steve alone in the heat of the sun.

He looked at his watch which showed 11.00 a.m., so he would climb at 11.30 a.m. Whilst waiting he suddenly remembered that his mother had told him that Sandy wanted him to ring when he could. It seemed like years since he had left his office and he wondered why Sandy wanted him to ring.

This, he would never find out, as unknown to him, Sandy was dead.

Sandy had gone round to Steve's house and told Steve's mother that he had been told by the office to take the MG for a wash and polish, ready for Steve's return.

He drove off, a life-time ambition realised, smiling at the girl sitting next to him as he sped along on the dual-carriageway, trying to impress her. She told the police later that he had stopped the car to put the hood down and as he got out and straightened himself up a bullet had smashed through his forehead, removing his brains through the back of his skull. He was dead before his body hit the road. The girl had seen no-one.

Steve looked at his watch and saw that it was time to start climbing. He had not told British that he had never lead in a climb and had always been on a rope held by the leader on the climb he was doing.

After about twenty feet he stopped and looked down. The view was wonderful and instead of feeling afraid, he actually felt a surge of adrenalin go through him that made him feel that he could tackle absolutely anything. He renewed his climbing full of confidence. He reached his companions without mishap and found that they had reached the base of the villa's walled garden. British signalled Aziz to climb up the wall over to the right and Steve to climb to the left. He himself would go straight up the centre. The wall was easy to climb, with lots of handholds and they all arrived at the same time. Steve looked to his right to British who signalled him to go over the top.

Steve slowly looked over the top of the wall and saw a beautiful large blue swimming pool, surrounded by a patio which was raised higher on the side nearer the villa. Steve could look into the villa because the patio windows had been opened wide, revealing a glass dining-table on which were two magnificent candelabra, glinting gold in the reflected sunrays off the pool He heard voices and he ducked down, heart thumping, as he held himself against the wall. '*Christ*' he thought '*we're sitting ducks. If anyone looks over this wall ...*' He looked down at the rocks two hundred foot below. '*Well* it's *not the fall that kills you, it's the landing;*' he remembered someone saying that in the bar of the Langdale Hotel, a couple of years back.

He looked across to British for comfort and to his amazement there was no-one left on the wall but himself. The voices hadn't got any louder so he risked another look, then saw British and Aziz, who had both climbed onto the roof via the water-drain channels that nearly touched the patio floor. British saw him at the same time and signalled him to hold his position.

The sun beat down on his back causing him to start to sweat with the heat and fear now the action had stopped. His knees were feeling the pressure of tension and then he experienced a violent 'knee-wobbler' which happens to climbers when legs have too much strain placed on them. All he could do was hold on and take more weight on his arms, gripping harder with his fingers on the rough stone walling.

The sweat was now running into his eyes, stinging, making him want to rub them. He felt as helpless as a newborn kitten, then his legs stopped trembling as he relaxed the tension. He played a mental game with himself of sending his mother a postcard reading 'dear mother having a lovely time. Had my leg over this morning and saw my first Spanish pussy, then had a most wonderful knee 'trembler'. Wish you were here.'

He was grinning to himself at this sexual wit when both his arms were violently gripped as British and Aziz seized him and hauled him unceremoniously over the wall, ripping his left trouser leg leaving a good piece of skin flayed off his left leg.

They ran across to the water drains where Aziz cupped his hands for Steve to put his foot in, then he heaved him up with all his might. Steve arrived on the low roof as if from a stage trapdoor. He was quickly joined by the other two. British looked at Steve's leg with concern at the blood that was oozing from the wound.

"Sorry about the rough handling, but we saw everyone had gone out of the front entrance to look at a car so we had to haul you in damn quick. Sorry about the leg." British apologised quietly, then said to Aziz, "The leg."

"No problems, Señor British," whispered Aziz. He whipped off his bandanna and tied it expertly round Steve's leg. "Thanks Aziz, I owe you one," Steve whispered gratefully.

"Is no problem," Aziz assured him. "I expert in many things. You buy Aziz large brandy when we finish, no problem."

British held his fingers to his lips for quiet. They held their breath as one man stepped onto the poolside patio.

"Lord Stuart McForson" British mouthed to them.

He was, Steve guessed, in his early sixties, with thinning grey hair, going bald in the middle. He was wearing a beige-coloured safari suit, which fitted him perfectly, despite his well-built frame. He wore a pair of snakeskin shoes and carried a copy of The Times under his arm.

The three of them lay flat down, as this just kept them hidden so long as no-one walked to the far side of the pool. This was Steve's first look at Lord Stuart McForson, the man who was the cause of this mission.

Lord Stuart flung his paper down on a poolside table.

"Kai," he shouted, "bring me the 'pipes'." There was a muffled reply as Lord Stuart sat down, surveying the glorious view, but without seeing it.

British had gone behind a chimney exit, busy extracting the tape recorder. "I'll set this running now," he whispered to them, "he might say something before the start of the meeting. It's got about ...," he looked at the tape, "two hours, that should be enough." He switched it on and said in a low voice, "This is Operation Precipice. Saturday 31st August 1974 at ...," he looked down at this watch, "11.50 hrs. Persons present so far are, Lord Stuart McForson and his body-guard, Kai Svenssen." He sent the tape recorder slowly down the drain channel on a piece of cord, to get as close to the conversation as possible.

Lord Stuart looked round as a man, wearing a loose-fitting blue pair of overalls, walked over to him. He had two guns, one under his left armpit in a holster and one strapped to his right thigh. He was carrying bagpipes.

"Just put them there, Kai." He indicated a low stone " This Times is two days old, it's bloody disgraceful if you ask me." He sounded disgruntled. "Why they can't make a special flight for newspapers and mail beats me ... get me a large pink gin."

Kai nodded his short, cropped head and left without a word.

Steve was impressed by Kai and by the two guns he carried. It was now noon and the heat was becoming a problem as they lay sweating, without any shade available.

"Christ, we're going to fry if his Lordship doesn't go inside soon," murmured British to them both. A horrendous sound split the air. They looked down and saw Lord Stuart had inflated bagpipes under his arm and while warming them up had started walking round the pool.

"Shit! If he looks up now we're in deep trouble," whispered British anxiously. "Keep as low as you can, shoot the bastard if he does look up and I'll try to get Kai, otherwise we'll all be blown away."

Steve and Aziz flattened themselves as low as possible, Steve with his shaky gun trained on Lord Stuart. Aziz slid a small throwing knife out of his front belt.

British crawled over to the front of the villa, ready to drop down and try to take out Kai, if necessary, but hoping to hell he wouldn't be faced with this deadly scenario.

Lord Stuart was, fortunately, concentrating on the chanter work, trying to remember the tune and had just started to play a tune that Steve recognised when Kai appeared with the pink gin indicating to Lord Stuart that he was wanted on the 'phone.

The bagpipes groaned as they deflated making Aziz look at Steve, astonished by this noise he had never heard before. British got up and did a crouching run on tiptoe, back over the roof and rejoined them.

"We have got to get off this roof, I'm sweating bloody

buckets," he gasped, as he grabbed the cord and hauled the tape recorder back up the drain channel. He switched it off. "Fat lot of good that was, what a waste of time ... not like this in the movies eh Steve?" Steve shook his head. "I reckon that if we drop over to the left we should be out of sight and be able to get in the shade. They have left the sun blinds closed that side ... come on," he ordered, leading the way as he spoke. The two men followed him, only too grateful of the chance to get out of the blazing mid-day sun.

They quickly slithered down the water-drain channel and as British had seen, they were able to utilise the shade of the over-hanging roof, unseen by anyone inside.

At the sound of a car British signalled to Aziz to work his way round to the front to check who was arriving.

Aziz slid off, hugging himself to the wall, then stopped to point at a gardener's water tap, set in the wall of the villa, giving the thumbs up sign, with a big smile.

British acknowledged the find and waved him onwards.

Aziz returned in two minutes and whispered to British that it was the American arriving, with another man.

"Good ... things are starting to happen. I've got to get this tape somewhere near them. Any smart ideas?" he asked, looking hopefully at his two companions.

"Through a window," suggested Steve helpfully.

"They all have bars on them, think again," British hissed.

"Señor ... Aziz think drop it down fire-hole on cord, yes?"

"Bloody good suggestion, Aziz. The fire-place has a big dried flower arrangement in it for summer ... right that's the plan, because I can't think of any other way."

British swung himself up on the roof, aided by the willing hands of Aziz, who was very proud that he had made a good suggestion. British checked that no-one had walked outside onto the patio, then tiptoed across to the chimney.

He rewound the tape, deleting what was already on it and switched it on. He looked down and realised that, due to the size of the fireplace, he could see all the way down to the bottom. He thought about climbing down, but discretion got the better part of valour. He lowered the tape down very slowly and, as he did so, he heard voices as people entered the room below. He tied the cord off to a radio aerial and rejoined the other two, in the shade.

The meeting was attended by Lord Stuart, Martin Silverman, Gus Hall and Lord Stuart's secretary, a Swiss-German lady by the name of Helga Boquarn, who was, British informed Steve and Aziz, believed to be Lord Stuart's mistress.

Kai had closed the front gates of the high wall surround and, believing them safe from prying eyes, busied himself pouring drinks for everyone.

They could not hear what was being discussed although at one stage the American's voice was raised to a high pitch and they heard him shout, "No way, Stu baby! I cannot raise that amount of money in the time you want it, it's just not possible, Goddamnit!"

The reply was shouted back just as loud by 'Stu baby', "If you can't take the heat, then get out of the kitchen or I'll find someone who can take the heat, and that's a promise, I assure you."

The voices calmed down and they heard nothing more for another hour. Suddenly Kai went out to the front and unlocked the gates and two cars roared off and all went quiet.

"Right," British whispered, "that's it. All we've got to do now is collect the tape and piss off at high speed. So give me a leg up." He put his foot up in front of Aziz, who cupped his hands and heaved British up onto the roof.

Steve had been bathing his leg wound with a water-soaked bandanna under the gardener's water-tap and now Aziz quickly rebound it for him, ready to move. They both had another drink of water in their cupped hands, then British joined them and also had a drink. The heat had been relentless for the two and a half hours they'd been there.

They were just going to climb over the wall when voices made them flatten out against the wall.

"Come along zen my little poppet ... you can rub some sun-cream on my back. I simply must get ze colour to show I've been to Spain ... so come along, my darlink poppet."

They saw a curly-headed blonde walk out of the villa to the poolside. She was around 5' 9" with a smallish bust and a lovely bottom, enhanced by a skin-tight white bikini. She was wearing high heels, which stretched her thighs into pillars of satin-white milk-chocolate. She strode over to a sun-bed, carrying a small tube of cream, then flicked her top off.

She sat on the sun-bed and applied the cream to her shoulders and round her pert breasts, starting to massage a nipple between thumb and finger. Her other hand slid over her stomach and down between her legs as she started to moan with pleasure.

"Hurry up poppet, my back will burn soon," she called out over her shoulder towards the villa, looking flushed now.

"I'll be with you shortly, my darling, but I must finish this paper to send to America first. You know my rule, business before pleasure." The reply was shouted from within. She mouthed the words he was saying to herself.

Increasing the amount of cream, she applied it angrily, pouting and muttering about being neglected by all ze rotten men she had ever met in her life.

To his embarrassment Steve got an erection, which amused the other two into making ribald comments on his manhood.

"Never mind playing with yourself and don't even think of her, 'cos she'd chew you up and spit you out in a ball of feathers. Helga is too much for you to handle ... and me I think," British advised Steve with a smile. "But as long as she stays there, we are in the shit and no mistake, and it's a long time 'til it gets dark," he said grimly, looking at his watch.

Helga suddenly got up, looking very annoyed and stamped off out of sight into the villa, breasts jerking up and down, nipples erect and ready for action, the cream making them glisten like silk.

They heard her shout and a reply was shouted back which was followed by the sound of a slamming door.

"Come on," British urged them, "it's now or never and for fuck's sake don't fall ... I hate paper work." They ran across to the wall and were just heaving themselves over when Aziz turned, ran over to the sun-bed, picked up her white top and stuffed it in his knife-belt. He then raced back and swung over the wall, grinning profusely.

"You mad sod!" exclaimed British. Aziz laughed as he waved his one free hand in the air.

"Aziz like very much." He took the top out of his belt and holding it to his mouth, he kissed it, then placed it back in his beltsaying, "Come ... we go damn quick," and they started their descent.

They arrived back at the cliff base without mishap and recovered their belongings from under the rocks.

"We are going back to Villajoyosa now, Aziz" explained British. "I will get in touch with you later with the 'Golden Eagle', if that's okay with you, my friend?"

British put his arm across Aziz's shoulder. Aziz nodded. "Si, Señor, Aziz very happy to work with you." He paused, "Even if no kill." He drew his finger across his throat from ear to the ear. "Buenos dias." He waved the white top in the air, then silently disappeared into the grove of trees from whence he had arrived earlier.

"Great guy, that Aziz." British watched him go, sounding full of admiration for his killer colleague. "I watched him kill a guard dog from 10 yards and, as the dog's handler bent over to examine it, finish him off as well, with two of the quickest knife throws I've ever seen. Not a man to make an enemy of, he's an animal really, but his sort are necessary to our work," he added as he saw Steve's incredulous stare on hearing this tale of death.

"Colonel Guntripp never mentioned anything like this to me," Steve said, in quiet protest to British.

"I agree with you," British said. "I reckon you were sent because nobody in our business knew you and that is why you were not trained ... to keep it that way. You were sent solely as a courier for this tape." He held the tape up to make his point. "And you were sent in via Valencia, instead of Alicante to keep you clean .... Pity about the Diplomatic Pouch though. I'll have to give that some thought later, so climb aboard I'm gasping for a drink." He looked at his watch. "Not bad timing either, we can get really pissed before the sun goes down." He laughed as he switched the scooter into life and the pair of them rode off, completely unaware that, up at the villa, Kai was sweeping the area with a pair of binoculars, mainly to keep a discreet distance from his employer, who was in the process of losing a lot of calories, with Helga astride him, riding him savagely, like a horse, demanding him to keep going until she came.

Kai was suddenly alerted by a scooter emerging from the grove down below with two riders on it. He focused in as much as he could and watched them ride round the various bends until they were out of sight.

He put the binoculars down and wondered what these two men had been doing, hidden down there. He decided to go down and have a look around, just as a matter of routine.

He entered the villa just as Helga was shouting, "Yes, yes, yes ... oh, fuck me, fuck me."

He walked silently to the Mercedes in the drive and triggering the remote gate control, glided the car out and down the winding track to the road. Turning left at the bottom he drove to the spot where he had seen the scooter emerge. He parked up and slowly walked into the grove, following the tyre tracks of the scooter, until he located the place where the riders had been parked. He saw now that three people had met there and he followed their trail through the small trees until it finished at the cliff face, underneath the villa.

Kai looked up at the cliff for a few minutes, then decided that he would check whether it was possible to climb it all the way to the villa. He climbed steadily, not noticing the searing heat in his concentration of looking for hand and foot holds, plus signs of any person having been there recently.

He reached the base of the villa wall and traversed slowly along until he found a small piece of cloth, clinging to the top of the wall.

He picked it off carefully and saw that there was blood on it and on the wall underneath. He put the cloth in his pocket and pulled himself up over the top of the wall. He was very angry with himself for failing to realise that his security checks of the premises had not taken into account the fact that anyone would be able to climb the cliff.

Helga, standing by the sun-bed was startled to see him suddenly appear. She was wrapped in a bath towel. "Zis is dangerous, no?" she gasped, "ze climbing could be kapput for you." She walked over and looked down. "Crazy loco."

Kai shrugged, not wanting to reveal the error of his security. "And," she went on, "have you seen my white sun-top? I'm sure I left it on here." She looked under the sun-bed as Kai shook his head. "Oh well never mind, it's most likely been blown away. My own stupid fault."

Kai left her settling down on the sun-bed and went to find Lord Stuart in the villa.

"Come in, Kai," Lord Stuart was relaxing on the bed reading a document. "Got a problem, then?" he asked as he saw the look on Kai's face.

"This sir." Kai threw the piece of blood-stained cloth on the bed alongside Lord Stuart, who picked it up showing distaste, that this had been put on his silk sheets.

"What is it eh?"

"I've just found it on the top of the wall over by the pool sir ... it wasn't there this morning."

Lord Stuart sat up abruptly. "What are ye' saying man?" He always went into Scottish dialect when he was upset. "Spit it oot now man."

"I believe someone has climbed the cliff this morning, possibly three men, sir. I saw two men ride away on a scooter towards Villajoyosa about ...," he looked at his watch, "forty minutes ago, sir, from beneath the cliff."

"Jeesus Christ man, Lord Stuart exploded, "I canna do everything m'self ... I employ ye to take care of me and the situation I'm in, so go and find the wee sassenachs and dispose of them, but only after you've gleaned the information they've gathered. So gang' with ye and put the job right." He waved his arm in dismissal and returned to his reading.

Kai left the room bristling with anger, his professional judgement had been questioned and he wanted blood.

CHAPTER 6
The Hunt

"Hello Mr. York," Eileen greeted Steve with a warm smile as he walked into the hotel reception. "I hope you had a nice time with Mr. Steele. You've certainly caught the sun," she added, noticing his face glowing red. "I'll bring you some cream for your face, otherwise you'll burn ... and," she added, looking over the counter, "I'd better bring some bandages for your leg."

Steve became aware that she was now looking at the green bag he was carrying. "I hope you've bought something nice?" she asked, looking him straight in the eye.

"Oh ... it's only something for my mother," he answered. Then quickly he added,"Don't I look at sight?"

Steve had looked across at himself in the large mirror by the counter and saw how rough he looked, with the bandanna still tied round his leg and with the healthy colour he now had, he looked like a vagrant.

"Thank you Eileen, I think the cream and bandages would be a good idea ... I'll go and have a shower first." He picked his room key up, then added, "No peeping this time." He laughed wagging an admonishing finger at her.

She smiled wickedly at him, "Spoil sport." She tucked her blouse tighter into her skirt, enhancing the outline of her breasts and cleavage. "I'll bring the cream and bandages in half an hour. Buenos tardes, Señor York."

Steve had now come down off the high state of adrenalin and became aware of pain in his leg, for the first time since he was pulled over the wall so unceremoniously by his two colleagues five hours ago. He limped off to his room watched by a smiling Eileen.

He entered his room and saw that a message had been slipped under his door. He walked in and threw his gun bag on the bed and read the paper. It simply said 'phone home.' There was no signature so he was confused. His mother did not know where he was, so he reasoned it must be from Colonel Guntripp. But what did it mean? Steve got undressed while he thought about this development, carefully untying the bandanna, which by now had stuck firmly to his leg. He ripped it off in one swift pull, wincing as he did so and the blood started to trickle down his leg again. He had his shower, then wrapping a towel round his waist and a clean handkerchief on his leg wound, decided to ring his mother.

"Hello Eileen, I want to 'phone my mother to make sure she's all right. Can you get me this number please?" He read out his 'phone number to her.

"I'll ring you back when there's a connection, Mr. York," she answered, then said, "I wondered who the message was for." She paused then added, "It came from London."

"I'm only guessing myself," he confided to her. "I just hope nothing serious has happened, like the dog dying, or the window cleaner hasn't been." He laughed nervously.

The 'phone rang after a couple of minutes. He picked it up.

"Your call sir," Eileen informed him briskly.

"Hello ... mother, it's Steve, what's happened? Are you all right?" he asked anxiously.

"Hello son," his mother replied, "I'm all right, but your friend Fred, from the office came round with some bad news so I thought you should know as soon as possible. I didn't know how to contact you, so it's lucky you rang me, son." She sounded upset.

Steve realised that the message must have come from the Colonel and his heart raced as he waited for news. It must be something very important for contact to be made.

"Well," his mother started, "that Sandy from your office came round and took your car to clean, or something. ... He told me he had permission," she added, as Steve groaned down the 'phone, "anyway, he's dead."

"What?" Steve gasped incredulously.

"Yes son ... he was shot." His mother burst into tears as she said it.

"Shot?"

"Yes," she wept, "the police think it was case of mistaken identity, and that it was you someone was trying to shoot. Oh son,"she wailed, "what have you got yourself into now?... Please come home," she pleaded with him. "I feel so nervous on my own," she said, stopping crying.

Steve was in a state of shock and tried to think clearly before answering his distraught mother.

"Now don't worry mother." He tried to placate her. "I should be home in a couple of days at the most ... just keep calm and keep Buster with you at all times okay? ... Have the police been round?" he asked tentatively.

"They certainly have son and I don't think they were too happy that I could not tell them where you were," she added. "In fact they were down-right rude about it ... and," she lowered her voice, "I think someone is watching the house, so please come home, I'm frightened son." She started to cry again.

"Don't cry mother," Steve implored her. "As I told you I

should be home in a couple of days ….. Have the police got anyone for the shooting?"

"No. I don't think so," she snuffled back.

"Right. I'll give Fred a ring, I'll ask him to come over and stay with you okay?" he asked with tenderness, feeling very protective of her and showing love for his mother.

"Thank you son." She sounded grateful.

"Chin up, and keep smiling, this will all be sorted out when I get home," he assured her but not reassuring himself.

He put the 'phone down and went and poured himself a large brandy which he downed in one gulp. The fire water hit him as it coursed its way down, bringing tears to his eyes as he tasted the subtle fierceness that his first Spanish brandy gave. He poured himself another and lay down on the bed, thinking about the demise of poor old Sandy.

'*Well*' he thought '*it could be worse, it could have been me.*'

He decided that he must get in touch with the Colonel, to see if he knew who was involved and how had they found out about Steve's involvement with the Department so soon; whoever 'they' were.

He picked up the 'phone and dialled reception. Eileen answered him and he gave her his office number to ring.

"Have you had your shower now, Señor?" she murmured.

"Yes," he answered. "All done and dusted and well into my second brandy," he informed her.

"Don't get drunk yet, Señor, I have to bandage your leg and put cream on your sunburn," she reminded him. "I'll get your number now, please replace your receiver."

The 'phone rang. "It's ringing for you," Eileen advised him.

"Hello," said a nervous-sounding voice. Steve recognised that it was Morris.

"Hello Morris, Steve Manly here ... what are you doing answering the 'phone?" Steve queried.

"Hi Steve," Morris answered brightly. "I'm answering the

'phone because everyone has gone home ... It's just gone six o'clock here," he reminded Steve.

"Oh Christ! Sorry Morris ... but is Fred still there?" he asked hopefully.

"Yes, he's playing snooker, I'll go and get him for you ... Terrible about Sandy isn't it?" Morris queried.

"Bloody awful," Steve agreed. "That's what I want to talk to Fred about, so jump to it my friend," Steve ordered him and heard Morris walking away to summon Fred.

He heard Fred returning with Morris.

"Hello Steve, nice to hear you, you old bastard, where are you?" Fred asked.

"I'm still in Spain and a good job I came here by the sound of it, eh?" Steve answered truthfully. "I'm ringing to ask you a favour mate."

"Oh ... yes," Fred sounded cautious.

"My mother is in a bit of a spin over this accident."

"Accident!" Fred protested. "Accident! He had his bloody head blown off, some accident!" he said vehemently. "And by the look of it, it was you who was the target, anyway."

"Calm down, matey, all I want you to do is go round to see my mother, she thinks someone is watching our house. Can you go and put her mind at rest for me?" Steve asked.

"When are you home?" countered Fred defensively.

"In about two days ... not long eh?" Steve answered as the door to his room slowly opened and Eileen tiptoed in, carrying a tray of bandages and cream etc. She put her finger to her lips and joined Steve on the bed, after placing the tray on the table.

"Yes, I can do that, no problem," Fred answered, much to Steve's relief. "I'll go round straight away."

Eileen leaned across and started to nibble Steve' s ear and her right hand rubbed across his towel, causing Steve to catch his breath as he replied to Fred, "Thank's Fred, I owe you one."

He gave a gasp as Eileen's hand slid under his towel and caressed his balls, then her fingers wrapped round his rapidly expanding cock and squeezed gently, while pumping slowly up and down.

"You got someone with you?" Fred queried as Steve's voice changed a note or two.

"No," Steve lied, "I've just had a mouthful of Spanish brandy, it fair takes your breath away ... I'll bring some back for you."

He gasped the last word as Eileen started to lick the end of his cock, then she smiled up at him and slowly wrapped her mouth round it and started sucking him.

"You lying bugger," Fred retorted, "you're at it now, you randy sod ... make sure you don't catch anything, that's all, otherwise Gloria will have your guts for garters." He rang off abruptly. Eileen stopped sucking and looked up at him.

"Who's Gloria?" she asked. "Do you want to ring her now?" she laughed, playing with his rampant cock.

"She's just a fellow worker in my office," he answered, lying back to enjoy this unexpected massage.

Eileen suddenly became serious, letting go of his cock she lay alongside of him and whispered in his ear. "How did it go today? Guntripp wants to know ... Steve," she added, to show she knew who he was.

"Brilliant day, actually," he answered and closed his hand over her right breast, stroking it round and round.

"We have got a recording of the meeting today that Lord Stuart McForson had with his financial adviser from America ... well, British has it at the moment," he added.

"Marvellous," Eileen breathed as she undid the buttons on her blouse. "I must take this off otherwise it will get creased and that would never do," she purred as she removed her blouse, revealing a black, silky bra that pushed her breasts together, making a wonderful cleavage. She folded her blouse neatly and placed it onto the bedside table.

Steve watched breathless as she took her skirt off revealing a tiny black pair of panties with lace edges that matched her bra. She stood with her hands on her hips, legs apart, showing little wisps of pubic hair peeping out of her crotch.

Steve reached forward to feel her but she brushed his hand to one side. "Not yet," she teased him, "I've got to play nurse, just look at your leg."

"Which one needs the most attention, nurse?" Steve joked as she went to get the tray. He watched as she bent over, her panties stretched tightly over her bottom, showing the cleft of her womanhood. She turned, smiling, with a bottle of iodine in her hand.

"I hope we're not going to hurt each other," Steve gasped as she applied the iodine swab on his leg.

"You men," she exclaimed, "you're all babies underneath."

Steve winced as the iodine stung his leg, his erection going down as fast as it had come up. She was obviously an expert at first-aid and soon had his wound cleaned and bandaged.

"There," she said triumphantly, "that wasn't so bad was it? ... Now we better put some cream on that face of yours."

"I'd like to put some cream on your face," Steve replied holding his cock suggestively.

"Put it down," she answered, "cheeky boy." She reached for the cream and applied it slowly and tenderly, saying as she did so, "This may peel in a few days, but you'll be all right."

Steve started to rub his hand hard between her legs, his erection returning with a vengeance.

"Gently now," she advised him, getting hold of his hand to slow him down. "I don't want to get sore ... not yet, we've plenty of time."

There was a loud authoritative knock at the door. Eileen shot off the bed, gathered her skirt and blouse and rushed into the bathroom, waving to Steve not to let on she was there.

Steve adjusted his towel and went to the door.

"Yes ... who is it?" he asked, snapping at the closed door.

"British."

Steve opened the door quickly and British stepped inside

looking rather flushed.

"Sorry to disturb you ... Matthew," he said looking carefully around, "but I have to sort a problem out right away." He walked over to the bathroom, hesitated momentarily then opened the door on an embarrassed Eileen.

"Thank goodness, it's you Eileen," British smiled. "Now you can stay and hear what I have to say to Steve, come and join us when you've got dressed." He closed the door.

"What the hell's the matter, British?" Steve queried.

"Kai, is what the matter is, he's in town and what's more I saw him examining my scooter very closely. Damnit," British punched a fist into his other hand. "I think he must have seen us on the scooter and followed us into town."

"Does he know who owns the scooter?" Steve asked.

"It won't take him long to find out I own it," British said grimly. "I'm quite a well-known figure here. I was stupid to ride it so close to the villa today, I must be getting old, not thinking of that." He sat down exhausted.

Eileen joined them from the bathroom having recovered her composure again, and fully dressed, sat on the end of the bed, attentively.

"Don't blame yourself, British," Steve replied. "You had me to look after too much to think straight ... but what should we do now?"

British turned to Eileen saying, "Will you look after the tape for now until this is sorted?" He pulled the tape from his pocket and handed it to her.

"Certainly," she replied calmly, putting it on the tray under the bandages. "I'll put it in the hotel safe, in the petty cash tin. I'm the only one with a key for it so it will be there until you need it."

"Good," replied British. "That's one problem solved but," he went on, "he will find out that you have been with me, Steve, so we have to assume that he will find out that you are staying here and come looking for you." He went over to the window and surveyed the court-yard.

"Should I check out then, British?" Steve enquired looking across at Eileen for support.

"No! We'll stay and face him here. I'll contact Aziz to get his arse over here, pronto." British stood up, said, "Adios" and left the room.

Steve looked at Eileen with deep concern. "Christ, this is good eh? We're in deep trouble now, I've see this Kai, he carries two guns, that we know of," he explained to her.

"Well," she said, "you had better get your mother's present out ready to greet him, hadn't you?" She laughed nervously at Steve's reaction to her suggestion.

"You know about that?" he asked resignedly.

"Sure, you didn't hide it too well when you came in, but the main thing is," she asked him, "can you use it?"

"I fired it a few times on the beach this morning," he answered truthfully, fetching the gun-bag and opening it for her to see. She took it out and examined the gun carefully. "Aah, a Smith and Wesson," she said, turning the gun over. "Why isn't it loaded?" she asked him.

"British made me unload it when we returned on the scooter," he informed her whilst looking in the bag for some ammunition.

She took the bag from him and extracted the clips of ammunition and loaded his gun for him. She snapped the safety catch on and passed it back to him.

"Don't forget to take the safety catch off if you have to fire," she instructed him. "And there are fourteen bullets in the magazine, so that should be enough to leave at least one of you lot dead," she said, handing him the gun.

"I'd better get dressed," Steve said walking over to the hanging clothes. "Mustn't be caught with my trousers down."

"What a waste," Eileen sighed as she watched him slip into his trousers, he tucked his gun into the waist-band.

She became serious again. "Now then we will have to have

a code between us should this Kai arrive in reception. Do you have any ideas?" she asked Steve, who could only shake his head negatively.

"You really are a baby in this line of work, aren't you?" Eileen remarked sympathetically. "Right, try this then. If he comes asking for you I'll tell him that you are in Room 68, next door and ring the 'phone once, got that?" Steve nodded in agreement. "Then it's up to you. But if I am under any duress, such as having a gun at my head, I will lead him to this door and say, 'room service'. He may make me say something else, but no matter, the thing is, the minute you hear my voice, you will know he is with me, understand?" she asked him, taking hold of his arm to make her point.

"What will you do, how will you escape?" asked a numbed Steve, pulling her to him in a protective manner.

"I do not know," she said slowly. "I may be killed, but whatever you do, kill him," she added vehemently. "I do not wish to die for nothing ... so kiss me, at least." She looked into his eyes passionately and their lips met, tingling with unseen little pulses, sending their nerve ends racing with desire and lust for each other. They broke from each other to draw breath. "Just my luck," Eileen whispered to Steve, "not to have you before I might die. Fancy me cradle-snatching at my age and I couldn't care less." She giggled, holding Steve tightly to her bosom.

"You're some woman, Eileen," Steve replied. "I've never met a woman who was prepared to die for her country," he said, cradling her face in his hands.

"Well we've all got to go sometime, one way or another, and at least my children will benefit if I die in Service."

"Children?"

"Oh yes," she explained. "I have three, all grown up now though, my husband was killed in Aden in 1964 ... that's ten years ago now," she said wistfully, twisting a lock of her hair in her fingers. "I was a normal housewife then ... how times and things change." Her voice trailed away.

Steve kissed her lightly on the forehead and walked to the door with her.

"Let's hope we can make love, manana," she said and walked away without a backward glance. Steve watched her go, full of admiration for this woman who was old enough to be his mother, yet so full of living and loving. He'd do his best to keep them both alive.

He checked his gun again, then finished off the second brandy that he felt he needed for Dutch courage.

His 'phone suddenly rang. He went rigid with fear, until it rang again. He picked it up and Aziz answered him with, "Buenos tardes, Señor, it is I, Aziz, most famous knife thrower in the world. Señor British has told me of our problem, no problem, I take care of heem." Steve could picture the finger going across the throat, "Yes?"

"I wish I had your confidence, Aziz, but I'm shit scared I don't mind telling you," Steve admitted to him.

"Do not worry, Señor, Aziz take care of you," he snorted with a fierce pride of his abilities to kill. "I go on roof above your head, then swing down like a leopard on his back, he not know what happen to him, he die quick." Aziz laughed crazily then rang off, leaving Steve to sweat it out for a while.

He heard a rustling noise outside his window, his heart pounded so loudly, he hoped no-one could hear it as he crept into the bathroom and slowly, ever so slowly, eased the blind back, his gun in front of his nose.

The elderly gardener was watering the hanging flower displays, unaware that a gun was trained on his head and a very itchy finger on the trigger.

Steve eased the safety catch back on, cursing the fact that because he had been given a secluded room he had forgotten that there were hotel staff going around doing their duties, as well as Eileen. He hoped none of them got in the way if any action started.

Over his head Aziz looked down, knife firmly grasped in his teeth, disappointed to see only the old gardener.

An hour went by and Steve was on his fourth brandy, now feeling completely fearless, muttering to himself 'come on you bastardo, I'm waiting to give you a nice shoot up the bum.' He giggled drunkenly to himself, flicking the safety catch off, 'there, I'm tooled up ready to blast you to hell, you swine' and with that he fell into a deep sleep.

"Señor, Señor, wake up!" He felt someone shaking his arm and woke with a start, clutching for a gun that was not there.

"Señor, I have your gun." Aziz held up Steve's weapon in front of his face. "I no wake you while gun in your hand Señor ... Aziz wish to live longer." He laughed at the look on Steve's face.

"What's happened?" he asked shakily.

"Kai, he go back to villa, no want to meet with Aziz, greatest knife thrower in ..."

"Yes, yes," Steve interrupted him in full flow. "Where's British gone now?"

"Señor British follow him to make sure he goes back to villa, come we go now, pack clothes."

"Why? Where're we going?" asked a surprised Steve.

"Aziz take you to Valencia, with tape, then Aziz get pesetas for drink damn soon off Señor British, okay?"

Steve jumped up relieved to hear he was returning home.

"Why has Kai gone back to the villa? I don't understand it, Aziz."

"Señor Kai was recalled on car radio by killer of music." Aziz pretended to play the bagpipes.

"Oh I see," Steve said. "Lord Stuart called him back, I wonder why?"

"Villa on fire," Aziz replied.

"On fire?" Steve queried him.

"Yes, I think Señor British did what you English call a divert and dropped a match in the villa garden," Aziz explained as the penny dropped for Steve.

"I see," repeated Steve, "he went and set fire to the garden, to cause a diversion, so that Kai would be recalled to deal with it ... brilliant thinking, eh?" he said to Aziz.

"No kill Señor," said a disappointed Aziz, patting his knives affectionately.

"Never mind, let's go and get the tape from Eileen. The sooner the better."

Steve packed his few things as fast as he could, then suddenly remembered his gun. What should he do with it? He tucked it in his waist band and they walked in silence to the reception desk. Eileen was nowhere to be seen and in her place was a very smart young lady who inclined her head to him and asked, "Can I help you, señor?"

"Where is the Señora Eileen?"

"She left a message for you to go to her quarters ... here is her key, Señor." She handed him the key to the penthouse. "You go up those stairs, Señor, all the way to the top, her apartment will be in front of you."

Aziz looked at Steve and said, "Jiggy-jig," smiling at him.

"Jiggy-jig, be buggered, Aziz. I want to get this over and done with ... off you go." He handed the key to Aziz, who raced off as fast as he could. He returned, breathing heavily within five minutes and handed Steve a black leather pouch bearing the gold portcullis crest on it.

"She was not there Señor, just this bag and a note for you." He handed Steve a note that was written in fine copper-plate writing.

"I am sorry I cannot say good-bye, but we will meet again I'm sure. Precipice is in the pouch, so put your gun and bullets in with it also, then you will be safe."

There was no signature. Steve put the paper in his pocket and opened the pouch and saw the tape was there. He handed both keys into the receptionist and left the hotel with Aziz, wondering where she had gone to so suddenly and why.

His thoughts were rudely interrupted as they stepped onto the pavement as Jaime stepped forward, grinning from ear to ear. "Jaime drive you," he announced proudly and promptly went to grab Steve's travelling bag. Steve looked questioningly at Aziz while hanging grimly onto his bag. Aziz positively beamed at Jaime before turning to Steve and informing him, to Steve's dismay, that Jaime was his cousin and they were making lots of pesetas together.

"I waited for your Señor, like you say, no problem."

Steve was amazed when he realised that Jaime had stayed waiting all day and night for him, as instructed by Steve, who had forgotten all about him, to his shame, in the excitement of the job he had been doing.

Steve walked reluctantly to the battered wreck that just passed as a car and climbed in. He wound the window down and the handle came off in his hand. Jaime laughed and punched the handle back on. "No problem."

Jaime walked round and got in as Aziz put his hand through the window and shook Steve's hand warmly. "It has been very good to work with you, Señor and Señor British send he regret he no here to say adios, okay?" He withdrew his hand quickly as the car burst into life with a deep roar and shuddering violently, set off to Valencia, throwing Steve back into his seat as Aziz vanished in the cloud of smoke and dust that spurted from the spinning wheels of Jaime's death-trap. This heralded another murderous drive with Steve clinging on for grim death, but happy to be returning home with a successful mission, albeit lucky, under his belt.

He opened his case and retrieved his gun-bag, opened it, took his gun out of his belt, unloaded it and placed it in the black pouch with the tape. He settled back to endure the rest of the hell ride.

They arrived at Valencia at 10.00 p.m. and Steve said good-bye to a happy Jaime, giving him all the pesetas he had left.

"Adios, Señor, hasta pronto," Jaime grinned, whilst checking the money he'd been given. He held a dirty hand out saying, "Señor return, see Jaime soon, si?"

"Not if I see you first you won't," Steve joked. "Hell will freeze over before then," Steve added as he slowly got his breath back.

Jaime made his exit saying to himself 'English joke, very funny, no,' and left amid screaming tyres and a cloud of burning rubber.

Steve stood and watched him go, then shaking his head, he tucked the pouch under his arm, picked up his bag and turned into the departure area.

"Over here, Mr. York," he heard his name called above the general hubbub of noise. He turned and saw Eileen beckoning to him across the concourse and he walked over and joined her. She held a plastic bag.

"I had to come and make sure you could get a plane at such short notice," she explained, giving him a little kiss on the cheek. "So we are to go to the cargo bays on this luggage truck." She pointed to a truck standing by reception, with a bored-looking driver, waiting for them.

Sitting on the truck, with his leg in plaster, was the courier who had been knocked down when Steve had arrived in Valencia, in what seemed days ago now.

"Wotcha, mate," the courier exclaimed, cheerily waving a cigar at him. "Got yer duty free's eh?" he asked patting a large bag which was alongside the briefcase handcuffed to his wrist.

Steve shook his head negatively.

"Blimey, you are new to this, ain't yer." He drew on his cigar. "This bloody leg ain't 'alf itchin', " he complained looking down at the offending leg. He went on "I'm having this off as soon as we get back to Blighty ... not the leg, ... the plaster." He laughed. "Get some English plaster on it ... I mean you never bleedin' know what these foreigners do to you eh?" He smiled as he made his point.

"This bag is your duty frees." Eileen passed the bag she was holding to Steve. "It's expected of all couriers," she whispered to him. "I won't come any further now you have a companion who obviously knows the system, adios." She pecked him on the cheek again and left him, as she walked gracefully across the concourse.

'Thanks Eileen' Steve said to himself as he climbed onto the truck behind the friendly courier.

"Girlfriend already," the courier exclaimed. "You're a quick worker ... and I see she got you a bag of goodies as well," he chortled. Can't be bad eh?" He leaned over to Steve. "The nickname's Honky, on account of the way I play the piano." He laughed and ran his fingers through the air as if playing an imaginary piano.

"The name's Matthew," Steve offered to a smiling Honky. "Pleased to meet you again ... I hope the leg is not too painful," he asked politely.

"Na ... my own silly fault mate," he laughed. "She was too fast for me, but ..., " he lowered his voice as the truck driver started to drive them off to the cargo bay, "she made it up to me y'know, came to the hospital yesterday to make sure I was all right . And I tell you what," he grinned, "It's bloody difficult to get a leg over when it's in plaster ... good job she was the athletic type. But the nurse wasn't very happy when we broke the leg support ... Christ, the pain and the pleasure, all at the same time, unbelievable mate, best physiotherapy one could have." He was still relaying the tale as they boarded the plane after a brief passport examination, by the same two officials who had checked them through two days earlier. They gave his black pouch only a cursory glance much to Steve's relief.

He settled back in his seat and was looking through his duty free bag when he heard Honky talking heatedly to an RAF officer further along the aisle. There seemed to be a crisis of some sort and Steve saw Honky wave his arms around then limp back up the aisle towards him.

"What's up?" he asked a red-faced Honky.

"No flights allowed out for twenty-four bleedin' hours ... can you credit it?" Honky slumped down into his seat, stretching his injured leg out down the aisle. "We're stuck on this bird for a day ... oh, sod it, let's get a bottle out and get pissed ... might as well eh?" He reached into his bag for a bottle suddenly looking a lot happier with life.

Their hangovers were just throbbing nicely when the plane roared into life and departed for Northolt, as predicted, just twenty-fours hours behind schedule.

CHAPTER 7
The Ryder Club

The dark blue Rolls Royce was waiting for him at Northolt.

"Cheerio Honky ... see you sometime." Steve shook hands with Honky. "Don't do anything I wouldn't do and if you do; be careful," he added with a wink.

"Blimey mate, you got a Roller?" exclaimed the astonished Honky as he saw the car standing on the runway. "We only get a black van." He nodded across at a funereal looking van waiting in the shadows of the Control Tower.

Steve watched Honky limp off and smiled to himself as he noticed that the limp became more exaggerated as Honky approached the black van, getting ready to tell his tale.

"Hello Mr. Manly." Henry had approached Steve whilst he watched Honky leaving. "Better late than never."

Steve was pleased to see Henry as he had been wondering what would happen when he landed. "Nice to see you Henry," he said as he handed his bag over, but kept the black pouch firmly under his arm. "A day sat on a sodding plane, bastardos. ... Where are we going?" he asked tentatively.

"Ryder Street, sir." Henry opened the car door. "But if you," he looked at his watch, "want breakfast, I can take you to your flat first if you require me to."

"My flat?" asked Steve as he climbed into the back of the

car, "What flat?"

"You have been given a flat because it would seem that the Colonel is well pleased with the operation results," Henry replied, starting up the car.

"Under my own name?" queried Steve.

"Oh yes ... your cover is no longer required, passport kapput," Henry informed him as they glided past the guard standing to attention, by the security gate.

"Will I be able to keep it as a memento, do you think?"

"Not for me to say ... but there's no harm in asking," came the answer. Steve was thinking ahead of when he might be able to return to Spain and liaison with Eileen.

They were travelling towards London as dawn was breaking, the sun peeping up over the horizon ahead of them.

Steve decided that he would like to see his flat and have some breakfast at the same time and was asking Henry to take him there when the car 'phone rang in front of him. He picked it up cautiously.

"Hello."

"Manly ... nice to hear you've got back, eventually," he heard the Colonel's voice, "and what a bloody awful time to arrive, it's before sparrow fart, don't y'know ... where are you now?" The brisk question was fired at him.

Steve put his hand over the mouthpiece to consult Henry.

"He wants to know where we are Henry."

"Tell him we are just approaching the Hanger Lane junction," Henry informed Steve.

"We're just approaching the Hanger Lane junction."

Steve passed the information on. "On our way to my flat for some breakfast, Colonel."

"Have breakfast! ... Have breakfast!" the Colonel exploded. "You get your arse down here to the Club, I want that tape as soon as possible, the Country's security depends on it ... and you want bloody breakfast!!" He rang off abruptly, leaving Steve feeling angry with himself, for forgetting the seriousness of the mission he'd been on.

"Forget the flat, Henry. Take me to the Colonel instead."

"Certainly ... was he upset?"

"Yes, and rightly so. I'm not used to this sort of life yet," he paused. "I'm not used to these hours of work. It's all so new to me, Henry, how do you cope?"

Henry swerved to miss a pedestrian running across the road.

"Stupid sod!" he rebuked the unknown runner. "He might have damaged the car if I'd hit him," he explained to Steve, who was resettling into his seat after the violent manoeuvre. "You'll get used to it after a couple of weeks," he said. "In fact, this job takes over your whole life so don't arrange any social activities, because you will let people down as the work demands." He hesitated then said, "Women simply don't understand this job at all and we cannot tell them what our work is, so my advice is don't have a serious relationship, because you won't have a cat in hell's chance of it working."

Steve sat thinking about Henry's statement. He felt high still on adrenalin and happy with all he'd done so far. No one would ever believe that, he, Steve Manly, was helping to keep the Country on its democratic course. He unzipped the pouch to make sure the tape was still there, then sat and watched as they swished through the outskirts of London, for the first time.

Henry dropped down through Shepherd's Bush, then to Knightsbridge, during which Steve saw the Albert Hall and a close up of Harrods, due to the build-up of traffic.

"How far now, Henry?"

"About ten minutes ... as the crow flies ... sometimes an hour." Henry added, "You can never tell with London traffic."

They turned down past Fortnum & Mason into King Street, then right at Bury Street and right into Ryder Street.

They pulled up outside a dark, red-brick building with a

stone porch on which was a cartouche inscribed 'The Ryder Club.'

Steve got out while Henry rang the door bell and after a minute the door entry 'phone crackled into life.

"Push the door, gentlemen, you are expected," came the instruction from the disembodied voice.

Henry led the way into the club reception area and they were met by the night porter.

"Good morning, gentlemen, may I take your bag sir?" He took the bag off Henry. "I'll put it here behind the desk and give you an identity tag for it," and while he fumbled around, a huge cat, with his tongue hanging out, strolled up to Steve meowing loudly and rubbed against his leg.

"What's its name?" Steve asked as he stroked the cat, who promptly rolled over on its back, tongue still hanging out.

"That's the Club cat, Marmaduke, sir."

"Why's its tongue hanging out?" queried an amused Steve, still tickling the cat into ecstasy.

"His teeth went so rotten we were going to have him put to sleep, but the members had a collection and paid for a vet to remove his teeth ... he's happy enough, although he can never keep his tongue in ... gives the mice a nasty suck though." The porter chuckled at his observation, then giving Steve his bag tag said, "Come this way, sirs."

He led them up a grand marble stairway with mahogany hand rails and deep-pile red carpet. On the final few stairs, the stairway divided, left and right. A display cabinet was screwed to the wall containing a couple of snooker cues and a white cue ball. Steve stopped to read the small engraved inscription under the display which proclaimed that these had once belonged to the great snooker player, Joe Davies. There was a small sign alongside, informing that the snooker room was to the right.

They were taken up the final few stairs to the left and into a large lounge by a now, heavy breathing porter, who gasped,

"The Colonel is over in the far recess, gentlemen." He turned and made his way back to the stairway, wheezing and coughing, then muttering an oath as Marmaduke raced past him, causing him to clutch the handrail quickly.

They walked across the lounge, obviously the nub of the Club, containing numerous large, red, leather armchairs, with small, round coffee tables placed at discreet intervals. The windows were from floor to ceiling and flanked by plush, plum-coloured tableau curtains, held back by gold-braided ties. The room was surrounded with numerous portraits, showing past Club Presidents and to Steve's left he saw there was a very small annexe, the entrance to which was guarded by a magnificent array of golf and snooker trophies set in a sparkling glass cabinet. Steve later discovered that this was a small bar for the restaurant that occupied the furthest part of the lounge they were passing through.

A small brass plaque, on the wall by the cabinet, was in honour of a Club member, who had, single-handedly, saved the Club's supply of Havana cigars during a fire started by an incendiary bomb, during World War Two.

The far end of the room was a small, discreet restaurant, masked off by a display of small palm trees which were placed to hide the various secluded alcoves, making the appearance of warmer climes.

Steve was suddenly very aware that he was in the very heart of the tradition of Gentlemen's Clubs and although he felt tense, he was happy to be a part of this life.

They smelt the cigar smoke just before they saw the Colonel, who was sitting reading a paper. He got up as they approached and held his large hand out to crush Steve's.

"Welcome to the Club, Manly," he boomed. "I hope you'll like being a member because I have put your name forward to the committee. In my opinion, you will be an asset to the Club, to become a member ... a mere formality of course," he added grandly. "When I propose someone," he paused then said abruptly, "you're incorrectly dressed y'know ... where's your tie, for Christ's sake?" He stared at Steve's open-necked shirt, "and what's happened to your trousers?" The Colonel pointed to the torn trouser leg.

"Sorry, Colonel, but I didn't know I was going to be brought here, and," he added defensively, "I have only just landed from Spain and it was rather hot there, sir." He looked down at his trouser leg, "This was a result of action in Operation Precipice, which I may add, with all due respect Colonel, ... I did not know I was involved with, until I got there." He hesitated, then went on, "I thought I was only going to receive and bring back information for you and not be thrown in the deep end of a very hazardous operation which could have cost me my life ... sir." He emphasised the 'sir' strongly, cross at being told off.

The Colonel glared at him for a moment then his face broke into a wide smile. "Well said, young man, I deserved that little rebuke, but as it is only," he looked at the clock on the wall, "07.30 hours we can forget Club rules for a few minutes."

He glanced at the pouch under Steve's arm and went on, "We do not normally allow brief-cases and the like, in the Club, unless in our private rooms, but time is of the essence in this case, so let's have a look at what you've got." He held his hand out and Steve passed the pouch to him. The Colonel looked at it closely then said, "This is not the pouch issued to you, who gave you this?" he asked quietly, leaning forward to hear the reply, showing a degree of concern.

Steve explained what had happened, stumbling slightly, he relayed that his inexperience had led to the change.

"Ah," the Colonel sat back, relief on his face. "Eileen, what a woman. ... Since her husband died working for me, in Aden, she's been a superb field operative for us. What did you think of British?" he enquired, gently opening the pouch at the same time.

"Great guy," Steve replied. "He gave me a gun and a quick lesson on shooting. ... That gun actually," he added, as the Colonel withdrew the green velvet bag containing his gun.

"Not loaded, eh?" the Colonel asked putting the bag carefully to one side.

"No sir," Steve assured him calmly.

"And this is the tape? He held it up to show Steve.

"Yes sir, it contains all the conversation of a meeting that Lord McForson had in his villa, with an American financier called Martin Silverman, who used to be an adviser to President Nixon. He was," Steve went on, "booted out by President Ford, last month, after President Nixon resigned over Watergate."

"Great stuff," chortled the Colonel. "Did you manage to hear any of the conversation yourselves?" he enquired as he turned the tape over in his hand.

"No, we couldn't get near enough because his secretary ..." he was interrupted by a smiling Colonel.

"The lovely Helga?"

"That's right, Colonel ... you know her?" The smile on the Colonel's face answered the question without a word being spoken.

"Then there was his bodyguard, Kai, who kept prowling around ... so we had a hard enough time not being detected. ... We think Kai spotted us leaving the area afterwards, which led to a bit of a hairy time until British caused a diversion." Steve sat back, flushed with the memory of the last two days' action.

"Good," replied the Colonel. "That bears out what British reported to me this morning. He was pleased, by the way, with your contribution to this operation ... well done, Steve."

The Colonel leaned across and patted him on the arm.

Steve felt full of pride as he received this unexpected accolade from both of them. Henry also mouthed 'well done' across to him.

"Right, I shall go and listen to this tape while you clean

yourself up ..." He looked to Henry. "Henry you must go and get Steve a couple of suits and a couple of shirts and ties ... no forget the ties," he corrected himself, "I'll give him a couple of Club ties. Go to our usual tailor in Jermyn Street, as soon as the shops open, yes?" He put his hand inside his jacket. "Get him a couple of pair of decent shoes ... can't let the side down." He glanced at Steve. "You're costing the department a small fortune, but we'll soon have you up to scratch." He laughed and looked for confirmation from Henry, who nodded acceptance of his task. "Charge it to this account." The Colonel passed a card to Henry and Steve saw the gold portcullis crest on it.

"Give Henry your sizes before he goes ... oh, and by the way, I've booked you into the Club here, for the next couple of days until you settle down. Actually we are concerned that a former colleague of yours appears to have been killed in mistake for you, so we are moving your flat location, as a precaution, until we know how they got on to you. It's a mystery at the moment," he hesitated. "We'll find out soon enough. See you at lunch downstairs, we have a very nice restaurant ... this here," he waved his fat hands round to the palm trees, "is only a bistro don't y'know, sausage and mash jobby, I call 'em school dinners."

He laughed and stood up, putting the tape in his pocket. He bent down and picked the gun-bag up and handed it to Steve saying, "You might as well keep this as your official piece and I'll arrange some more lessons for you as soon as possible. We have a gun range under the Club y'know ... see you at 13.00 hours ... and you, Henry," and he was gone in a cloud of cigar smoke, leaving Steve and Henry sitting looking at each other, both happy the Boss was happy.

"It seems that you've had quite a show in Spain," commented Henry. "Well done, Steve and welcome to the side."

Steve was embarrassed by this and stood up saying, "I

only did what I was told and only nearly shit myself a couple of times." Henry replied that a man who is not scared at sometime in his life, is a real idiot. This statement was comforting to Steve and they made their way down the stairway to the reception.

"I want to have a look in the snooker room, Henry," Steve requested as they reached the small landing.

"Okay," Henry replied. "There are no lights on, so if you stay by the door I know where the switches are, hang on." Henry disappeared into the dark while Steve stood waiting. After a moment, there was a small curse as Henry bumped into an obstacle, followed by a triumphant "voila!" and the room was flooded in light. Steve saw that the room contained three large snooker tables, each with its own set of lights suspended above it. The tables were surrounded by small, cinema type chairs, raised up about a foot high to enable the occupants to have a clear view of the tables. Above the chairs were some large paintings, depicting various scenes of men enjoying themselves with drink and women. The pictures had all been painted, Steve was told by Henry, by a Club member, who was an artist of some repute.

"It's very grand for a snooker room," Steve remarked as he looked round.

"Oh yes," agreed Henry. "We have a professional marker as well ... you should see the money that's played for here, you wouldn't believe it ... they bet a hundred pound a point, making the black ball worth £700." Steve looked at him in astonishment and muttered, "By heck," shaking his head in wonderment at the revelation that anyone could have so much money and gamble it on snooker.

"That's not all," carried on Henry. "On the third floor we have a professional gambling club, with off-course bookies and direct lines to the race-courses ... I'll show you when you are accepted properly into the Club."

"You are a full member then?" Steve asked him.

"Yes, because although you thought I was a chauffeur when you first saw me…."

Steve interrupted him with, "Sorry about that, Henry, I'd no idea at the time."

Henry went on, "Well, in fact, I am a specially trained field officer in all the necessary arts of self-defence, driving and small arms firing. By the way what have you been given, then?" he asked inquisitively pointing to the bag.

"Smith and Wesson," Steve replied, opening the bag to show him. "What do you carry then?" he returned the question.

"Heckler Koch, 18 rounds of 9 mm, but I can convert it into a full-automatic submachine gun if I fit the shoulder stock on, giving me a rate of fire of 2,200 rounds per minute." Henry proudly patted the bulge on his left breast, "And it's mostly plastic … see." He pulled his gun out, just as the night porter, who was just going off duty, came into the room to see why the lights were on. He flung his hands in air and gave a strangulated cry of, "Don't shoot, don't shoot, I'm only an old-aged pensioner and I haven't seen a thing," he gasped.

"Put your hands down, you silly old sod, I'm only showing it to Mr. Manly," Henry explained hurriedly to the shaking old man, who slowly put his arms down and left the room hurling abuse over his shoulder. People had no right to do that to him. He'd fought in the first World War and he shouldn't be treated like this, and wait 'til the committee hear about what you buggers were doing with guns in the snooker room and incorrectly dressed with no tie on. The sound of his tirade grew quieter as he receded down the stairs.

"Oh bloody hell," Henry snapped, putting his gun back in his holster. "I'd better go and square up the old bastard before I get reported … come on Steve," he instructed an amused Steve, "otherwise I'll be barred for a month." He switched off the lights and they followed the porter down the stairs and were just in time to stop him relaying what had happened to the day-time commissionaire who had just come on duty for 08.00

hours.

"Now, my dear fellow," Henry put his arm around the still shaking porter, "I reckon you need a nice bottle of scotch to take home for your missus ... yes." He hugged the porter to him tightly, as if in friendship and the bulge of his gun dug hard into the porter's ribs.

"Yessir," the porter agreed immediately. "Thank you very much sir, she'll like that sir, she will indeed," he agreed, keeping his eyes averted from Henry's.

"Well then, take a bottle of whisky out of your night stock cupboard, there's a good chap and I will sign the bill, okay?"

The porter did as he was bid with a bemused commissionaire looking on. The porter produced a bottle and Henry signed for it, releasing the porter to leave, clutching the bottle to him like gold-dust.

"What a decent old boy," Steve exclaimed as he watched him go through the revolving swing doors that had just been opened for the day. "It was good of him not to take it further, eh?" he looked at Henry.

"Decent be buggered," muttered Henry in Steve's ear. "I just pressed my gun in his ribs to give him a little reminder that I would be upset if I was reported, " he said happily. "But it has cost me a bottle, so you owe me half, because it was your fault I took it out in the first place ... yes?" he looked at Steve enquiringly.

"Fair enough, but you'll have to wait 'til I get paid, I'm skint, I gave all my pesetas to a crazy Spaniard."

"Fair enough," agreed Henry. "Now give me all your sizes and I'll go and get your kit for survival in Gentlemen's Clubs ... I bet there were none in the one-horse town you come from." He laughed as Steve wrote down what sizes he required.

Steve passed him the paper and Henry gave a bow and left, leaving Steve getting his room key from the commissionaire.

"There you are sir, can you please sign the book." A book

was spun round on the desk for him to sign. Steve remembered the last time he signed a register, for Eileen and wouldn't do that stupid trick again, he thought to himself signing the book with a flourish he spun it back to the waiting commissionaire confidently.

"Thank you Mr. ... er ... York, I thought you were Mr. Manly, sir." The question came from a puzzled man.

"Oh sorry , I'll sign again ... I am Mr. Manly, I've just had a long conversation with a Mr. York in Spain," Steve lied to him, once again annoyed with himself for being so stupid.

He was passed the key to room 32 which he was informed was on the first floor and that he could use the lift which was located round the back of the stairway.

Steve handed in his bag-tag, retrieved his bag and walked to the lift, admiring this wonderful place, so full of history. He found the lift and whilst waiting, he saw that there was a small passage-way leading to a pair of impressive glass doors. He couldn't resist the temptation to have a peep through them, so he made his way up the passage-way to the doors. He pushed them open slowly and saw that this was yet another bar, with lots more small pictures around the room. His eyes were drawn to a magnificent gold clock which had a surround of feathered wings, topped by an Eagle's head with piercing black eyes, high on the wall above the bar. He suddenly realised that the clock was no ordinary clock, as the hour's figures were on the wrong side of the clock, which was indeed, going backwards. The scrolled wooden sign underneath it was inscribed 'The Eagle's Nest.'

'*Well that's different*,' he thought to himself and made his way to the lift which had arrived during the time he was in the bar. He got in and saw that the lift actually had a brass handle, like a tram, with which to select the floor required. There was a brass handrail underneath this handle. He turned the handle to 1, then pressed a green button that was alongside it. The result was startling, the lift acted almost like an ejector seat and he arrived at the first floor in two seconds flat, spread out on the floor like a stranded whale.

He then understood what the brass hand-rail was for. "Jesus Christ," he muttered to himself, struggling to his feet as the doors snapped open. He stepped out, glad that there was no one there to witness his undignified arrival. *'I wonder how the old boys of the Club manage to use this lift without getting put in hospital,'* he thought to himself as he arrived at the door to room 32.

The room was small, containing a single bed, one chair and a cracked wash-basin in the corner. There were a couple of old threadbare towels laid on the bed with a small piece of soap placed on top of them. He put his bag in the tiny, single wardrobe and read all the information notices regarding fire precautions and do's and don'ts, that were pinned to it.

He looked in vain for a telephone, to give his mother a ring before she stuck pins in his photograph for not ringing home.

He was told later that telephones were not put in on purpose in order to keep the room costs down, for the mainly retired Life Members that used the Club. Life Members paid a one-off, set fee and did not pay anything else for as long as they were members, which curtailed investment in the premises somewhat, as there were a lot of them, he was to be informed later.

Feeling tired he lay down, fully dressed and fell fast asleep. He was woken three hours later by Henry knocking on his door. He opened the door to find Henry hidden behind a huge pile of bags. Henry staggered into the room, promptly falling over the bed, landing in a heap and uttering deep meaningful words of disquiet, much to Steve's amusement.

He picked himself up as Steve thanked him and started opening the bags excitedly.

"Right," said Henry, "these are your suits, one pin-stripe and one mohair, perfect." He held them up to show Steve.

"Here's your shirts, with," he advised Steve, "double-cuffs

... Gentlemen never have single cuffs you know ... plus," he said, pulling a small box out of his pocket, "two sets of cheap cuff-links." He passed the box to Steve triumphantly. "You'll have to get your girlfriend to buy you some better ones for Christmas ... these shoes are the best money can buy ... I wouldn't mind having them myself," he added grudgingly as he handed them over. "And here's a couple of Club ties the Boss left for you in reception."

Steve saw that the ties had been embroidered with a replica of the Eagle Clock that he had seen in the bar.

"That clock is in the bar downstairs," he remarked to Henry, showing him the ties.

"Trust you to find the Eagle's Nest so soon," Henry replied. "That's where we all meet, prior to lunch in the main restaurant," he advised Steve with enthusiasm. "That reminds me, don't forget we are meeting at 13.00 hours and it's now mid-day. I'll see you in the bar 'cos I have the day off now, to help you settle in. Aren't you a lucky sod then?" He laughed and left Steve getting changed. He made do with a strip wash at the small cracked sink, that did have, however, piping hot water.

He had quite a job putting his cuff-links in, never having used them before, but he managed it after a few minutes. His black shoes were the finest Jermyn Street could offer, all hand-stitched, leather soles and shining clean.

He opened the wardrobe door to see himself in the long mirror he'd noticed when he put his bag in, but the door fell off in his hand and it took him some time to re-hang it with the aid of a strong nail-file.

At 12.45 hours he was ready. He left his room and went via the stairs to the Eagles' Nest, not wishing to risk the lift again. The bar was still closed so he went to the public 'phones that were situated by the lift doors and rang home.

"Hi mother, Steve here, how are you keeping?"

"Oh it is nice to speak to you son, where are you? Still in

Spain?" she asked with a tenderness that put Steve on his guard, waiting for the 'barb' to be added.

"I'm in London now, mother, in a rather exclusive Gentlemen's Club, in the West End," he told her proudly.

"I'll believe you, thousands wouldn't," came the stock reply he'd expected of her.

"I am mother, it's brill. I wish you were here to see it ... and I've been given a whole new wardrobe of clothes and shoes as well because I did so well in Spain," he enthused to her.

His mother took no notice and said, "She's been on the 'phone again."

"Who?"

"Her," came the stark answer. "You know who, so don't play the innocent with me, son, it doesn't become you," she snapped at him. "Fred's been round and done some shopping for me, unlike some I could mention." She sniffed down the 'phone. Steve wanted to ask her about the 'phone call as he assumed it was Gloria calling, but he thought he'd better let it lie and asked, "How is Fred mother? Tell him I owe him one when I get home."

"And when will that be then?" his mother flashed at him.

"I really do not know at the moment, but I'm having lunch with my boss shortly," he added.

"Oh, la-de-da," she mimicked him. "Having lunch with your boss now is it? Never mind that your mother hardly has anything in to eat, you just think of yourself, son, like you always do ... I pity that poor woman who keeps ringing up for you ... she must want her head examining," and with that tirade, the 'phone went dead.

Steve looked at the receiver in his hand, nonplussed. How could his mother be like this, when not twenty-four hours ago he had been risking his life for Queen and Country?

He replaced the receiver slowly feeling quite pensive, when he was suddenly slapped hard on the back. He turned round angrily and in front of him was a beaming Colonel who said, "Bloody marvellous tape, we are ahead of the game now and no mistake. You're all going to get a little bonus next week ... we'll let you live longer." He roared with laughter at his own joke. "The Scottish usurper thinks he can take over the Country by attacking the Houses of Parliament and Buckingham Palace, at the same time. Well, we'll show the scum-bag whose running this Country and it isn't that good friend of the people, Henry Worthington, no sir!" He scowled at Steve then said, "Let's go in the bar and celebrate." He led a slightly bewildered Steve by the arm into the Eagle's Nest for the first, but not the last time.

They settled down in one corner of the now-packed bar and the Colonel waved a command to the bar staff and two gins with tonics appeared, as if by magic, borne on the tray of a smiling waiter.

"Good afternoon, Colonel, nice to see you again."

"G'day David," the Colonel grunted back. "This is a colleague of mine, Mr. Manly ... so look after him when he comes in, won't you? He is a new member."

"Certainly, sir, pleased to meet you Mr. Manly and if there is anything you want please see me." David warbled away, smiling all the time, then bowed his head and withdrew back to the bar.

"Good chap that," the Colonel admitted. "Very helpful." He picked up his glass, "Here's to you Steve m'boy, may we have a long and fruitful partnership."

"Cheers," reciprocated Steve, then asked. "Excuse me for being a bit thick, Colonel, but who is Henry Worthington?"

"Henry Worthington," repeated the smiling Colonel, "is the name we keep on our files, for Harold Wilson, the Prime Minister. Bloody silly if you ask me, because I reckon everyone in the National Press knows who Henry Worthington files refer to ... some secret," he chuckled finishing his drink and signalling for another.

Henry came across the room accompanied by a tall, well-built, swarthy man with a small beard which made him look like an Arab and introduced him as Craig Martell.

"Pleased to meet you, Craig," Steve stood up and shook his hand, while the Colonel waved acknowledgement to Craig and remained sitting down. Steve sat down again and had a sip of his drink.

"Now Gentlemen," the Colonel began, having looked around to make sure no-one was near enough to overhear him. "This is the latest knowledge we have on our Scottish friend ...thanks to our men in Spain, and young Steve here," he nodded his appreciation at Steve. "We now know that he intends to make a coup of the Country by attacking Parliament and Buckingham Palace with an armed force, crazy as it may seem. We had found out about the plot two years ago when we were investigating Mr. Worthington's involvement with the Ruskies." He paused and glanced round at them all, "And we dismissed this as too bizarre to be workable. However, during the last six months we became aware that this was serious operation not be laughed at and due to," he looked at Steve, "some excellent trace work being done, we were able to tap certain lines and intercept mail. That leads us to believe an attack is now a serious proposition. We have learned of an American involvement to provide as much money as possible, if not arms as well, to install Lord McForson as King.

We have not, to date, located the main case of his operation in Scotland. In fact we have lost two operatives on the investigation already. One was found dead on a Scottish golf course, near Edinburgh, with a crossbow bolt through his neck and one ear cut off. The other," he looked round at them, "is a puzzle, because he was found knifed to death in a beauty spot, near Ridgeborough, Leicestershire. He also had one ear cut off."

He paused as David brought another round of drinks, then carried on when David left them again. "We do not know why our second man was near Ridgeborough ... you replaced him actually, Steve," the Colonel said almost apologetically to Steve, then went on, "but we do not know of any hit man who cuts an ear off their victims ... any ideas gentlemen?" They all picked their drinks up as if on cue, to think about what the Colonel had just said.

Craig spoke for the first time, slowly and deliberately and Steve recognised from his accent that he came from Liverpool. "I worked out in Africa some years ago ... you remember Colonel?" he asked the Colonel, who grunted. "Yes."

"Well, I came across a mercenary soldier who used to cut an ear off each soldier he killed because he was paid a bounty on each ear he produced, one for each kill."

"That sounds like our man, Craig," muttered the Colonel, "well done, now who is he?"

"I'm trying to remember his name," said Craig furrowing his brow in thought. "I know he was a Swede, but what was he called?" he drummed his fingers on the table top.

"How about Kai?" Steve's heart was pounding as he offered the name to the waiting group.

"That's it ... Kai," agreed Craig nodding assent. "Have you met him at all?" he queried Steve.

"Yes, two days ago on an observation job for the Colonel ... he is Lord McForson's bodyguard."

"And you lived to tell the tale," Craig said grimly.

"Well done, both of you," enthused the Colonel. "That's what these meetings are all about, to share our knowledge right down the line. My God, men, this is the first indication we've had that his Lordship has moved his base of operations south of the Scottish Borders."

He was almost talking to himself by now and pulled himself up as he carried on talking to them. "Up until now, Gentlemen, we thought the only problem was the alliance of Henry Worthington with the Russians. Now we also have Lord Longford entering the frame, by convening a conference next

Saturday at Central Hall in Westminster. He is going to be the chairman and apparently this may lead to the formation of a group of people pledged to overcome the nation's economic difficulties."

He was scowling round the table at each of them in turn. "So here we have Lord Longford sticking his oar in, and at the same time, there are two other parties for us to worry about. Colonel Stirling and his GB 75 organisation, plus General Sir Walter Walker, whose Civil Assistance group intends to take over essential services in the event of crippling strikes."

"How many people do these organisations have then?" asked Steve, who had no idea there was anything like this going on in the country and was amazed about this revelation.

"Well, we believe that the support for Lord Longford's meeting is around the 800 mark," the Colonel replied, "which is neither here nor there. But Sir Walter reckons that if all the groups he knows, like the Unison Committee for Action, based mainly in the North of England, and the Association of Ratepayers' Action Group, were to form regional volunteer forces in England, similar to the old B Specials in Northern Ireland, then there could be as many as six million people involved, one way or the other ready to step in and take over the running of our Country. Now are you getting the picture, Manly?" the Colonel asked Steve intently, leaning forward for Steve's answer.

"Yes, Colonel, I am and I'm sorry to keep on asking questions, but six million? Wow! It's all so new to me," Steve replied, grateful that he was not being talked down to by the Colonel. "But are we supporting the Government to see that these guys don't take over, or what?"

"What our job is at the moment, is to," he looked round at the expectant faces, "stop these people joining forces, thereby making a formidable force ... Lord McForson lays claim to the Throne of England, as King Stuart I, with no authenticated claim possible from his lineage," he added.

"We've already checked it out ... he's just a power mad, silly old fart, who was no problem until he got that financial backing from America, last week. We are now looking at someone who would make the perfect figure-head, for the Unison of Groups to present to the people, and ensure public backing, if the time comes Gentlemen." The Colonel stopped to have a sip of his drink while this information sank in.

"Bloody hell," the expletive came from Craig, "even I had no idea about all this going on." He looked across in support of Steve then said, "What's the first plan then Colonel ... knock off the ring-leaders?"

The Colonel smiled as he heard the question. "Violence is not always the way," he paused. "But the first priority is to remove Lord McForson from the equation by any means at our disposal ... if you get my drift?" He looked at them all expectantly. "We cannot allow Lord McForson to be given the opportunity to become King Stuart I, yes?" he tilted his head forward looking at the table as they all nodded in agreement. "Right then," he turned to Henry. "I need you to drive Steve back home to Merseyside ... tomorrow, first thing. I need him to do some more special traces." He turned to Steve. "That is, if you're agreeable Steve. We don't know yet who killed your colleague Sandy, so it could still be dangerous. At least you have a gun now and know how to use it. Just take care ...we need your specialised tracing skills ... they are invaluable to us," he added looking at Steve with an expectant smile creasing his fat face.

"Certainly Colonel," Steve replied. "I'll do my best and keep my eyes peeled for further information about Sandy." Steve gave a big sigh and said, "I'm ready for a game of golf, it seems years since I last played."

"Wonderful!" exclaimed the Colonel. "I'll put your name down to join our little Golf Society. I don't play myself," he patted his rotund stomach affectionately, "as you can see. But our little circle of golfers are able to fly anywhere in the world to play golf, without raising suspicion ... it's the best cover story we have, y'know," he explained enthusiastically as David came to them and announced their table was ready in the restaurant.

They finished their drinks and walked through into the most magnificent restaurant that Steve had ever seen. There were three large sparkling crystal chandeliers, suspended down the centre of the room, which gave the appearance of a myriad of chandeliers in the mirrored walls that surrounded the restaurant, making it look absolutely palatial.

Standing to attention in the centre of the restaurant was a chef, dressed in gleaming whites and at his side a huge trolley on which there was an ornate silver dome.

He nodded to the Colonel as they passed him on their way to the only table set in the mullioned bay window.

The meal they had was the best Steve had ever eaten and they had a different bottle of wine with each course. They ended the meal with everyone having a large Baron Otard XO cognac, served from a black, gold-inscribed bottle, which, according to the colonel, "Was the only cognac to be aged at the Chateau de Cognac."

Steve drank his brandy and wondered what his friends back in the old snooker room in Merseyside would say if they could see him now. His thoughts were rudely interrupted by the Colonel announcing that they were all going upstairs to the lounge for another couple of drinks. The Colonel signed the proffered bill and they all rose, to a man and followed him up to the lounge.

Steve selected an armchair and dropped into it with a sigh of relief having eaten, and drunk, far in excess of his usual intake.

"You'll get used to it, Steve." Henry dug him playfully in his ribs. "Make the most of it while you can, eh?"

"Craig," the Colonel said, "I want you to take Steve down to the gun gallery and let him shoot the gun he's been given ...

he's a bit rusty. ... Oh, and also get him measured up for a shoulder-holster at the same time ... he can only stick it in his waist-band at the moment and we don't want him shooting his damn wedding tackle off, eh? Ha Ha," the Colonel shook with mirth at the thought.

"Will do Colonel," Craig agreed. "We'll set a day."

"Good man," replied the Colonel, who then shouted, "where's my bottles, a man could die of thirst here."

"On it's way, Colonel," Steve heard a woman's voice reply and two bottles of Lanson Black label arrived, carried by the most gorgeous woman Steve had ever seen.

She had flaming red hair and sparkling green-hued eyes, with full luscious, shiny red, bow-shaped lips. She wore a tight black skirt that showed the outline of her suspenders and black, high-heeled shoes that seemed to stretch her long legs even longer. A pristine white blouse was tucked firmly into the large, black plastic belt that nipped her waist in and seemed to push her bosom outwards, forming a deep cleavage of firm flesh, outlined by the white satin, lace bra that was struggling to contain her breasts. Round her neck, on a silver chain, she wore the tasting cup of a Sommelier, which nestled in her cleavage.

"Here you are Colonel," she teased him, leaning over and kissing him on the forehead with a laugh.

Everyone was mesmerised by her bottom, which clearly showed, not only her suspenders, but the outline of a tiny 'G' string. She turned round quickly and they all had to look away, as if disinterested.

"Who's this then, Colonel?" she asked, looking at Steve with a little mischievous pout of her full, shiny, red lips.

"Steve, meet Geraldine," the Colonel obliged her. "The best sommelier in the City," he added smoothly.

"Pleased to meet you Steve," she gushed. "Any friend of the Colonel is a friend of mine." She leaned over to kiss him on the cheek, and all eyes in the bar swivelled round to admire her beautiful body, and dream of Heaven.

"Pleased to make your acquaintance, Geraldine," Steve stuttered. He felt totally overwhelmed by the sheer sexuality of this woman as her scent wafted over him, in a cloud of promises, promises.

She smiled, as if she knew what he was thinking, which made him blush for the first time since he was an adolescent schoolboy.

He watched her return back to the bar after first arranging both bottles, deep in the ice while David made a performance of polishing each fluted glass before placing them carefully in front of them all.

"Some woman, that is," the Colonel said admiringly. "I wish I was as young as you Steve ... I think she likes you, you lucky young devil," he admitted smiling at Steve. He extracted a bottle from the ice and poured them all a glass of bubbling champagne.

"Here's to tossing the caber right out of England." He stood up holding his glass high and said, "This side of the table would like to take wine with the other side of the table." They all stood up and clinked their glasses in response and the day dissolved into night.

The next day, whilst he was sitting in the back of the Roller on his way to Merseyside, he vaguely recalled being put to bed the night before and the perfume on his clothes left him in no doubt as to who had put him to bed.

CHAPTER 8
The Alibi

Steve slept for most of the homeward journey and woke just as they turned off the M6 motorway, towards the Lancashire coast. He saw the time was 10.00 a.m. and made a quick decision.

"Henry ... I might as well go straight home and unpack, it won't take me long, then if you don't mind, you can drive me to work and I'll be able to show the bastards what a big man I am now, turning up in a Rolls Royce, bloody wicked eh? Henry," he chortled aloud.

"You're a real swanker and no mistake Steve, only I would forget the 's' if I worked with you, and by the way did you manage to kiss 'The Red Admiral' then? You lucky sod," Henry retorted, in good humour, as he swerved the car to avoid some children running across the road playing chicken. "Stupid little sods they could get themselves killed running front of me like that ... I wonder where their parents think their little darlings are playing right now?" he grumbled to himself.

"What the hell are you talking about?" Steve answered a smiling Henry. "Have I kissed 'The Red Admiral'? Do you think I'm bloody queer or something?" Steve demanded.

"Oh never mind Steve, I just wondered, that's all," Henry replied making Steve very suspicious.

"Come on" Steve cajoled him. "What are you talking about?"

"Forget it, I shouldn't have mentioned it ... it's just something that I've never done myself, you'll know what I mean, if you ever get the chance." Henry left it at that, which left Steve wondering what on earth kissing a bloody communist was all about, and feeling annoyed with Henry for not saying what he meant.

"You're bloody well cracking up mate," he said to the back of Henry's head.

"Bollocks," replied a smiling Henry.

"Do you know there is a man, in my old office, who would get on with you like a house on fire ... you both have to same command of the English language ... none." Steve retorted to Henry.

Steve decided to sort out the bag that contained his duty frees as he'd only managed to have a cursory look until now since Eileen had handed it to him at the Valencia Airport.

He was pleasantly surprised to find a large box of Cuban cigars, a couple of silk scarves and two packs of assorted bottles of scent. He found a small message written on a picture postcard of the airport, saying, 'I hope these are all right, I got you two of everything because I didn't know how many girl-friends you have back in England.' There was a lipstick imprint of a kiss at the end of the message, but no signature.

Steve thanked Eileen silently in his mind and resolved that he must go to Spain as soon as he possible could.

They glided smoothly up outside Steve's house just as his mother was coming out of the front door. Steve quickly took the cigars, a scarf and a pack of scent out of the bag, leaving a scarf and a pack of scent in the bag, to give to his mother as a present.

"Hello mother!" he shouted to his stunned mother who had just turned from locking the front door and was confronted with seeing her son emerge from the back of the Rolls Royce. Steve strode swiftly up the path and hugged his mother, who promptly burst into tears.

"Hey, come on, there's no need for this." He put his arms round her shoulders, comforting her. "I've brought a pressie for the lovely Señora, from sunny Spain ...ole."

"You fool," she smiled through her tears. "I'm just pleased and relived to see you, that's all." She turned and unlocked the door as Henry walked up the path with Steve's bag and black pouch.

"Hello Mrs. Manly," he greeted her and gave her a little peck on her cheek.

"Well, she countered, brushing the tears away, "at least you kept your promise and brought him home in one piece ... thank you." She pecked his cheek in return.

"Come in and we'll have a nice cup of tea." She swept into the house ahead of them clutching the bag Steve had given her.

Steve, smiling, looked at Henry and said, "Smooth bastard, she likes you, there's not many get invited in for tea."

"Just my natural charm, pal," Henry replied as he shut the door. "Where do you want this?" he hissed at Steve holding the pouch out to him.

"I'll shove it under my bed for the moment ... if she knew what was in this pouch she'd throw a fit and no mistake."

Steve went into his bedroom with Henry following on, when a flying but happy Buster launched himself on the defenceless Steve, smothering him in a barrage of excited licks and wagging his tail furiously.

Henry, on seeing how big the dog was, backed off, holding Steve's bag in front of him like a shield. Steve laughed trying to control his dog. He gasped, "Don't worry Henry, he's a softy really."

Henry was not so sure and stood his distance until Buster calmed down. Buster left Steve and investigated the person who had come into his master's bedroom.

"Stroke him," suggested Steve ,"and you'll be his friend."

Henry obliged until Buster rolled over asking for his tummy to be tickled. "There you are ... what did I tell you? Let's go and have tea."

Buster raced past them both in order to get there first, knocking Steve sideways in his exuberance.

"Crazy pooch," he joked as they walked into the kitchen where his mother was putting slices of cake out onto a plate, alongside which was a plate of Bath Olivers.

"Come along," she said happily. "Let's go into the lounge. I want to hear all about your new job and your Spanish trip, then I'll tell you about young Sandy, poor boy." She gathered up the tray and led the way to the lounge, hindered only by an excited dog, who'd realised that the biscuit barrel had been opened.

She passed the tea to them both and offered the cake and biscuits, which were eagerly accepted, as they had not had any breakfast in London due to the early start.

"Right, now, tell me everything." Steve's mother settled back in her armchair expectantly while casting a critical eye over her son's new clothes.

"There's nothing much to tell really," Steve started slowly, pretending to be laid back but frantically trying to pick his words carefully. "I went to Spain, as you know, to do some research for my new department and I finished what they wanted me to do earlier than I expected. I was flown back yesterday morning and taken by Henry to meet my new boss at a Gentlemen's club called, The Ryder Club ... near Fortnum & Mason," he added, name dropping to give credence to his story.

"Why?" His mother asked sharply, putting her cup down and looking hard at her son.

"Why what?" he answered defensively.

"Why have they picked you to do this work?"

"Because, mother," he answered, "the person who was going to Spain was murdered in Ridgeborough, and I was sent in his place simply because I was available at the time, and that's the truth,, isn't it Henry?" He looked at Henry for support.

"That's right Mrs. Manly ... Steve just happened to be available ... anyone could have been sent, including me," Henry explained as he crammed cake into his mouth to avoid talking more on the subject.

"I do not believe a word of it," his mother proclaimed at length. "Replaced a murdered man ... hah!" She gave a little sarcastic laugh. "Next you'll be telling me that poor Sandy was murdered by mistake for you because he had your car ... you're getting like a Walter Mitty, you really are." She smiled now. "I reckon there's a woman at the bottom of this ... you want to tie a knot in IT." She glanced down at his trousers. "Just like your father ... men." She returned to drinking her tea, happy at her judgement.

Steve looked at Henry and raised his eyes in relief that his mother was best thinking 'a woman was at the bottom of it all'. He'd try to keep it that way as long as he could

"Tell me about Sandy then," he changed the conversation.

"Well," she started, "he came round and told me that he had been told by your office to wash and polish your car ... so I gave him the keys." She looked very sad with her eyes starting to fill up with tears. "I do wish I hadn't, perhaps he would still be alive," she added sniffing.

"Carry on mother, it wasn't your fault," Steve placated her, putting his hand on her arm.

"Well, the next thing I know is, the police are at the door saying there had been an accident and they were arranging for the car to be driven back here, as it had not been damaged in the accident at all. The girl who was riding with Sandy told them whose car it was ... his poor mother, I do feel sorry for her, they won't release his body until they know who did it.

All we know is he was shot. I can hardly believe it could happen here."

She blew her nose. "Then I thought someone was watching me, it was awful son," she sighed. "Thank goodness your friend, Fred came round to look after me ... he's been marvellous to me ... have some more tea." She poured them both another cup of tea as she carried on. "The police want a word with you as soon as possible, but I told them you were out of the country at the moment, but they still want to see you."

"That's okay mother, I'll pop in and see them," he assured her. "Who was the girl he had with him?"

"I believe her mother works at your office but I don't know who ... she's still in a state of shock, Fred tells me."

"So long as you are all right mother, that's what matters," Steve asserted. "Now Henry and I are going to the office and I am back home for a while, so you have nothing to worry about, all right?"

"That's a relief to know you will be staying home son," she smiled. "I want to know how you acquired that suit and shirt, they must have cost you a fortune?"

"Not really mother, just perks of the job," he explained lightly. "Anyway where exactly is my car now?"

"Fred took it to put it in the office garages because they did not know how long you would be away," his mother replied, "and I couldn't tell them," she added sniffily.

"Okay mother, I should be home around six tonight." Steve stood up and Buster leapt up and danced all round the room, ready for walkies.

"Stay," Steve commanded him sternly. "You daft bugger."

"Steve, I've never heard you swear before and I do not like it," his mother rebuked him. "Buster has been as good as gold and it's been a good comfort to have him with me at night." She leaned down and stroked Buster's head. He promptly rolled over in submission.

"Okay, let's go Henry," said Steve walking to the front door. "I'll buy him a sheep's head as a treat for being such a good boy, see you tonight, mum."

Buster seemed to know they were talking about him and jumped up, resuming his enthusiastic dance up the hallway.

"Goodbye Mrs. Manly, see you again." Henry pecked her on the cheek again.

"Do call me Hilda," she gushed. "There's no need to stand on ceremony here," she added smiling profusely.

"Okay Hilda, see you soon," Henry said, as requested and they left a happy woman to take Buster a walk.

Their arrival at the office coincided with lunchtime and many of the workers saw Steve arrive in style, to his absolute delight.

"Come on Henry, I'll show you our snooker room. It's not a patch on the Club snooker room though," he explained to Henry. "However, you'll meet my pal, Fred." Steve led Henry through the main entrance passing the little office Morris worked in.

"Well look who it is." Fred beamed as he saw Steve enter, "To what do we owe this honour, m'lord?" He bowed his head in mock respect to Steve.

"Hello you old toss-pot." Steve shook his outstretched hand. "How's yer piles?" he asked jokingly.

"Bloody itching, if you must damn well know ... who's this?" Fred grinned at Henry, "Another mug to buy your drinks?"

"This is Henry, who I work with in London ... Henry meet my pal, bollock brain."

"I've heard a lot about you Fred," Henry replied. "I hope it's all true!"

"Arseholes," came the stock reply.

"That's m'boy." Steve laughed as Fred ran true to form, then said, "Thanks Fred, for keeping an eye on mother. Much appreciated. I owe you one ... by heck, I only go away for a few days and Sandy gets himself killed. What's the score on that now then, Fred?" he asked grimly. "And who the hell was he with anyway in my car? I didn't even know he had a girl-friend."

They went and sat down at a small table while the rest of the players resumed playing. They discussed the various details of what had gone on while Steve was away.

"Your mother was no problem and I didn't see anyone watching her when I checked ... and Sandy really bought it, he had half his head blown off with one shot, the Police said he didn't know what hit him."

"Poor sod," Steve murmured.

"The girl that was with him, Sue, works in our post-room with her mother, Pauline, you know ... the one with the frizzy hair." Steve nodded. "But she hasn't come back to work yet due to the shock she had, seeing him killed."

"I'm not surprised to hear that Fred, I'd be off work if I saw someone lose half their head and no messing, mate," Steve agreed vehemently. Then he leaned forward and whispered, "How's Gloria?"

"She's off work with stress, or something. I'm not sure what, she's not been in since you left." Fred added, "I think she must be lovesick for you or ...," he added wickedly, "maybe it's morning sickness." He sniggered to a startled Steve.

"Bloody hell! Don't even joke about it, you rotten sod. I hope your poxy piles explode," Steve retorted angrily as he tried to straighten his tie.

"Well that's a nice way to talk to your mate, I don't think," grumbled an upset Fred. "Just because you've got promotion and posh clothes, you think you are superior to all of us now. I'm surprised you bother to speak to us at all!" With that remark, Fred got up and left the room leaving everyone astounded by his outburst.

"Come on Henry." Steve stood up. "Let's go to my office

for a coffee ... cheerio everyone, see you around."

There was a babble of goodbyes as Steve and Henry left the snooker room for the last time.

Steve felt for the first time that people were genuinely jealous of this promotion and transfer to London. He remembered how Gloria had 'gone funny' when she heard the news of his promotion and now Fred had reacted the same way. *'Well sod him ... sod them all, with their petty little minds, in their stupid little domestic worlds. He didn't need them any more, his world was far too exciting now,'* he thought to himself as they arrived at his office, which Steve found to be unlocked, much to his annoyance.

"I'll put the kettle on and make a coffee," said Henry.

"Good man," replied Steve who was not really listening as he had seen there was a 'tube' message lying on his desk. He picked it up and saw that its arrival time was printed at 11.45 a.m. He glanced at the wall clock which showed 12.30 p.m. He unscrewed the top to get the message out.

Colonel Guntripp had sent two bits of paper with a couple of lines of information on to be dealt with as soon as possible.

"Look at that Henry." He threw the papers on his desk in disgust. "I've only just got back and he wants me to get started right away ... what a pain."

Henry finished putting the kettle on and walked over to read the two bits of paper.

Steve noticed another piece of paper in the 'tube' and picked it out. He read it with dismay. "He wants you back in London, Henry, as soon as possible."

Henry read his instruction and fed it straight into the shredder and destroyed it, without saying anything for a few moments, then said, "Right, I'll have a coffee then I'm off ... that's the way our work goes, isn't it?" He smiled, "At least I've got a Roller to do the journey in."

They sat and had their coffee not saying anything until Henry spoke, his voice no more than a whisper. "The person who shot Sandy wanted you, so keep your wits about you, trust no-one. Can't you think of anyone who is new to the offices or has just appeared, say, in your pub?"

Steve shook his head. "There are only a couple of people who knew what I was doing and this has happened so quickly I cannot believe it can be anyone here at all. And, don't forget, the people here knew who Sandy was, they wouldn't have confused him for me."

I guess you're right there Steve," agreed Henry rubbing his chin thoughtfully. "But that would mean it is someone passing information from the London end ... jeez, that's bad news," he exclaimed as they realised the seriousness of this deduction. "We've got a 'sleeper' in our midst."

"Sleeper?"

"Yes, someone is working against us, yet is accepted as one of us, the bastard. Whoever it is, we'll have to be careful. I will have a good look at our end of the operation and do a double check on all our 'Box 500' clearances, when I get back," Henry informed a very shaken Steve.

"Bloody hell, Henry, it's bad enough coming up against the likes of Kai, without someone on our side trying to blow me away. Some promotion this is." Steve ran his hand through his hair agitatedly. "What the hell do you mean check 'Box 500', what's that mean, when it's at home?"

"It means," explained Henry patiently, "that I will check all our personnel for their political aspirations. In other words, what political parties have they ever been involved with, right back to their student days ... you never know, one might have slipped through our vetting procedures."

"Let me know as soon as you can because at this rate I won't live to spend my first pay cheque." Steve gave a nervous laugh. "No wonder everyone drinks and smokes so much in this game," he observed wryly.

"You will be fine," Henry tried to calm him down. "Don't tell anyone about this." He paused and looked straight in

Steve's eyes, "Not even the Colonel, because," he went on, seeing Steve react sharply to the suggestion, "when he's tanked up in the Club he does say things that should not be said, because he feels safe to do that in that environment. Personally I think he should not take risks like that."

Henry patted Steve on the shoulder and rose to leave.

"Thank you Henry, keep in touch, because I don't know how long I am going to carry on here. I really enjoyed my few days working in the organisation properly and I can't wait to get back to London. Here ..., " Steven spread his arms, "seems like a back-water of still-life to me, now I've had a taste of how exciting life can be."

"Sometimes, Steve," advised Henry, "it's better the devil you know than the devil you don't ... take care." He shook hands. "I'll find my own way out," and with a wave he was gone, leaving Steve looking down at two bits of paper.

Steve worked until 5.00 p.m. keeping well away from the snooker room. In fact, he decided to keep his contact with staff members down to a minimum to avoid the back-biting and jealousy. He even made his way down the back fire escape to get to the garage for his car.

The little M.G. was sparkling clean and Steve remembered that Sandy had taken it for a wash and polish that fateful day. He climbed in, pulled out the choke and started her, smiling to himself as she roared into life straight away.

He drove round to the police station on his way home to inform them he was back should they wish to see him. He was asked by the Desk Sergeant if he wouldn't mind waiting to see Detective Inspector Cutts who was investigating the murder.

"Bad business, sir, we're not used to having shootings in this neck of the woods," he said shaking his head.

Steve sat in the waiting area until, after five minutes, a tall, balding man, wearing baggy trousers and a black roll-neck sweater under a well-worn leather bomber jacket, entered. He came straight over to Steve and showing his I.D., card under Steve's nose introduced himself, "Hello, Mr. Manly, I'm Dectective Inspector Cutts, in charge of the murder of Mr. Beach."

"Who?" queried Steve.

"Mr. Mungo Beach," the D.I. replied. "But everyone seems to only know him by his nick-name of Sandy, refers to Sandy Beach, it seems better than Mungo, I suppose, " he mused.

"Sorry Inspector, I had no idea of his real name," Steve apologised. "I only met him at work two years ago and I only ever knew him as Sandy."

"Anyway, sir, thank you for coming in to see us, we just need to clear up one or two points about this murder with you. We believe that whoever shot Mr. Beach believed they were shooting you. We have not yet found the gun but we have been told by ballistics that, from the bullet they recovered from Mr. Beach's body, we need to look for a sniper rifle, an Enfield Enforcer with a telescopic sight. We were also told by the young lady in the sports-car that the car belonged to you, yes?"

"I don't own it, Inspector," explained Steve. "The car is really owned by the department I work for, so it is, in fact, a Government car," he announced proudly.

"What sort of Government work do you do sir? Perhaps there may be a connection here." The Inspector opened his notebook again.

"I forward information to doctors around the country, giving details of the latest medical treatment available and then patients can be treated with the best medicine," Steve explained glibly.

"And they give you a sports car ... for doing that?" The Inspector gave a little grunt of amazement. "I'm obviously in the wrong career, sir." He then asked Steve, "Can you think of anyone who would want to hurt you, for any reason at all, someone's boyfriend ... or husband," he added, as he saw Steve react to this suggestion.

"No," Steve lied, pretending to think. "No I simply cannot think that I've upset anyone enough to shoot me, I mean, it looks like a good marksman did this ... not a jealous husband, don't you agree?"

"I think you're right, sir. It was a single shot right between the eyes, from 200 yards or so. I was just thinking out loud," the Inspector countered. "Anyway sir, all we need to know is where were you on Saturday, the 31st August, around 11.00 a.m?" He gazed hard at Steve.

"No problem at all, I was in Spain on business," Steve answered happily.

"Yes," the D.I. took his note-book out and flicked through the pages until he found the relevant pages.

"Ah yes ... your mother told us you had gone to Spain." He hesitated, then said, "We need to see your passport and we need details of your flight, with the names of anyone who can verify that you were in Spain ... shouldn't be too difficult, should it sir?" He looked at Steve with an encouraging smile.

Steve had gone cold with shock as the realisation suddenly hit him, that there was no way he could prove he was in Spain. Because of the assumed identity he'd gone with, and due to the nature of the work, no-one would be able to give him an alibi.

"Are you all right sir?" he heard the Inspector asking him with concern in his voice.

Steve, pulling his thoughts together replied, "I'm fine Inspector, I'm just a bit tired from the trip. I only got back late last night," he lied, his mind racing with the problem that now faced him.

"Right then Sir," the Inspector went on, "all we need is to see your passport as soon as possible ... say tomorrow morning, here, at 10.00 a.m."

"Certainly Inspector, until tomorrow." Steve held his hand out and shook the Inspector's heartily, but left the station with his mind in a whirl, thinking of what to do next.

He sat for a few minutes in his car trying to work out what to do, then, making his mind up, started the car and raced back to his office, as fast as he could drive.

He arrived at his office to find Morris just locking the main front door. He looked in amazement at Steve's arrival at that time of the evening and pulled the door open for him.

"What's up with you Steve? Have you left something behind?" he enquired as Steve pushed past him.

"Sorry can't stop Morris ... things to do, no rest for the wicked y'know." He made light of his return and walked quickly to the lift, leaving a bemused Morris re-locking the doors.

Steve reached his office and went and sat at his desk. *'Calm down now'* he told himself. *'Have a cigar.'*

He went through the cigar ritual, lighting it with the cedar-wood wrapper, as he'd been shown, then sat back, enveloped in a cloud of smoke, thinking to himself. He leaned forward and, picking the receiver up, dialled the Ryder Club, drumming his fingers impatiently on his desk top.

"Hello," he said as he was answered. "May I speak to Colonel Guntripp please?"

"The Colonel has already left, sir," he was informed, making him think fast of alternatives.

"Is his driver, Henry, there please?"

"He's driving the Colonel, sir."

"Damn ..." Steve was starting to panic now. "How about Mr. Martell, is he still there?" Steve asked hopefully.

"I'll go and check in the lounge, sir, hold on," and Steve heard the 'phone being put down and the sound of feet receding into the distance. *'Come on ... come on.'* Steve was so wound up now that he stumped the newly-lit cigar out fiercely into the ashtray. He heard the sound of someone breathing heavily as they picked the 'phone up.

"Yes, he's still here sir and he's picking the lounge 'phone

141

up now sir. Good Evening."

Steve heard a double click, as one 'phone was picked up and the other put down.

"Hello, who's that?" The cautious voice of Craig came like a ray of sunshine to Steve who blurted out, "Thank Christ you're there Craig. It's Steve, Steve Manly, I met you yesterday with the Colonel," he explained. "I really wanted to speak to the Colonel, but cannot find him, so I'm hoping you can advise me ... yes?"

"Hold on Steve, I'll have to talk on scramble, just a minute." Steve heard a couple of bleeps, then Craig came back on. "There, that's safer ... now what is the problem?"

Steve relayed to him the problem he had with the police enquiry and was at a loss to know what to do. Craig did not answer Steve straight away and there was silence for a minute until Steve couldn't contain himself any longer.

"Are you still there?" he asked as his heart pounded fit to burst.

"Well, my advice is to tell them you have had your passport stolen ... make them believe that you think the person responsible for the shooting may have had something to do with it."

"Brilliant," Steve agreed, relief flooding through his body. "What about my alibi,then?"

"Married woman," came the instant reply.

"Married woman?"

"Yes, tell them you went to Spain with a married woman and she is married to a local dignitary and not only that, but her husband is on the Police Committee. That should put them on hold." Craig laughed at his ingenuity.

"Bloody marvellous Craig," Steve said, thankful that he had at least some answers now and even if the Inspector didn't believe him, they could prove nothing.

"Did you exchange money for pesetas in Spain, because the receipt will have a date on it, to help prove you were in

Spain?" Craig suggested.

"No," Steve said ruefully, then he remembered his duty frees bag. "I was given a bag of duty frees though," he told Craig excitedly. "Is that any good?"

"That's it then Steve, you've cracked it, because they always give a sales receipt for them ... you've held onto it haven't you?" Craig asked sharply.

"I think so," Steve said, thinking hard. "It must be in the bag I gave my mother when I came home."

"Then I should get your arse home, right now, because once you find that receipt, that's your proof you were in Spain on that date, you're as good as in the clear."

"Thanks Craig ... I owe you, you've got me off the hook, thank Christ, I really thought I was in 'dickie's meadow' as we say up North." Steve said thankfully.

"Anytime Steve. I know you're new to this work, we've all got to learn the ropes quickly and at least you asked for advice before you really dropped in the shit." Craig rang off chuckling to himself.

Steve drove home, hoping that his mother had not thrown the bag away, with the receipt still in it.

"Hello son," his mother looked up from her knitting, as he walked in, brushing aside the rapturous welcome from Buster. "I'll get you some tea ... you did say you would be back for 6.00 p.m. and it's now ...," she looked at the clock on the mantlepiece, "7.30 p.m. I suppose you went for a drink?" She rose and walked into the kitchen as she was speaking.

"No. I didn't actually ... I went to the police station to, as they say, 'help them with their enquiries'," he replied, glancing round the room to see if the bag was there.

"I'm glad to hear that," she replied from the kitchen. "The sooner they find out who did it the happier I will be, I don't like the thought of a murderer walking round here ... I mean it could be anybody," she said dishing out a plate of hot Shepherd's Pie for him. "Come on eat it while it's hot." She

143

placed the plate on a tray. "You can have it on your knee, then you can sit and talk to me." She fussed around getting a knife and fork and condiments ready for him.

"Mum," he started to say, but his mother interrupted.

"Mum, is it now? ... What trouble are you in? You always call me mum instead of mother, when you want something. I can read you like a book." She folded her arms under her bosom, then, clasping her hands together she waited.

"Well, you know that bag that I gave you from Spain? Have you still got it?" he asked hopefully.

"Yes son, it's here." She reached down by her chair and produced the bag from behind her knitting bag, much to Steve's relief. "Why?"

"I want the receipt out of it, that's all mum, for the accounts department," he added and started to eat his tea.

He watched out of the corner of his eye as she rummaged in the bag until at last she pulled out a small piece of paper which she held up to show him.

"Is this it?"

Steve nodded and took it from her. He gratefully read the till receipt for the gifts that had been bought by Eileen, at Valencia airport. The day, date and time were clearly printed.

'Great stuff,' Steve thought to himself. *'Because even the police would realise that he must have been there to have bought presents that day. Eileen, I really owe you for this'.*

"Why are you smiling ... am I tax deductible then?" His mother was at a loss as to why he was so happy with just a till receipt. He just smiled at her.

"Oh! Get on with your tea and stop annoying me," she rebuked him and resumed knitting again, the needles flashing and clicking at a fast rate, with a contented Buster lying across her feet.

The next morning he arrived early at work, parked the car in his bay and went straight to his office, causing a startled

Morris to say, "What's up?... Wet the bed?"

"Very funny Morris," Steve answered back over his shoulder as he walked quickly past.

"She's not in today y'know," Morris shouted after him.

"Even funnier ... don't give up the day job," he advised Morris, thankful the lift had arrived to whisk him away.

He put the kettle on for a coffee, then threw the crushed cigar into the rubbish-bin, thinking *'what a waste of a good cigar'*, but he placated himself that last night his adrenalin was really flowing under tremendous pressure to provide himself with a fictitious alibi. He looked at the wall clock which showed 8.15 a.m. *'Good'* he thought *'I've got over an hour or so to clear these papers, then go and see the Inspector.'* He suddenly felt happy with the way things had turned out and, indeed, looked forward to the confrontation with the Inspector.

He sat sipping his coffee, deep in thought, when the 'phone ringing made him jump, making him spill a little of his coffee onto his hand.

"Blast," he said as he picked the 'phone up.

"Pardon me!" he heard the Colonel's voice boom down the line.

"Sorry Colonel ... just spilt some coffee," Steve explained getting a tissue from his drawer.

"I hear you've run into a spot of bother about Spain? A bit of a rum do, what?"

"You could say that Colonel, but with the help of Craig, I think I've cracked it." He explained softly, cradling the 'phone in the crook of his neck.

"Two words of warning, Steve," the Colonel countered quietly. "Don't treat the police as fools, because people lie to them every day of the year, so bear that in mind. The other problem is that you cannot get the Department involved, got it? You don't exist on paper and we do not know you." The Colonel emphasised his last three words, then went on, "Apart from the fact that you push paper around in a back-water office on Merseyside and you may be interested to know that Matthew York was killed off last night, in a road accident, got that?"

"Yes," was all Steve could bring himself to answer.

"Good man, we'll carry on giving you trace work for the time being, but you won't be coming to London until this is resolved, or it simply dies down. You will retain the promotion, car and office though. We are just putting you on ice ... anyway, good luck Steve, keep me informed," and the 'phone went dead.

Steve replaced the receiver slowly, not feeling at all as happy now, as he was before, he really was on his own, damn it!

"Hello, Mr. Manly, glad you could make it." Detective Inspector Cutts held a hand out in greeting and went on, "Have you brought your passport then?"

"No ... afraid not, Inspector. I can't seem to find it at all." Steve sounded apologetic. "I last remember having it at Euston Station when I bought a rail ticket," he added.

"That's a shame sir. Let's hope it turns up then ... have you got your rail ticket then?"

"I threw it away when I got home ... sorry Inspector."

"We're not doing very well, are we sir?" The Inspector was now studying Steve closely. "How about the people you were with in Spain, then?" he queried.

"It's a bit embarrassing Inspector." Steve felt himself going red in the face as he carried on lying. "I went with a married woman and not for work."

"A married woman eh?" The Inspector paused, "That explains why you did not leave a contact number for your mother or your office. Assumed name?" he prompted Steve.

"That's right, Inspector," Steve carried on explaining, his heart rate rising by the second. "She's married to a local dignitary, in fact he is also a member of your Police committee

146

panel, so you can see I'm not in a position to divulge her name." He felt the sweat starting to trickle down his back.

The Inspector's face lit up into a big smile. "That's all right sir ... I've a good idea who you mean, because she only arrived back from a seminar abroad, this morning," he told an astonished Steve, who couldn't believe his luck that there was an unfortunate woman who had unwittingly helped him with his alibi.

Steve immediately took advantage of this by producing the receipt for the duty frees "I've got a receipt for the duty free gifts that I bought at Valencia airport, on the day in question." Steve gave it to the Inspector, who examined it closely.

"I see you bought perfume, silk scarves and some cigars ... well, I'll keep this receipt, if I may sir," he smiled at Steve. "This places you definitely in Spain on the day of the shooting, as far as I'm concerned, thank you for your co-operation."

He walked to the door and opened it for Steve to leave. "Take care sir," he smiled knowingly. "You know we haven't caught the killer yet, so be careful, call us if you get worried about anyone or anything, cheerio." He closed the door behind Steve, who walked out to his car, a very relieved man indeed.

He returned to his office and dealt with the remaining traces quickly and put them in the special 'tube' marked with the gold portcullis. He walked to the dispatch tube in the next room and fired it off with a quiet whoosh. He suddenly wondered who did receive the messages he sent when the Colonel was away in London. He resolved to ask him after informing him of the result of his interview.

"Hello, Guntripp here," the Colonel barked.

"Manly here again, sir," Steve replied. "Good news, the police seem to have accepted my alibi, plus, I had an amazing stroke of good luck as well, so there is nothing to worry about now, Colonel," declared Steve happily.

"Oh yes there is something to worry about," replied the

Colonel. "Do you remember the trace I gave you on your birthday, re a Bob Cowle and you gave us a McIan?" He paused to let Steve remember.

"We now know he is working for Lord McForson and listen to this, he is living near Ridgeborough, not far from where our man was murdered ... so far, so good." The Colonel's voice went quieter.

"This is being scrambled for security. We suspect that there is an operational headquarters for Lord McForson in that area and I want you to go to Ridgeborough and join up with Henry. It's an easy drive up the M 1 for him, couple of hours at the most. He'll have British and Craig with him and we've also rented a secluded farmhouse for you all to live in, on the outskirts of the town."

Steve heard him draw on a cigar, cough and then resume, "I think the four of you should manage the job ... drive over in your car, there's lots of out-houses for you to keep it in."

"When do you want me there?"

"Saturday, the 7th, meet them at the Town Hall. You can park in the square outside ... about 10.00 a.m. Lord Longford is having his meeting at Central Hall, Westminster, that day, and I want you all in position. Any questions?" he added quietly.

"None at all Colonel, except ... can you tell me who reads the messages I send in the 'tube' when you're not here? And can Henry bring more bullets for my Smith & Wesson? I mean, I feel that I need a bit of practice," he confided.

"The bullets are no problem at all, consider it done." There was a moment's silence then, "Your messages are received by one of our people that we have had to send from London, to replace Sandy."

Steve gasped as he heard that Sandy was an operative. "Yes, he was the best mole we could have, no-one suspected him, until he got shot that is. We believe now that he was the target and not you. The fact that he was driving your car was excellent cover for whoever did it ... we'll get the bastard."

The line went dead as usual leaving Steve slightly shaken at the speed of events and the fact that Sandy was an operative.

Steve worked the rest of week in a state of anticipation, keeping to himself, although he did try to ring Gloria at home. All he heard was an answer-phone asking him to leave a message, so he rang off quickly.

He packed his car early Saturday morning, hampered only by Buster wanting to help him by running between his feet and giving little excited yelps of joy thinking he was going for a ride.

"Stop it, you daft bugger, you'll have me over if you're not careful," he scolded Buster half-heartedly.

"Why don't you take him with you," his mother appeared at his side, "I'll be all right and I'm sure Buster would be good company for you while you are doing your medical research in Manchester."

Steve felt a little uncomfortable, having told his mother that he would be away for the next couple of weeks, or so, doing medical documentation research. He hated lying to her but it was for her own safety, he reckoned.

He looked at Buster, who stared back with big mournful eyes, as if he knew he was going to be left behind.

"There's no way I can take him mother ... I'd like to but ...Mum," Steve said hesitantly, "do you remember when I rang you from Spain ... you said that Sandy had rung and wanted me to contact him at the office."

"That poor man." His mother sighed. "Yes, of course I remember ... why?"

"Did he give you any idea what it was about?" he asked hopefully.

"He sounded rather excited." His mother looked thoughtful. "He said he had discovered something that he had to tell you urgently and he wanted you to contact him as soon as possible, that's all I can tell you," she explained.

Steve wondered what on earth could Sandy have found out that was urgent enough to make him reveal he was working for the Colonel.

Steve started the engine and with a quick wave to his mother and a miserable Buster, he set off to Ridgeborough.

HALL
FARM

CHAPTER 9
Hall Farm

Steve arrived in Ridgeborough just before 10.00 a.m. only to find that a street market was in full swing in the square and there was no room for parking at all. He left his car on a piece of derelict building land nearby. *'So much for the best laid plans'* he smiled to himself as he strolled back to the extremely bustling square. He saw a large building with a clock tower which dominated the square and made his way over to it. He entered through the large, plate-glass swing doors etched with the crest of the town.

He looked to his left and saw a small reception desk behind which sat a very pretty receptionist who smiled warmly at him as he strolled over to her.

"I'm supposed to meet come colleagues here at 10 o'clock." He looked around as he spoke, trying to see if they were already there.

"Have you tried the coffee lounge, sir," she smiled as she pushed her long dark hair back from her forehead and pointed across the room to a door on the far side. "They may be in there, and if not," her eyes twinkled at him, "I'm free for coffee in 10 minutes." Steve felt himself going red as he said, "I might well take you up on that, it's the best offer I've had all day." He laughed and winked at her which made her smile even wider.

"All right," she grinned, "you're on ... I only hope they are not in there now." She paused. "It's not often we get such a well-dressed man in here." She gave him an appraising look. "Are you on holiday?" she asked, giving a cheeky wink back at him.

"No. I'm here on a course at the University for a few weeks, with some colleagues," he replied, straightening his tie. "I'd better check the coffee bar." He turned and walked away as she answered the persistently ringing 'phone.

The coffee bar was empty, so he ordered a coffee then, picking a table which gave him a full view of the entrance, sat with his back to the wall. He picked up a paper from the next table and started reading.

"Your coffee sir," he heard a woman's voice from the other side of his paper. He put the paper down and saw the pretty receptionist standing in front of him, holding two mugs of steaming coffee.

"Not here yet then?" she enquired.

He shook his head.

"Good ... may I join you?" she asked demurely, putting the mugs down on the table.

"Of course you can, feel free." He stood up and pulled a chair out for her to sit on. "How much do I owe you?"

"The coffee is my treat," she replied. "You're a real gentleman aren't you?" She smiled as she sat down, smoothing her skirt down fussily. "There aren't many round here I can assure you," she added. "I hope I don't seem too forward," she explained, "but when you walked in you were like a ray of sunshine, looking so clean and smart and your shoes must have cost a fortune." Her voice trailed off as she became embarrassed by offering such a forthright opinion to a complete stranger.

"You don't miss much," Steve teased her. "I bet your husband is well-looked after," he added, noticing her wedding ring.

"Oh him!" she began, covering her ring with her other hand. "He goes his own way ... we hardly talk to each other anymore ... we just share the same house, that's all." She picked up her coffee and sipped it slowly.

"I'm sorry to hear that," Steve answered sympathetically.

"It's not nice for anyone when a relationship breaks down, I should know ... it's happened to me," he explained gently as he reached across the table and tried to hold her hand.

She snatched her hand away quickly and looked round at the two lady servers who were stood talking in the coffee bar service area.

"Sorry," she said, "but they watch me all the time ... they love gossip." She giggled. "They're trying to work out who you are ... nosey devils."

"Sorry ... er, what's your name?" he asked. "Mine's Steve."

"Nice to meet you Steve," she gazed at him. "Mine's Barbara." Her eyes were sparkling at him, causing him to catch his breath as his heart skipped a beat.

"That's a nice name, Barbara," he repeated it slowly, "do you live locally then?" He decided to get some local knowledge while he had the chance.

"Yes, I've lived here all my life."

"Do you know of a mansion round here that is most likely set in its own grounds owned by a Lord McForson?"

"Oh! yes," she answered enthusiastically. "Everyone knows that, he's a local celebrity round here you know ... do you know him then?" She sounded incredulous.

"No," he replied. "I have only heard of him." Steve answered carefully, as Barbara carried on explaining, "He owns a large mansion, about ten miles west of here, toward the M 1 ... it's a huge place, more like a fortress than a mansion." She spread her hands to show the size. "It's called Black Lake

Mansion. It's in the middle of Black Lake Park ... on account that there's a lake called Black Lake, in the Park." She giggled, putting her hand over her pretty mouth.

Steve was starting to warm to this lovely woman by the minute, she seemed so relaxed and cheerful all the time.

"How do you know all this?"

"Well ... up until a few years ago the Mansion was owned by a lovely family called the Appletons, and I worked for them as a secretary, until ...," she looked down at the table, "until they lost money on the Stock Market and Lord McForson bought it from them ... it was all very sad, they were lovely people," she added thoughtfully.

"You mean you actually worked in the mansion?" Steve asked and now it was his turn to sound incredulous.

"Yes, for about three years, but Lord McForson brought his own staff from Scotland with him. So I was released," she snorted, "surplus to requirements."

"So you know your way round the park and mansion then?" Steve could not believe his luck.

"I was actually running the estate for the Appletons, so I had to have maps of the park."

"Have you still got them?" Steve asked quietly.

"Yes ... oops, I must go," she apologised, "my coffee break is over." She stood up. "Nice to meet you Steve." She held her hand out and Steve held on for a second longer than necessary, and looking into her eyes, he asked, "Where can I contact you, Barbara? ... I'd like to see you again," he added. "I think you've got lovely eyes."

She smiled, saying, "I work here three times a week," and with that she walked through the entrance to the reception leaving Steve admiring her legs and lovely round bottom.

He sighed and had just picked up his mug when British, Henry and Craig all walked into the room. He stood up.

"Hello British, I didn't think I would see you so soon," he remarked as British crushed his hand in welcome.

"Nice to see you Steve," British chortled. "I hear that your colleague, Matthew York, is dead." He laughed. "What a game we played didn't we?" He sat down at the table while Steve shook hands with Henry and Craig.

"Nice to see you both and," he looked at Craig, "I owe you for your help with the little shooting problem I had."

"That's all right pal," Craig grinned. "When it comes down to it, we're all on our own when things go wrong. So we have to help each other, 'cos no other bugger will. Get the coffees then!" he exclaimed sitting down swiftly into the chair just vacated by Barbara. He noticed the coffee mug in front of him had lipstick on it. "Christ you're a quick worker, who's this then?" He picked up the mug to show the others.

"Listen, I've been working while you lazy sods have been cruising up the M 1," Steve quipped. He went and ordered four more coffees from the now, very attentive ladies behind the counter who were trying to work out if they were mature students or lecturers at the University.

"I reckon we should have our coffee and then go to ..." British took a piece of paper from his pocket, "Hall Farm, which is apparently twelve miles west of here, back towards the M 1,we can discuss how to find our target and take it from there." British put the paper back in his pocket.

"I already know where our target is," a proud Steve told them. "Lord McForson lives about ten miles west of here, towards the M 1 ... a huge place, more like a fortress than a mansion called Black Lake Mansion. It's in the middle Black Lake Park, on account that there is a lake called Black Lake, in the park." Steve repeated what Barbara had said to him, word for word, much to their amazement.

"Well done Steve," British congratulated him warmly, while the other two nodded in agreement.

"Let's have our coffee and get to base as soon as possible." Again they nodded in agreement. British looked at Steve, "Well ... how?"

"Sheer talent," Steve smirked as he realised that they were puzzled as to how he got the information for them. "And what's more we will be going past the very Black Lake Park in question to get to our farm ... it was the pretty woman in the reception here who told me all about the Mansion because she used to work there." Steve lowered his voice to them.

"Great going Steve," said Craig. "We're off to a flying start now ... can she help in any other way?" he queried.

"She said she had a map of the grounds."

"A bloody map of the grounds?" they all chorused quietly.

"Yes," Steve enthused. "But I'll have to take her out for a meal before I can get my hands on it," he went on with a smile, "so who's got the petty cash then?"

"You jammy bastard, I bet it's that pretty long-haired receptionist here, isn't it?" guessed Henry, "her lipstick matches the coffee mug that Craig held up before." He sat back pleased with his deduction.

Steve answered with only a smug smile.

"Let's go folks ... we've work to do." British rose as he spoke. "Where's your car Steve?"

"On a building site."

"You get your car and join us outside ... we're in an old Land Rover with a canvas hood, you can't miss us."

"Well," Steve asked, "shall I take her out for a meal? It would make our work a hell of lot easier to have a map, wouldn't it?" Steve pursued his case.

"All right go ahead," Henry butted in. "Here's some money." He gave a small clip of notes to Steve who tucked it in his inside pocket without looking at it.

They all stood up and walked into the reception area. Steve went over to Barbara and waited while she finished talking on the 'phone, while his companions watched from a distance. She put the 'phone down and looked up at him giving him a big smile.

"I see your friends have arrived then."

"Yes, thank goodness," he laughed, then asked hopefully, "I want to take you out for dinner tonight, if that's all right with you?"

She shook her head slowly but still smiling said, "Sorry ... not tonight, I'm washing my hair,but," she went on wistfully, "if you only want the information on Black Lake Park you don't have to take me out to get it ... I've got it all here, in my old work folder."

She reached down under her counter and produced a battered old green A4 folder, held together with an elastic band. She handed it to Steve saying, "I don't want to know what you are all up to, but good luck." She touched his hand gently as he took the folder from her. Her smile had lost the sparkle.

"I can't thank you enough Barbara," Steve said earnestly, "but you must let me take you out for a meal if only to help me spend this." He produced the clip of money from his pocket.

"Come on," he pleaded with her, "let's have a bit of fun. Life's too short and it's only the Government's money anyway," he added and her smile regained its sparkle.

"In that case," she asserted, "although I don't know you at all, I'll take a risk this once, so pick me up outside here 8.00 p.m. tonight ... yes?" she asked.

"No hair wash?"

"Not now," she laughed. "You'll have to suffer me with un-washed hair, if you don't mind?" She touched his hand again, fleetingly, sending a tingle right up his arm.

"See you at 8.00 p.m. then you chose the restaurant ... see you." He squeezed her hand and returned to his curious colleagues.

They went outside and Steve showed them the folder containing the maps and other information.

"Well done Steve," British said slapping him on the back, "the sooner we get to base the sooner we'll have a plan of action."

Steve retrieved his car and drove round through the thronging crowds and met them outside as arranged. They set off with Steve following the Land Rover.

They drove for about 20 minutes through very beautiful countryside until they saw a sign saying 'beware of the deer' and beside it, pinned on a high dry-stone wall, was a notice declaring that Black Lake Park was closed to all visitors.

They drove on for another half a mile then came to a T junction. Straight ahead was a large set of iron grille gates with a gate-house guarding the entrance. They could see a driveway which swept away through pine trees until it was out of sight. A large 'CLOSED' sign was pinned on the gate.

A signpost at the side of the road indicated that to the right was the M 1 and to the left was a cart track, unsuitable for motor vehicles. British turned left and drove on until they were out of sight of the gate-house then pulled over to the side of the track, with Steve struggling to keep the M.G. going over the high ruts in the track, just behind him.

They all got out and looked at the wall which stretched as far as the eye could see in both directions.

"This is Black Lake Park," British declared. "Someone give me a hand up onto the wall."

Henry cupped his hands for British to put his foot in and lifted British until his head was above wall height. He stayed motionless for a few seconds then indicated for Henry to lower him.

"Well that's a bit of a bugger," he said dusting himself down. "There is, it appears, an electrified fence, running parallel to the wall, but it's too far away to jump over, from the wall, sod it!" he exclaimed. "Well that's our first problem boys, but once we are in, there seems to be lots of trees for cover. Mind you," he went on, "I could also see what looks like a sentry tower, let's hope it's simply a fire-watch tower and not manned, otherwise we may get our arses burned." He joked grimly as they resumed their drive to the farmhouse.

Hall Farm was a large three-storied house, fronted by a long gravel driveway which swept round the side and into a courtyard surrounded by out-buildings, just as the Colonel had described to Steve.

They drove straight into a huge barn with Steve thankful to end the hard drive he'd just had and he switched off the ignition gratefully.

"Not the sort of car for this terrain eh?" Craig smiled sympathetically down at Steve.

"You're damn right about that." Steve hauled himself out of the M.G. "But it pulls the birds," he rejoined as he walked slowly round inspecting it. "Look at all the shit it's picked up," he groaned whilst kicking some dirt off with his foot.

"Never mind," replied Craig laughing at him. "You'll have time to clean it before you take her out tonight, once we've had our ops meeting. Gather round everyone," he suddenly shouted, clapping his hands loudly for attention.

"We've got our little pinkies to do especially as our base is so close to our target." He paused shaking his head. "I can't believe the Colonel could make a mistake like this ... however," he took a deep breath, "we have to make the best of it ... I'll do you first Steve." He turned back to the Land Rover and took a small first-aid bag out of the map shelf. He opened it and placed its contents on the bonnet of the Land Rover, he turned to Steve.

"Right, place your hand here, front up," he indicated the bonnet, next to the first-aid box, "and hold it still okay? ... It won't hurt," he laughed seeing the look on Steve's concerned face. "All I'm going to do is paint the end of your fingers, with this little brush." He showed Steve a small make-up brush. "This 'New Skin' puts a second skin over your finger-prints, so that when we leave this place, the bastards won't be able to trace who was here understand? It dries almost straight away," he explained to an incredulous Steve as he brushed both of Steve's hands.

He repeated this operation on Henry and British, then he asked Steve to do his fingers for him.

They stood around talking for a few minutes waiting for the 'skin' to dry then Craig said to Henry, "Get the clothing and boots out. We're putting on a change of clothing that you will not take off until we leave this farmhouse," he told Steve, as Henry unloaded a large canvas holdall.

"And the Scavengers will see to the rest," British advised Steve, "and we wear these combat-boots from now on." He passed pair of boots to Steve. "These are yours we knew your size from the Ryder Club visit, when you were kitted out ... see."

He turned the boots over and showed Steve the sole of the boots. "The pattern is the same on all our boots ... we try to confuse the buggers." He laughed, "Especially if you can manage to walk backwards every now and then ... just swing round a tree, that should do it .. mind you," he added, "I don't know if it works, but it amuses me to think of our trackers trying to figure out two tracks leading to a tree, then, kapput nothing." He chortled at his sense of humour.

"You are barking mad, British," Henry declared, whilst balancing on one leg, pulling on a black boiler-suit. "Who, in their right mind would play games in a combat zone? ... Bloody crazy." Henry joked.

"I'm not bloody crazy," retorted British. "A little irritable first thing in the morning, maybe, but not crazy." He threw a discarded shoe, humorously, at Henry.

They all finished putting their boiler-suits on, then piled their clothes and all their personal effects into the canvas holdall and put it back in the Land Rover.

Henry issued them all with black balaclava helmets to complete their all-black outfit.

"You are completely invisible British," advised a laughing

Henry, who added, "apart from your white beard and white hair."

"Bollocks," replied British, "you won't see me when I'm really ready for action."

"Come on, let's unload and get inside. I was given a key by the Colonel," Craig interrupted the general banter.

They all helped to retrieve two large boxes with rope handles, from a trailer already parked in the barn. Steve looked inquiringly at them. Henry caught his eye and said, "All the gear we should need for the job ... we had it sent ahead, couldn't go in the Land Rover," he added, "not with all of us, no room."

"Christ, it weighs a ton," Steve gasped as he took hold of one side opposite Henry, while holding his travelling bag in his other hand.

"Are you a man or a mouse," quipped Henry, as he lifted his side up.

"Eek, eek," gasped Steve. "If I get a hernia there may be trouble ahead." He heaved the load up and they walked over to the back door, following Craig and British carrying the other box.

Craig unlocked the door and they found themselves entering a large kitchen which had a huge, black-leaded oven range dominating the far side. They dropped their loads in the middle of the floor, thankfully.

"Right ... you two," he looked at Henry and British. "Sweep the house and check for a look-out position as high as you can ... we should be able to see quite a distance."

They both nodded and opening one of the boxes removed a small black box from which Henry pulled out a small aerial. He then switched it on at the side. Steve had never seen this before and asked what it did, to a bemused Henry.

"I'm going to 'sweep' the house for 'bugs'," he replied, "just to make sure no-one has planted a listening device anywhere ... can't be too careful in this game."

British also got a 'sweeper' and the pair of them started to go round the kitchen with Steve watching in amazement.

"Steve." Craig interrupted his thoughts. "Can you go and secure the barn then have a look round the out-buildings to make sure no-one is around, okay? And take your gun."

"Sure thing Craig," Steve answered pleased to be able to do something positive.

Steve opened the green bag and took his gun out and laid it carefully on the table, he then took his one remaining clip of bullets out and saw he had only five left.

"Christ!" exclaimed Craig who was looking on. "Is that all the bullets you've got?" He sounded incredulous.

"Well, I did ask the Colonel for more and he said he would send some more up with Henry," Steve replied defensively as he put the clip in his gun.

"Sorry Steve ... getting wound up too soon," Craig apologised. "I'll check Henry has them, while you are securing the outside ... see ya." Craig turned and left Steve tightening the black belt over his boiler-suit.

Steve slipped the gun into his belt, wishing Henry had got him a holster before he shot his 'wedding tackle' off, as forecast by the Colonel.

He stepped out into the farmyard which was bathed in the evening sun and walked slowly to his right towards the first dilapidated out-house. He pushed the rotten wooden door open and looked all around the small room, but it only contained a pile of sacks in one corner. The largest rat he'd ever seen, disappeared into it. The sudden movement caused him to involuntarily go for his gun.

He smiled to himself *'slow down you silly sod'* he told himself and left the rat in peace.

He closed the protesting door and strolled to the next building, the door of which was a stable-door. He quietly opened the top half but saw only empty horse stables. He closed the door and secured it with a hasp and staple.

'So far so good,' he thought as he scanned the yard very carefully and became aware that he was being watched from the farm. He gave the thumbs up to Craig to let him know all was well so far. Craig acknowledged with a wave and faded out of sight. He checked a couple more out-buildings then went into the main barn where their cars were parked. He entered, feeling quite relaxed, when from the pile of straw bales at the far end of the barn he heard a sudden rustle of straw, followed by a guttural curse and a head appeared over the top of the bales.

Steve's heart nearly stopped beating with fright and he threw himself behind the M.G. trying frantically to pull his gun at the same time.

"Don't shoot, don't shoot, Señor, we are on same side," a foreign sounding voice implored him from above.

Steve looked over the top of his car, but the head had gone out of sight.

"Who are you ... show yourself ... and move real slowly if you want to stay alive," Steve shouted, his voice breaking slightly with the strain, as he pointed his wavering gun at the area where he had last seen the head. His heart was pounding so loudly he felt it could burst. 'Pull yourself together' he breathed to himself, 'keep alert,' as he slowly knelt up, both arms outstretched, resting on the car bonnet, pointing the gun at the top of the bales.

"No shoot Señor," the disembodied voice said again. "I am sent by the Colonel to make food for company ... is true," the voice protested, "I show myself ... si?"

Steve realised that this person knew who they were and relaxing slightly stood up as two hands appeared over the hay bales.

"Okay ... pal ... but take it easy," Steve advised the person. "I've got an itchy trigger finger."

"Si ... I understand Señor," came the now assertive reply and Steve saw the intruder stand up.

"Don't move ... pal, let's talk." Steve walked out from behind the car but kept his gun trained on the person.

"What's your name?"

"Santiago Montana, Señor."

"Well then, Santiago ... you'd better get your arse down here, but real slow, okay?" Steve commanded him in as tough a voice as he could muster, given the circumstances.

Santiago made his way to a small ladder leaning against the hay and slowly climbed down, as instructed.

Steve backed away, keeping the distance between them as Santiago, reaching the floor, turned with hands up, towards him.

Steve was confronted by a swarthy, broad-shouldered man, with a florid face and heavy jowls. He had short, jet-black, sleek hair and was smiling widely, showing two rows of perfect white teeth. The linen jacket he had on was straining at the seam, trying to contain his bulging arms.

"Señor" he asked quietly, "may I take my arms down now?"

Steve was just going to answer him when from behind him he heard a footstep, then, "Santiago ... you old bastard, what are you doing here? ... It's all right Steve, he's one of us," Craig shouted as he rushed past and embraced Santiago who embraced Craig back joyfully, almost lifting him off his feet, shouting loudly "Ole ... ole, Señor Cragg, you El Perro," and the pair of them did a wild impromptu dance round the barn floor.

Steve replaced his gun in his belt, making sure the safety catch was on, relieved that all was friendly and watched the two of them going wild until they calmed down enough to explain their happiness to Steve.

"This is Santiago," Craig introduced Steve who shook hands with a still beaming Santiago. "Best field chef I've ever met and he can shoot the eye of a goat out at a hundred yards. He and I go back a long way." Craig turned to Santiago. "What are you doing hiding in bloody hay then, Señorita problems, eh?"

"No, Señor Cragg, I sent by Colonel to look after farmhouse, but you no here when I arrive with the trailer. I no have key, so I wait and fall asleep, I no hear when your cars arrive ... too much vino tinto." He shrugged his massive shoulders apologetically.

"You ... waiting for a key, I can hardly believe it," Craig answered. "You normally just bulldoze your way in, what's up with you, old age?" Craig joked.

"No ... I told not to 'make waves', Señor Cragg, so I not batter door down," Santiago answered, waving his large hands around in explanation, "or shoot bloody lock off," and he produced a gun so quickly that Steve didn't even see where he had got it from.

"Not lost your speed though, eh? Bastardo." Craig laughed as Santiago replaced the gun in his jacket pocket. "Good job I came along when I did eh Steve?" Steve readily nodded his agreement.

"Come on Santiago," Craig said as he turned to leave the barn. "Come and meet the rest of the guys ... you carry on Steve and we'll see you later."

Santiago retrieved a suit-case from the trailer and joined Craig, his massive frame swaying as he walked flat-footed across the farmyard. He was still laughing and sharing old times with 'Señor Cragg.'

As Steve watched them go he suddenly felt very tired as the shock of this event came home to him. *'Could I really have tried to kill someone, if necessary?'* he thought to himself. *'Or I could have been killed myself, Santiago was fast with his gun.'*

He sat down on a bale and rested for a while, before completing his patrol with nothing to report when he got back to the farmhouse.

They were all sitting in the kitchen listening to Santiago

recount how he was assigned to this job and, indeed, he was making love to 'his little flower' when the call came.

"My leetle flower no like Santiago going, so she speet on me and no wish to see me again ..." He drew a finger across his throat then laughed. "But she will wait for me, I verrry good to her ... and her leetle sister." He rocked with laughter again, as he out-lined the curves of a woman with his hands.

Craig, having the green folder that Barbara had given Steve earlier, in his hands, stood up and called them all to order. He wanted to start the ops' meeting. They all looked at Craig expectantly.

"The order is," he began as he emptied the folder onto the table, "to kill Lord McForson before he receives the finance from the American, Martin Silverman ... who I believe some of you gentleman have already seen in Spain, yes?"

Steve and British nodded their agreement as Craig spread the folder paper over the table.

"The reason we need to do this, according to the Colonel, is that Lord McForson claims that he is a descendant of James VI of Scotland and I of England, his lineage being from a child that was stated stillborn in 1568, but actually the child, a boy, survived." Craig paused to let this information sink in.

"Is it possible?" Henry queried, echoing a question they were all thinking, except for a bored Santiago, who just sat trimming his nails with the scissors of his Swiss Army knife.

"The experts, again according to the Colonel, say it is not possible," he paused, then went on, "but the point is that certain Amercans do believe his claim." He pointedly emphasised the 'do', "And are now willing to back him if a new government takes over by force. He would become King Stuart 1st of the United Kingdom, silly as this may seem. This is not a new claim by any means, Lord McForson has stated his claim for years, but without the financial clout to do anything about it, until now."

"Do we know how big his outfit is?" asked British.

"All we know is that he has a small force that he had trained, up in Scotland ... we think around fifty men."

"Where are they?" asked Steve.

"That's for us to find out," Craig answered grimly. "They may be here in Black Lake."

"Bloody hell ... fifty men and only five of us!" drawled Britis

"Not quite, I'm afraid," Craig informed them. "There will be only four of us ... Santiago is here only to cook for us and give back-up here at the farm as soon as we go into action ... then he leaves us for sunnier climes."

"Lucky bastard," British moaned. "I'd sooner leave for sunnier climes and make my sandcastles in Spain."

"Bollocks! ... You know you like the action, otherwise you wouldn't be here." Henry grinned as he spoke.

"Santiago will make dinner," announced Santiago as he stood up. "I have already the food ... be ready one hour," and with that he went to the far end of the kitchen and lit the gas range.

"Right, gentlemen," Craig carried on. "Let's study this map of Black Lake." He spread the map out on the table and they all gathered round to study it closely.

"This stream runs right through the estate," Craig traced the route with the tip of a knife. "It goes into the lake, going under the railway viaduct, then exits down a series of water-falls and through a power house making their own electricity ... very organised." He commented, "No wonder he bought this place. He must run the electric fence off it as well." He peered at the map. "Obviously that was added after this map was made. We can assume the fence runs all the way round inside the wall. There must be weak point where the railway goes in, and out, of the estate," he pointed to the railway, "here ... and here. There seem to be only two gate-house entrances, one of which we know is closed for normal use. I don't see the fire-tower marked on here, so it looks as though it is a later addition, which means, " he asserted, "that it is a look-out tower... Blast ... there must be more than one, that's for sure," he maintained, speaking softly.

"So the first thing we must do tonight is to a circuit of the estate and look for weaknesses, because, gentlemen there will be some I assure you. So we will have something to eat courtesy of Santiago, then a couple of hours sleep." He looked at his watch. "It is now 19.30 hours, are we agreed?"

They all checked their watches with Steve the only one having to adjust his watch, much to the amusement of British who chivvied him to buy a proper watch.

Craig went on, "We will leave at 02.00 hours and I reckon we should only take two hours, to complete as dawn is breaking."

"Why go at 02.00? and not as soon as it goes dark?" Steve interrupted, perplexed about the late start.

"Because," sighed Craig, "it is a well-known fact that security men are at their most relaxed, semi-dozing, if not sleeping, between the hours of 02.00 and 05.00 hours. I believe it has something to do with the temperature of a person's body-clock. Most people who die during the night, die during these hours." Craig told an amazed Steve. "Any more questions?" Craig looked round them all.

"What about my meeting with Barbara to-night?"

"Cancelled," came the curt reply, "duty first, so you will give the petty cash back and just dream ... when, and if, we get back to London. Just send her a present and say thank-you for the information, Steve. Hard luck old son." Steve was patted on the back. "That's the way it is in this business," Craig added, when he saw Steve's unhappy face. "Just think of staying alive, not fucking, okay?"

"Okay," agreed Steve, who then asked, "where's the 'phone, I'd better ring mother to let her know I'm all right?"

"Ring your fucking mother!! You don't half ask some

stupid questions!" exploded Craig. "I'm not sure why you are with us on something like this ... I suppose the Colonel has a motive .... but really, Steve, forget homelife, at least while working, you can make it up to all the women in your life, when you go home ... they'll only be mad at you for a while." He softened his tone. "We all go through it for the Queen and Country, y'know."

"I ask questions when I don't know," Steve said defensively. "Otherwise how will I know ... I haven't been trained like you lot and I, like you, don't know why I'm here either, I'm a pen-pusher out of his depth," mumbled a now deflated Steve.

"You are doing all right," British and Henry said, almost together. "Keep asking questions and you have more chance of survival," added Henry helpfully.

"Sorry Steve, just getting a bit tense," Craig apologised as British and Henry scowled at him. "Anyway, that's it for now, so we'll eat, then rest, until 02.00 hours ... oh and don't forget your night-scopes, that's all." Craig swept up all the papers back into the fold and left the kitchen.

"Night-scopes?" Steve whispered to Henry.

"Image enhancing night vision ... helps us see in the dark, see ya," and Henry departed leaving Steve deep in thought.

"Señor Steve," Santiago interrupted his thoughts, "you like a small Tequila, pep up?" A bottle was thrust in front of him by a smiling Santiago. Steve shook his head, then asked, "Have you had your fingers done yet?" thinking of the finger-prints on the bottle.

"Señor, look." Santiago put the bottle down and showed Steve his scarred fingertips, as if they had been burned. "Acid, Señor, I do it to myself many years ago, now, no problem." He roared laughing. "No prints, no hang for sheep, or babies." He roared again at his wit, and went back to his cooking.

Steve shook his head in amazement thinking, *'they're all bloody crackers in this game.'*

Santiago produced a superb meal, only upset because no-one could have wine with his culinary delights and they all settled down to rest until 01.45 a.m. as instructed.

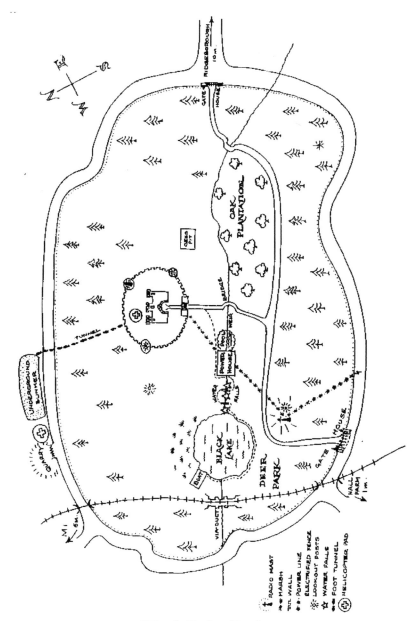

Black Lake Park

171

CHAPTER 10
Black Lake Park

"I propose, that as the Black Lake is so near, we proceed on foot, and circumnavigate the whole Park," Craig told the assembled company. They were all dressed in black and carrying their night-scopes, strapped to their belts. They had checked their guns and each had a small knife strapped to his thigh.

"We will look for anywhere where we might make an entry into the Park, but I do not want to alert them in any way, do you understand?"

They all nodded and Craig carried on, "When we get back we will have a de-briefing session, before we hit the pit. Now while we are out there we might run into local people, could be a courting couple or poachers, anyone, and you must not get involved at all," Craig stressed, looking round fiercely at everyone, " in fact you must run away, if there is any chance of contact."

"Run away?" they all mouthed the words to each other.

"Yes, run away, disappear as fast as you can, it won't be difficult, it's as black as a badger's arse out there."

"What if we come across their guards, then?" asked Henry as he took his knife out to test the sharpness of the blade. They all looked at Craig with fierce interest.

"Do what you have to do to get away as quietly as you can,

otherwise shoot the bastards, then get your arses back here as fast as you can." He looked at them all in turn, "If any of you hear a shot, then you must return here pronto," he added.

"Pronto," echoed Santiago, "and I, Santiago, will wait for you all, I watch from the high vista." He pointed up at the ceiling, "And if any Perro follows you, I keel," he ran his finger across his throat.

"Thank you, Santiago," Craig cleared his throat, trying not to laugh at this show of dramatics, then carried on, "and no stopping to look for each other ... got it? As Santiago has just said he will watch for our return, so make the whistle or he might blow your fucking heads off ... and before you ask Steve ... this is the reed to blow when you get back near the farm." He handed Steve a small piece of card that had a tiny strip of copper across a hole in it and said, "Try that."

Steve put it in his mouth, failed to get a sound at his first try, but managed a thin high pitched whistle with his second, much to his relief.

"Right, let's go for a stroll," Craig commanded. "You catch the arrow, British." British nodded assent.

Steve had just time to ask Henry what 'catch the arrow' meant, and Henry told him it referred to cowboy films when the rider at the back always got the arrow first.

They all trouped out of the backdoor and into the inky, black night, watched by Santiago, who was silently wishing them luck whilst squeezing a small cross in his hand and crossing himself repeatedly.

They went in single file, like a black snake, across the farmyard, and along one side of the cart-track that they had arrived down yesterday. Craig led with British 'catching the arrow,' stopping and turning every now and then to listen intently, then running silently to catch up with them again.

They reached the end of the track and saw the Black Lake Park perimeter wall across the road. Craig halted them and they all crouched down by the wall, virtually invisible.

"I reckon that if we go to the right first, the way we came yesterday, we can suss the gate-house out and also have another look at that watch-tower we saw. So keep well into the wall," he said this mainly for Steve's benefit as the others were already against the wall, but Steve was standing slightly away. On hearing the command he went as close as the others.

They set off walking in the long grass, having an occasional stumble over a stone or root, until they came to what appeared to be a stone parapet. They looked over and saw it was the railway, running underneath the road.

"Can you see the bloody electric fence anybody?"

"No," came the whispered reply from British. "My bet is that it terminates either side of the track, otherwise the railway workers would set it off when they do the track maintenance ... it could be a good way in," he added.

"Let's press on then ... that's a good start," Craig whispered back sounding very pleased with himself.

About fifty yards further on, they came to two huge solid wooden gates that were chained together with two huge padlocks which had turned rusty with non-use.

"Give me a leg up," Craig asked Henry, who cupped his hands together and hoisted Craig smoothly up the side of the gate. Craig carefully looked over then suddenly ducked.

"What's up Craig?" British whispered.

"Something is moving by the trees, so I'll just have a look through my imager night-scope." Craig untied his light and slowly straightened up and looked over the wall again, and then lifted the imager to his eye. The others waited patiently and Steve tried to keep as calm as he could although again his heart was racing like mad.

Craig lowered himself as Henry let him down slowly. "Panic over boys," he said quietly. "It's a herd of fucking deer. There is also a drive going as far as I could see and about forty yards along to the right, there seems to be a sub-station, with a power line looping across behind the pine trees. I suppose it

174

joins to a pylon which must link with the Power House, by the Lake ,... so far so good." He brushed himself down and with a curt, "Let's go," set off along the wall again. They all followed, semi-doubled up.

Half a mile further on they came to a small bridge where the stream from the estate ran under, but the electric wire line was suspended across it and they could hear it humming away, like an angry bee.

"There's another possible," Craig murmured, as he looked over the wall, courtesy of Henry again. "Only wet." He strained to look to his left, then suddenly croaked, "It *is* a bloody look-out tower. I can see the people in the viewing hut and ...," he paused to put his scope to his eye again, "I can see a search-light. ... Oh! Fuck me," he said in exasperation, "If there's one here, they must have more round the other side. ... Sod it," he grunted as he climbed down. He clipped his scope back on his belt, then beckoned for them to follow him.

They pressed on until they came to the junction where, to their right, was the road they had driven in on from Ridgeborough. It then turned right and ran straight on in front of them, following the wall, to the M 1, according to the road sign.

The metal gates still had the 'CLOSED' sign fixed to it and the gatehouse was unlit and deserted.

They had a problem now, because they would be exposed as they tried to cross past the gates. They decided the best method was to crawl on their stomachs as fast as they possibly could, and blessed the fact that the moon was not out that night. Also, according to Craig, the guards should be dozing by now, as it was 3.00 a.m.

Once decided, they executed the move as fast as they could, and Steve, although he hurt his knees and elbows, was as fast as the others, which pleased him greatly and he silently rubbed his hurting places, without saying a word to anybody.

"Christ, that hurt," British exclaimed, rubbing himself

furiously on his legs.

"Time to lose some weight, I'd say," Henry chuckled quietly in British's ear, which only produced a string of whispered profanities from British, as they crouched around Craig.

They all froze, momentarily, as they heard a rustling noise to their right, relaxing only when they saw a fox running across the road, nose down, hoovering all the scents up in his quivering nose. The fox suddenly stopped, put his nose in the air, gave a quick look both ways and raced back the way he had arrived.

"Thank Christ guards don't have noses as sensitive as old foxy, or we'd be in deep trouble," murmured Henry watching the fox run to cover.

They filed off, following the wall for half-a-mile which swung round to the left for another few hundred yards before bending right.

They were jogging along, on the balls of their feet when Craig stopped and sank down, waving them down as well. Ahead of them, outlined above the top of the wall was what appeared to be a look-out tower, which they all studied through their night-scopes.

"I reckon that's a fire-watch tower, I don't think they would put a manned security tower next to the road, otherwise it would alert the authorities that there was something going on in the Park," British whispered to Craig.

"I reckon you're right ... I can't see any movement ... can anyone?" he asked the group, who all agreed with British.

Clipping the scopes back on their belts, they proceeded as before. The road slowly swung to their left then ran straight on as far as they could see, with pine trees either side, making it resemble a black tunnel.

Craig spotted a break in the trees, behind the wall and asking for a leg up off Henry, scoped the area, then dropped down excited at what he'd seen.

"I can see the Mansion on a rise, so I want all of you to have a look."

The Mansion stood on a hill that was surrounded by a perimeter wall, with two towers perched high on its East and West corners. The East tower was topped by a large communication tower, with flashing beacon.

"Why do you reckon they have a beacon?" mused Craig, to no one in particular.

"Aircraft ... helicopter!" exclaimed British. "Of course, he'll have a bloody helicopter, as sure as eggs is eggs."

Armed with this information they carried on jogging along the black road until British hissed, "Car coming."

They ran to their right across the road and climbed over a small, dry-stone wall, crouching as low as they could, in the long damp grass.

The car passed without problem, but, as they waited, they suddenly became aware of the ground trembling beneath them.

"What the fuck's that?" Craig muttered, listening intently as the sound faded away.

"It sounded like an underground train to me," Henry said.

"There can't be ... we're not near the railway yet ... that's another quarter of a mile to go yet," Craig said thoughtfully, "according to the map, anyway."

"I agree with Henry," British said, "and I reckon it was heading towards the Mansion ... what do you reckon, Steve?"

Steve nodded agreement, having kept to himself since Craig had been angry with him for asking too many questions.

"We'll keep this side of the road until we reach the railway," Craig decided. "It'll be harder going, but we should reach an old quarry shortly, according to the map anyway ... there might be a connection."

A hundred yards further on, their way was blocked by a high-wired security fence, forcing them to return to the road. They were aware that the night sky was starting to lighten behind them, dawn was approaching fast as they doubled their speed, much to Steve's consternation, as he was already feeling the pace of the journey.

"There's the old quarry." Craig stopped them to peer ahead through his scope. "Supposed to be disused now, but we'll take that with a pinch of salt," he added grimly.

They passed the quarry at the double, noting through the wire mesh that there were a couple of lorries parked inside the compound. Once they had passed it, British made his way back, to look again at the lorries, at Craig's request.

"I reckon the quarry is in use again," he told them when he returned. "But I can't see any digger, J.C.B.'s ... so I don't know why the lorries are there at all," he added.

"We'll assume then," Craig said, "that the quarry is linked up to the Mansion, for reasons unknown as yet, by that train we heard. What a stroke of luck we heard that,... we need all the luck we can handle." He turned and led them forward until they reached another bridge over the railway, the electric fence diving into the ground as before, and re-appearing on the other side.

"This is the other side of the estate, so we can't be far from completing the circuit now, lads," Craig encouraged them.

The road turned right now, away from the wall, carrying on towards the M 1, leaving them to follow the wall to their left, back on the cart-track again.

They found the stream entering the Park on its way to the Black Lake and they could see it passing under a viaduct that carried the railway across the estate. The day was now getting very light as it was 4.30 a.m.

"We should have no problem now," Craig said. "There's nothing left to see ... so let's bugger off back to base ... the faster the better."

He had no sooner said it when they heard the un-mistakable sound of a helicopter.

"Down," Craig snapped. "Foetus position, pile together, so no arms and legs showing, just be a black blob," he commanded as he rolled himself into a ball and they all squeezed tightly together, hiding their faces.

The helicopter passed somewhere overhead and they only moved when the sound had died away.

They unwound themselves and adjusted their equipment.

"What do you reckon?" Craig asked British.

"I think it was headed towards the quarry."

"I reckon that as well," agreed Henry.

"So do I," Craig agreed. "Let's get back to the farm ... I'm fucking well starvin'," his scouse accent came to the fore, "and Santiago does a mean breakfast."

They needed no urging on as they made their way back to where they had started along the wall, two hours earlier. They turned away from the wall, heading back to the farmhouse in ever lightening skies.

They stopped, after entering the farmyard for Craig to blow his reed to let Santiago know they were there.

"Ole, buenos dias, Señors," Santiago's voice came from behind and above them. They all spun round to see Santiago, standing on the roof of the barn, gun in hand, smiling down on them. "I see you, plenty running to have Santiago's food, si?" he laughed at his little joke, then putting his gun in his jacket pocket, climbed down a drain-pipe showing an agility that belied his size and joined them in the yard. "I see big helicopter, Señor Cragg, very low ... he see you?" he asked showing concern.

"No. I don't think so, otherwise he'd have circled for another look ... let's eat." He put his arm round Santiago and they made their way across the yard gratefully and into the warm farm kitchen. Santiago crashed around in a flurry of pans, pausing only to put an apron on. It amused Steve to see a trained killer in an apron.

"I good cook, Señor Steve," Santiago had caught Steve

smiling. "I take care be clean, no Mexican tun-tum." He rubbed his hands over his stomach. "I'll show you how to cook, if you ever come to Puerto de la Cruz."

"Sorry Santiago," Steve apologised. "I wasn't laughing at you ... you move well for a big man, that's all and I do wish I could cook so I might take you up on that offer." Steve added, "But where is Puerto what-ever?"

"Tenerife, Señor, very nice, very warm all year round." Santiago carried on laying the table as everyone went to wash, shave and shower.

Santiago laid on a huge cooked breakfast, after which, despite them all starting to feel sleepy, they had a de-briefing session. Everyone put their own ideas forward on how to tackle the problem now that they had seen the perimeter of Black Lake estate.

"We can go in as a team, or in pairs, or single," Craig suggested. "What does everyone feel?" He looked round the table. "I favour pairs myself," he added, leaning forward on the table.

"Sounds good to me ... I'm for that, " agreed Henry.

"And me," British informed them, then they all looked at Steve for his input.

"Well," he started hesitantly, "not having the experience, having only been on one operation," he looked at British, "I'll go along with what you all decide is the best way of doing the job." He slumped back in his seat.

"Fair enough, Steve," Craig replied. "Who goes with who then?"

"I'll team with Steve," British advised them. "We've already worked together in Spain and I'm happy to be with him ... that'll leave you and Henry together, and I know you've been operational on the same case in the past."

"Excellent," Craig agreed smiling. "Now, what about this operation ... any ideas?"

"Get on the railway line, go under the road, through the

tunnel, then along to the viaduct. Abseil down to the stream and follow it to the power-house, blow it up, then wait for the bastards to come out shooting," Henry suggested fervently.

"Ang on der partner," Craig's scouse accent interrupted the blood-thirsty Henry, "think you're fucking James Bond ... you'll get us blown away. Ta very much for your idea. I liked your plan up until ... then blow the fucking power house up ... you mad sod," he admonished Henry.

"Well," said Henry, on the defensive now, "we could put explosives in there ... we've got plenty here and use a delayed timer, to make a diversion for us all."

"Now you're talking," Craig was more enthusiastic about this plan. "What do you two think?" he directed his remark to British and Steve who looked at each other for mutual agreement.

"We like it ... because," explained British, "that would also create a diversion for us as well. So if we can time our operation together, so much the better, yes?" he looked at Steve for support.

"I think ...," Steve was wary of not showing himself up, "I think British and I could go in through the main entrance and go up the driveway to the mansion and suprise them ... 'cos they won't expect that." He stared down at the table while this idea hit home.

"Go through the fucking main entrance, walk up to the mansion and surprise them ... have I heard you right?" Craig said in a condescending voice.

"Yes."

"You'd be fucking dead before you got through the gate, dick-head," Craig admonished him severely.

"I disagree," Steve answered, aware that British had closed his eyes to await his revelation.

"Go on ... amaze me," Craig countered, putting his hands behind his head.

Henry decided he needed another cup of tea and leaned

across and poured himself another in anticipation of a serious argument.

"Well," began Steve, "I noticed that the vehicle which passed us on the road ... when we heard the train," he explained, "was a milk-van, which set me thinking that the mansion would have to have deliveries of food and milk, yes?" They all had to agree with him so far. He went on, "Now, I reckon that the milk delivery would be around dawn and they will automatically let it through the gates, when they see it on the security cameras. If the two of us waited by the gates, we could tag on behind it, and be shielded, all the way up to the back-door, so to speak." He relaxed back in his chair. "Or am I being a mad sod as well?" he asked sarcastically looking at Craig.

"Bloody good idea, partner," British enthused. "I reckon it's so risky that they would not expect anyone to try to follow a vehicle through the front ... it's brilliant, well done." British held his hand out to Steve who shook it happily.

"I admit I've guessed the delivery will be early," he admitted, "but I'm willing to do a stake out early tomorrow morning to check the arrival time. I think the delivery will be at the same time each day, and if they have a large number of men, I think it will be a large enough vehicle to cover British and myself. Can I have some more toast please, Santiago?" he asked a startled Santiago, who had sat listening to the meeting intently drinking his tequila, with salt and lemon.

"Si, Señor mad sod." He sprang up and started the toast.

"You know Steve," Craig admitted slowly, "I would never have thought of that method of entry, which means, in retrospect, that they would not expect it either ... well done, Steve." Steve was positively glowing with pride now.

"I'll go for that, and if the delivery time is right for us, we can all get into the estate at the same time, from opposite ends and with the help of the explosion diversion, we should be able to at least get to Lord McForson," he declared, smiling for a change. "So an early start for you tomorrow, Steve ... but right now I'm going to have a large whisky. I need it to relax, then we can hit the hay until to-night ... meeting finished."

Santiago carried over a bottle of whisky and some glasses on a tray and the toast for Steve.

"Thank you Santiago," Craig said and poured himself a large whisky, with a splash of water, while the others followed suit, rapidly.

"May I ask one question, please?" Steve queried.

"Go ahead," replied a happy Craig sipping his drink.

"How do we get away afterwards?"

"Ah," Craig sighed, staring at his glass closely. "A fucking trouble maker ... good question though, eh, boys?" he enquired round the table, then said, "I simply don't know ... okay?" He sounded tired for the first time.

"Fine ... just thought I'd ask," Steve raised his glass and standing up said to them all, "this side of the table would like to make toast with the other side of the table ... to our success, gentlemen and stuff 'em all."

They raised their glasses and downed their drinks in one.

"Come on boys," Craig said, as he refilled his glass. "A bird canna' fly on one wing alone." He laughed, "It's an old Scottish saying," as he swilled it down his throat.

Steve was astounded how fast these men could drink once they finished being on duty. A feat that, in a short time, he would be able to match.

"Who's staying on duty then, while we're sleeping?" British asked, as he swiftly knocked his third drink back.

"Santiago," Craig answered happily, pointing at Santiago.

"Señors, Santiago guard every bastardo while they sleep," he said, as he downed another tequila. "Salu, Santiago never sleep on duty," he added confidently glass in the air.

"That's true," admitted Craig, "he can drink all day and night and still be alert, never met a man like him ... I'm done for, I'm off to my pit ... hell, it's 9.00 a.m. see you all at 18.00

hours." He stood up with an effort. "Christ, I'm stiff now, getting old, where's my zimmer," he joked as he departed and went upstairs, leaving the three of them all starting to feel tired.

"Well done Steve," British congratulated him warmly. "For an untrained operative I think 'the boy dun good', we'll be a good team." He paused. "Don't worry about how we get out of this, you and I have got a lot a women to love yet and the Devil takes care of his own, night or day." He corrected himself with a laugh.

"Cheers British," Steve replied. "I appreciate what you've just said, because I was just thinking I should have stuck to normal office work, instead of this sort of work," he added more to himself than anyone else.

"Bollocks," British threw back at him, "you enjoy it," and left Steve sitting with Henry and Santiago.

"Another drink, Steve?" Henry asked.

"Just the one then, if you insist," Steve agreed.

"You're easily led, aren't you?" Henry quipped merrily as Santiago produced another bottle after pronouncing the 'rights of the bottle' was in order.

Steve didn't remember going to bed but had a very bad headache when he was woken by a smiling Santiago, bearing a steaming mug of tea, which he carefully set down on the little wooden, bedside table.

"Buenos tardes, Señor Steve ... te."

"Gracias Santiago ... I feel awful," Steve admitted as he struggled to sit up.

Santiago produced a hip-flask and poured a generous helping of whisky into Steve's tea saying, "Hair of el perro ... you feel better soon."

"El what?"

"El perro, the dog," Santiago explained patiently.

"Thanks ... I hope it works," Steve said and he drank the

tea as quickly as possible.

Thirty minutes later he was feeling a lot better and after a sharp, cold shower he joined the others in the kitchen. They were already eating their breakfast/dinner.

"Hi Steve," Craig welcomed him. "Get some food inside you ... you've got a long night. We are going to get all the equipment out and give it a check over. The viaduct must have a hundred feet drop at least, so we have to make sure we have enough rope, otherwise we're in the shit, or the stream," he joked. "What time are you thinking of getting to the location then?" he asked Steve.

"About dawn, I think," answered Steve as Santiago set a huge plate of fried bacon, eggs, sausages and fried bread in front of him. Steve carried on, "About 4.00 a.m. and as long as it takes."

"Don't go in your black outfit. Henry has a camouflage boiler-suit and a small net to go over you. You must find a spot where you can lie down ... all day if necessary, so don't have anything else to drink from now on. Then you'll not be wanting to have a piss at the wrong time. Believe me, Steve, there's nothing worse than lying down for a few hours, awash in your own piss, I tell you from experience." Craig ribbed his chin thoughtfully.

"I hadn't thought of that," Steve said gratefully. "What about food then?"

Craig passed him a bar of chocolate. "Here is a strong laxative, take it now," he advised, "and you should be cleared out by mid-night, big shit, no Steve."

"What?"

"Never mind, it's part of a joke about constipation, I'll tell you it one day," Craig promised. "Only half the bar mind okay? Otherwise you'll never leave the bog for a day."

Steve finished his meal then had his chocolate and wandered out to the barn to watch them checking their equipment. Ropes were stretched out across the barn floor, and on top of a sack, a pile of screw-thread karabiners .

Henry saw Steve had come into the barn and signalled him to join him outside. Mystified Steve followed him outside. Henry walked across the farmyard, in the warm evening sunlight, and went over to the low wall. Henry pointed over the wall at some sheep which were standing harmlessly grazing in front of them. He put a finger to his lips for quiet and drew his gun out of his holster and took slow, careful aim at the nearest sheep, then pulled the trigger.

Steve watched as the sheep seemed to literally disintegrate into a ragged bundle, with bits of it flying everywhere, and Henry laughing like an hyena.

"What the fuck was that?" Craig shouted as he ran across the yard from the barn, followed closely by British who was pulling his gun out, thinking they were under attack.

Craig looked over the wall at the disintegrated sheep, then back at Henry who was still having hysterics.

"You've shot a dum-dum, haven't you? You daft cunt. The farmer will be bloody upset now. Why did you do that?" he angrily asked Henry.

"Only a bit of fun Craig ... just showing Steve what a dum-dum bullet can do," Henry retorted. "There's no harm done, the old sheep didn't feel a thing," he added, sliding his gun back in it's holster.

"How many have you got?" Craig asked him crossly.

"I only filed the one, just to show Steve that's all, keep your hair on, I'll pay the farmer for his manky old sheep."

"That is not the point and you know it. We are supposed to be at the University on a course, how do we explain to the farmer about one of his sheep being turned into chicken feed?" Craig had calmed down by now as Santiago joined them to look across at the remains of the sheep.

"No problem, Señors," he beamed. "Santiago make good stew with heem, farmer no find, sheep he run away okay? I get basket to put heem in straight away." He turned and ran back to the farm so that he could remove the evidence.

"Sorry partner," Henry said to Craig. "I was getting bored, so I decided to show off okay? Forgot I was in England." He ambled back to the barn, passing an elated Santiago running with a basket to gather his fresh sheep up.

"Mad sod," Craig said, "but I think we are all mad in some way ... if a farmer comes round, we know nothing."

They stood and watched Santiago fill his basket with glee, before they returned to join Henry in the barn.

Steve sat in the kitchen, semi-dozing, until 3.30 a.m. then having changed into the camouflage boiler-suit, set off for his observation stint, having duly emptied himself on the toilet, thankful he had not eaten the whole bar of laxative.

He felt extremely thirsty but was told by Craig to only wet his lips with water, before he left.

Craig had told him that if he ran into trouble he was on his own, and that he must not, under any circumstances, reveal why he was there. Should he have to do a runner, he was to go to the railway station waiting-room and they would contact him there. No one would take any notice of a dirty git, in a boiler-suit, Craig assured him, just keep the gun hidden away.

Steve reached the small bridge, where the stream exited from the estate, at exactly 4.20 a.m. He left the track and climbed over the small wall onto the banks of the stream.

He studied the terrain through his night-scope and could see the tree-lined road from Ridgeborough and faintly he could make out the gatehouse entrance of the estate.

He remembered that Craig had looked over the wall and spotted a look-out tower, so Steve had to look for more substantial cover as the grass would not conceal him from a tall vantage point. He turned to view the course of the stream, with his scope and spotted what appeared to be the outline of a clump of bushes, about fifty yards down-stream.

He followed the course of the stream, cautiously keeping

as low a profile as he possibly could to the bushes.

He picked a spot beneath two thick bushes, which should give him excellent cover from the tower but also give him a good view of the road and gatehouse.

He looked at his watch, the luminous hands pointing to 4.30 a.m. and looking to the east he saw that the night sky was starting to cast off its dark mantle, as the day-star started to rise, spreading a warm glow on the distant horizon.

He lay down on his stomach and pulling the camouflage net over himself, settled down for his first ever observation stint, wishing that one of the others were there with him, in case it all went wrong.

He had checked his gun and placed it by his right hand, when he became aware of the damp wetness of the early morning dew, seeping through his clothes. *'Fuck it'* he thought. *'I should have brought a sodding ground-sheet'.*

Thirty damp minutes later he replaced his scope with a pair of binoculars that Henry had given him, as the daylight improved.

Two vehicles had driven up from Ridgeborough, but each had followed the road past the gatehouse and driven straight on towards the M 1.

Steve lay thinking of all that had happened to him in such a short time, from his birthday on June 14th until now, the 9th September ... three months only, but what a three months.

Steve smiled to himself, shifting his position slightly, as he had been lying there for an hour and it was now 5.30 a.m. He popped another wadge of Wrigley's gum in his mouth, chewing slowly to enjoy the flavour.

He felt at peace with the world and, he suddenly thought, his bank balance was building up for the first time in his life. Maybe trying to become a golf professional wasn't the wisest thing to do, especially as the Colonel had already said he could join a Golf Society that would let him play golf all over the world.

He was jolted out of daydreaming as he heard a horn hooting twice. He saw that a milk float had stopped in front of the gates which were now slowly swinging open in response to the horn blasts and the float trundled through as soon as they were wide enough.

Steve looked at his watch, 5.35 a.m., elated that his hunch had paid off. He was just going to leave his cover when he heard a man's voice shouting,

"Come here, Sam ... you daft bugger."

Steve froze as he heard the rustling of grass and twigs behind him, then a brown and white Cocker Spaniel, burst through the bushes and came racing towards him, nose twitching in excitement.

Two wood-pigeons rose up from a bush, a few yards from Steve and the dog shot off after them, barking happily.

"Stupid dog," Steve heard the man say to himself as he approached where Steve lay, frozen by fear initially, but now gripping his gun close to his chest.

Steve saw the man's wellington boots stop in front of him and saw the end of a double-barrelled shotgun hanging down on one side. Steve held his breath and waited for shouts of discovery, but nothing happened for a few seconds, then he heard the sound of rain on the bush and his net. He realised, with disgust, that the man was urinating on him, soaking through his clothes, like the dew had, only warmer.

The man's attention was on his dog as he urinated, luckily for Steve. He shouted after his rapidly disappearing dog, "Sam, come back yer daft bugger, we want rabbits, else no supper for you." He shook himself, zipped up and went after his dog, still muttering oaths to himself.

Steve lay there for five minutes, in case the man came back, the urine going cold on his back, then slowly turned over and sat up, still under the net. He secured his gun under his boiler-suit, and sat there, wondering how to leave his hide to get back to the farm now that it was broad daylight. He had not thought of this when he had come up with his master plan.

'What a stupid pillock I am,' he angrily pushed the netting off his head and looped the binoculars round his neck, then slowly rose to his knees.

The milk float waddled out of the gates and set off towards Ridgeborough at a fair old speed, as it was slightly downhill for a mile or two. Steve stood up looking to his left for the watch-tower. To his relief he could not see it, so by the same token he reasoned, they couldn't see him.

He rolled the wet netting up and stuffed it down a rabbit hole. *'Sorry Mr. Rabbit'* he thought *'but my needs are greater than yours.'*

He walked briskly back along the stream, pausing only to pretend to be a bird watcher and looked across the fields with his binoculars at a flock of passing birds. He could see the man and his dog, two fields away, rooting in a hedgerow.

He turned and retraced his steps to the track.

The Land Rover came hurtling round the bend ahead of him and shuddered to a halt as Craig hit the brakes hard.

"In!" he shouted at Steve, who leapt aboard gratefully. Craig turned it round in one manoeuvre, running up the grass verges on both sides of the road, throwing Steve from side to side, making him cling on to stay in the vehicle. It clattered back along the track to the farm where Craig swung it straight into the barn and screeched to a halt. British, who was waiting by the doors, swung them shut behind them.

"Any luck?" Craig barked.

"Yes" Steve gasped, still recovering from the speed of the ride. "05.35 it arrived, blew the horn twice and drove straight in."

"Good man," Craig was now smiling as they climbed out of the vehicle, "anyone see you?"

"I don't think so."

"You smell awful," Craig wrinkled his nose. "Did you fall

in a cess pit or something?" he asked, looking Steve up and down, noting Steve looked wet, as well as smelly.

"I was pissed on."

"Pissed on?"

"You heard ... some bastard rabbit shooter pissed on the bushes that I was hiding under, but I was so well camouflaged, he didn't see me." Steve saw Craig start to smile as British joined them both.

"You've been pissed on?" British repeated what he had just heard. Steve nodded glumly, awaiting ridicule.

"Well done, partner," British declared proudly. "That means you hid yourself so well that you couldn't be seen from three or four feet, bloody brilliant ... I'd shake your hand, but you're a shit heap." British stepped back from a beaming Steve and added, "If I were you, I'd go and have a bath now and have a rest ... we are having an ops meeting at mid-day to arrange the timing of our mission ... see you then."

CHAPTER 11
Operation Monarch

Steve awoke refreshed after a good sleep and going down to the kitchen, found everyone there, except Santiago.

"Now then gentlemen," Craig had stood up when Steve entered. "We will now formulate our action plan which we will call ... Operation Monarch." He looked round for some comment and receiving none, proceeded. "We are instructed to kill Lord Stuart McForson, by any means possible. If we are caught and, if still living," he added, "brought to trial, each of you are on your own. Do not expect any help from the Colonel, or any government department ... because we do not exist, not officially anyway."

He leaned forward and picked up a piece of paper and held it up. "This is to make your last Will and Testament ... y'know ... who you want to get your ill-gotten gains." He coughed to cover a smile. "When completed, give them to Santiago. Oh! By the way, he is look-out on the roof of the barn, at the moment."

He passed them all a sheet of paper, an envelope and a pen. "Santiago has his instructions what to do should none of us manage to get back from this mission."

Steve felt a chill run right through his body. *'Bloody hell,'* he thought, *'this is getting a bit too real now.'*

"You okay Steve?" asked British who was sitting by him. "You look a bit white!"

"I'm fine," Steve assured British. "I suppose it is just like Operation Precipice, without the climbing," he joked.

British patted him on the back. "We'll be fine, just remember to keep your head down and run bloody fast when necessary," he countered Steve's query.

The kitchen went very quiet for half-an-hour, as they all started writing their wills out. Each pausing to think about who to nominate their belongings and monies to.

Craig collected them all after each will had been witnessed by Santiago and placed them in a black briefcase that had the portcullis crest impressed on it, in gold.

"Santiago will take these to London ... if required," Craig explained, then added to Steve. "He'll go in your M.G. ... the Land Rover can't be traced, but your M.G. can. Any questions so far?" He looked round at their attentive faces.

They all shook their heads, looking at each other in agreement. Craig unrolled a large makeshift map and draped it over the large bread-bin on the table.

"I made this map from a small one that was in the folder we were given by the lovely Barbara." He picked up a bread knife to use as a pointer.

"Here, gentlemen, is the railway line," he prodded the map with the knife, "which I propose that myself and Henry will proceed along until we reach here." He put the point on the viaduct where the railway crossed the stream. We will then abseil down ... how far do you reckon Henry?" he turned to Henry quizzically.

"80 feet, give or take a foot, I reckon 100 feet of rope should make it all right," Henry answered, looking down at his finger-nails, in a matter of fact sort of way.

"Well ... if you're wrong, we could make quite an impression on this mission." Craig smiled at his little pun, then went on, pointing the knife to the relevant areas. "Then we follow the stream down to the lake, go round the lake, here," he pointed to the north side of the lake, "and follow the three waterfalls, to the power house ... here." He paused to sip his coffee.

"Water takes the shortest way down," observed British, "so how can you be sure you can just trot down them?"

"Because there is a fucking path all the way down, alongside the stream here." Craig stabbed the map so hard with the knife, the map and bread-bin, fell off the table.

"Only asking," replied a peeved British as Craig bent down and recovered the bin and map and placed them back on the table.

"Sorry British," Craig said. "It was a good question. I forgot you hadn't see the original map."

"How long to there, then?" British accepted the apology.

"One hour precisely," Craig answered curtly, then relaxed and added, "give or take a minute or two. By my reckoning we should be there at 05.00 hours if we start at 04.00 hours. We will place...," he corrected himself, "I mean Henry will place the explosives in the Power House, or all round the outside, if we don't have time to get in and set the time for ...," he looked at British. "What do you reckon you need?"

"Steve says the milk float goes in at 05.35 hours. By the time we follow it up to the Mansion, assuming it arrives at the same time, of course, then we have to find the Master bedroom, etcetera; I reckon you can set the time for 05.50 hours ... that should do it." British looked at Steve, who being out of his depth, simply nodded his agreement.

"Well done British ... got that Henry?"

"Yes ... 05.50 hours, on the nose," replied Henry, swinging his feet up on the table, arms behind his head.

"Dawn will have broken by then," Craig advised, "but the

194

guards will be just waking up, after another peaceful night of doing bugger-all for their money ... boy are they in for a surprise!" He laughed grimly, as Steve blurted,

"Will Lord McForson have Helga with him ... do we shoot her as well?" Steve was absolutely horrified as the thought of killing a woman entered his mind. The others just stared down at the table for Craig's answer.

"Try not to shoot her, if she is there, but if it can't be avoided," Craig shrugged his shoulders in answer. Then to change the subject, "You should be more concerned about the whereabouts of that bastard, Kai, he won't be far away from his Lordship, I assure you. He'll come out shooting so I suggest that you, British, can guard Steve's back, while you, Steve, pump as many bullets as you can, into the bedroom that British decides is the right one, as soon as you fucking enter. No asking questions. No, good morning sir, are you Lord McForson? shit ... get it? We'll give you Henry's Heckler Koch, with that fire-power even you can't miss." The others all smiled encouragement at Steve.

"I'll go for that," British agreed, "even Steve can't miss a bed with that gun."

"Is the fire-power," Steve asked breathlessly, "the gun with 2000 rounds a minute, give or take a round?"

"If you put the shoulder-stock on," Henry added.

"Christ ... can I try it first?"

"In the barn later," agreed Craig. "And now we come to the difficult bit." He looked slowly round at them all. "How do we get out of the place once they are all alerted ... any ideas?"

"Run through the deer park ... with so much movement amongst the deer they would have difficulty spotting us," Steve offered, hoping he'd got the solution.

"No," Craig disagreed, "because that would mean leaving the Park in the direction of the farm .. and we don't want to lead them there. Good thought though Steve," he added. "Anyone else?"

They all fell silent as they tried to work the best way out of this situation and what options were open to them. At length, British got up and went to the map, picking the knife up as he did so.

"I reckon that you," he looked at Craig and then to Henry, "and Henry ... after planting the explosives, carry on across the pool here." He pointed to the small pool on the map. "And follow the stream down to where the approach road, to the Mansion, goes over it ... here. Steve and I will join you and then we could all go together downstream and exit the Park under the wall here." He pointed to where the stream ran under wall out of the Park. "With any luck we might reach the clump of bushes where Steve here got pissed on." Steve grinned sheepishly, "They're about fifty yards further on. We could stay there until dark or until Santiago could pick us up." He stared round at them all. "Any helicopter search wouldn't see us, well, that's what I think, anyway." He went and sat down.

"The idea that we all leave together appeals to me," Craig answered this proposed plan, and seeing all the others nodding their consent, stood up. Looking at his watch he said, "I have 14.00 hours on my watch ... that's 2.00 p.m. to you, Steve," he joked aside to Steve. "We will meet in the barn at 03.30 hours, leave at 04.00 hours. British and Steve should enter the Park at 05.35 hours precisely, okay? ... If the milk-float does not arrive by 05.45 Henry and I will force an entry into the Mansion before the explosion and do the job ourselves. Hopefully it won't come to that," he added.

"Too bloody true," agreed Henry fervently crossing himself as he checked the time on his watch closely.

"Henry," Craig said, "can you check the ropes and climbing gear we need and explosives ... I'll carry the gear if you carry all the explosives?"

"Yes, you carry all the explosives Henry," mimicked

British laughing, "that's you all over."

"Bollocks ... I have to set them, so it makes sense for me to carry them ... arsehole," Henry answered amicably, not rising to the bait British was throwing to wind him up.

"I will inform Santiago what our plans are ... can you take watch Steve, while he makes us something to eat? ... I could eat a sick donkey," Craig grinned as he folded the map away.

"Where's the Colonel?" Steve suddenly asked as the thought struck him.

"In his beloved Club," Henry answered. "Out of the firing line, awaiting news of our mission, with a large drink in one hand and a large cigar in the other, no doubt ... or even," he touched the side of his nose, "kissing the Red Admiral."

"What is the Red Admiral, then?" Steve asked perplexed, but bringing a smile to everyone's face as they heard the question.

"You may find out one day," Henry laughed, "so I won't spoil it for you," he laughed mysteriously.

"Oh sod you then ... I don't want to know, anyway." Steve felt annoyed at his lack of knowledge on this subject, then turned to British, "Can you show me this gun then? I'd better at least pull the trigger first."

"Let's mosey on down the old corral," British drawled in a western accent, "and let's fly some lead, partner."

They were walking across the farmyard when Steve asked, "What exactly is a dum-dum bullet? Henry used one on that sheep, how does it work?"

"You file a cross into the nose of the bullet," British explained, as they waved up at Santiago, who was lying just below the apex of the roof, cradling a rifle in his arms.

"Ole, Santiago," they called up to him.

"Ole, Señors," came the instant reply and a wave, from a smiling Santiago.

"Ole, Santiago," they heard Craig shouting behind them, "food before we all die of starvation ... pronto, por favor,

Henry will cover."

"Si, Señor Cragg ... Santiago make good food pronto."

They entered the barn, sliding the huge doors open, letting the afternoon sun flood in as British carried on, "Then , when it enters the target, it leaves a small hole, then sort of explodes, making a bloody big one on exit ... understand? It's banned throughout the world because it is not classed as sporting. Bloody politicians know nowt tha' nowst," British mimicked a Yorkshire accent as he withdrew a gun from a compartment under the Land Rover.

"This is a Heckler Koch ... we'll shoot at the far end of barn, into those bales," he pointed to the far end of the barn at a stack of straw bales.

"What about all the bullets afterwards?" Steve asked, remembering the incident on the beach in Spain.

"You're learning fast, Steve," British said patting him on the shoulder, "but we have no worries on that score, because they'll be swept."

"Swept?"

"Yes ... when we bugger off back to London ... hopefully. A specialist cleansing team will be sent in, to clean and clear away everything possible, including all tyre tracks. They're a very efficient bunch of blokes. We call them The Scavengers."

"Sounds very efficient to me," Steve replied.

"More than that," British went on, as he loaded the gun, "when they leave, a party of under privileged children will be given a free holiday straight away, so the place has children running all over it for a week, before it's handed back to the Estate Agent. The government pays for all damage they do to the property. Brilliant, eh?" He smiled at Steve as he handed him the now-loaded gun.

"What kind of bloke is a Scavenger?"

"Not the sort you'd want your mother to meet, that's for sure ... they're the rejects of society. But once they've sworn allegiance to the Queen and Country, they are fiercely patriotic and operate a code of silence, second to none."

Steve was astounded by all this information. He was fast coming to understand that, at twenty-three years of age, he really knew nothing and again gave a fleeting thought as to why he had been involved in these sort of missions when he obviously was not fully trained.

British fired the first burst of bullets, the sound of which nearly made Santiago fall off the roof, as he was precariously balanced on the edge, making his way down.

"It's okay, Santiago," Henry placated an angry Santiago, "practice fire ... sorry, we should have warned you."

Santiago reached the yard and tossed the rifle to Henry and went up to the farm house muttering to himself about 'Inglaises, bastardos.'

Henry swung the rifle over his shoulder and climbed up to his position, passing an empty half-bottle of Tequila in the rain.

Steve learned, in the next thirty minutes, just how devastating the weapon was he'd been entrusted with on this mission. British showed him how to load the clip of 18 bullets into the handle of the conventional pistol.

"I thought this gun had lot of fire-power?" Steve queried, turning the gun over in his hand.

British took the gun from him, and producing a small shoulder-stock from the Land Rover told Steve all about it as he fitted it to the gun.

"This makes an internal adjustment to the firing mechanism, which turns it into a fully-automatic, submachine gun, with the firing rate of 2000 rounds plus, per minute, like we told you earlier. Look," he showed Steve, "it's made mostly of plastic ... gives it great lightness for our job. It's the military version of the civilian version."

Steve had never seen anything like this in his life and British told him to keep the stock on while working out how he could carry it tied on his waist.

They were all assembled in the barn at 03.30, fully kitted out. Henry had a canvas pouch attached to the left side of his waist, containing the explosives and detonators and draped around his shoulders he had a large coil of nylon rope, almost hiding the gun sitting on his right hip.

Craig had numerous slings and karabiners tied round his waist, plus, on his gun-belt, he had four hand-grenades.

Craig called for all their attention by clapping his hands. "The timing is very important but ...," he hesitated, "we cannot foresee on these missions, therefore, we must stick to our schedules, as near as we can." He looked at British and Steve. "I mean that, if we failed to blow the power house up ... you two must carry on, without the aid of the diversion. The guards should still be relaxed after a calm night, so you will have the element of surprise on your side ... but get the bastard, understand?" He emphasised the 'get.' "If however, the milk-float fails to get you into the Park, for whatever reason, both Henry and I will run to the Mansion and try to get the job done ourselves. You two can wait by the stream exit to give us covering fire, if necessary, right?" He stared round at them all as they showed they understood the instructions.

"I suggest that we all have a piss now, we don't want to be caught having a 'jimmy riddle' ... might get it blown off and that would never do. You'd have nothing to play with in your pits." Craig gave a little chuckle at his witticism, then went on, "And don't forget to use your whistle when you return or Santiago might get you with 'friendly fire', he'll be extremely jumpy by then."

They were all relieving themselves when Steve's alarm went off, on his wrist watch, at 04.00 hours. Craig checked his and said, "Let's go," and they all left the barn in single file, as before, with Craig leading and British 'catching the arrow,' as before.

Santiago, watching them go from above, crossed himself in silent prayer, then took another swig of Tequila to calm his nerves. An owl also watched them go waiting to go into the barn with a mouse hanging from his beak for its babies.

They reached the wall of the Park without trouble and turning to their right, they ran as lightly as they could following the wall until they reached the railway line.

Craig looked over the parapet at the railway line, the lines gleaming up from the dark recesses.

"Fuck me!" he exclaimed in dismay. "It looks further down then I remember, we could break a leg dropping down there."

"Donna worry, Señor Cragg," Henry did his Santiago impression. "I, the great Houdini, have the very method to hand." He took out a small bundle of what appeared to be wire. "25 feet of electron ladder, wide enough for a boot," Henry explained, "strong enough to support an elephant see ... duralamin rungs and wire with a one-ton breaking strain." He unrolled the ladder, which gave a metallic clink as he did so.

"Quietly now," whispered Craig, as they lowered it over the bridge. "Hold it down, you two," he told British and Steve, "while we climb down. I hope there's not a fucking train due," he added as an afterthought.

"We're safe enough with British as the anchor man anyway, he could hold a tug-of-war team," Henry quietly stated.

"Bollocks ... I'm all muscle, that's all," British retorted then added, "just watch you don't get a train up your arse ... mind you there's enough room for one." British rocked with silent laughter at the thought.

Steve listened to all this humour, not understanding how they could all be cracking jokes on a mission that they could die on. It was simply beyond his logic. He was, however, going to learn the value of this attitude, in the months to come.

They held onto the ladder as Henry, being the lightest,

went over the top first. Craig saw Henry reach the bottom and look up at him.

"Okay, here I go ... so hang on to that fucking ladder."

"Sodding well get going ... we've got the strain," British whispered urgently to Craig, who did as he was told.

Craig had more difficulty with the ladder than Henry, due to the fact that his feet were wider on the ladder rungs, making it hard to get them in and out of the narrow rungs. He swore softly to himself at the effort involved. He eventually made it and they felt the ladder go slack as Craig released his hold on it. They eased the ladder back up carefully and watched the two dark figures stepping from sleeper to sleeper until they faded from sight into the darkness.

British rolled the ladder up tightly and they hid it in the long grass, because it was of no further use to them.

They followed the cart-track along the wall, past the old gatehouse and then past where the power line joined to the electric fence. They couldn't see it but could hear the humming wire. They reached the stream's exit and following it down to the same bushes where Steve had hidden earlier, made themselves as comfortable as possible, waiting for the arrival of the milk-float.

Craig and Henry walked the sleepers until they reached the viaduct. Henry searched for a suitable belay point for the rope but failed. He whispered to Craig that they would have to tie the rope to the railway line.

"I cannot see any other way to do it, can you?" he asked Craig.

"No," agreed Craig, "but what if we double the rope round the rail and then go down on a double rope, we could pull it down after us?"

"Not enough rope," whispered Henry as he started to thread the rope under the rail. "We'll have to leave it tied to the rail, mind you," he added, "they might think we are going to come back this way and rappel up it, so that will keep some of the bastards occupied, I reckon."

"Quite right," Craig agreed and started to lower the rope until there was no rope left. He looked down into the dark void, but could not see the end of the rope at all.

"Can you see the fucking end, Henry, 'cos I can't?"

Henry tried to locate the rope end but failed in the darkness.

"You go first, Henry," Craig advised, "then if you've got the distance wrong and you break a leg, don't come running to me."

"Oh, very funny, I'm laughing all the way," Henry retorted, as he stepped into the two small loops he'd made with a sling off Craig's waist, pulling them up his legs as far as they could go.

He clipped the rope through the karabiner on the sling and climbed onto the parapet. He tested that the rope was taking the strain all right then said, "I can rappel up again if the rope isn't long enough, but we would not have time to blow the power-house then. So I'll just go for it." And with that he leaned out into the void and started to walk down the viaduct wall.

Craig rested his hand on the rope lightly, feeling it stretched tight over the brick-work until 20 seconds later it went slack to the touch. He leaned over and pulled the rope up a few inches to make sure Henry was clear. He clipped himself onto the rope and climbed onto the wall, comforted that he had not heard Henry fall off.

The last fifty feet were free-fall and Craig arrived, in a rush, at the side of a jubilant Henry.

"Twenty feet of rope left, not a bad guess eh?" he said, as he helped Craig off the rope. They set off following the stream down to the Black Lake which they reached with only wet feet to complain about.

"Looks very menacing, doesn't it?" Henry observed,

looking across the dark expanse of water, rippling in front of them. "Which way do we go now?"

"To the left, because there should be a boat-house, according to the map," Craig answered. "Maybe there's some sort of boat, then we won't have to go right round the lake, which on the map looks marshy to me and we'll save time, so let's check it out."

They went no more than thirty feet before the outline of the boat-house came into view. The large wooden entry doors had heavy duty chains through the handles with rusty padlocks securing them. Craig tested them gently.

"No chance of breaking these ... not without making a hell of a racket at least," he observed wryly.

"I'll shin along the roof and look over the entrance to see if there is a boat ... give me a leg up." Henry offered his foot to Craig who heaved him up the wall until he got a firm grip on the roof edge and managed to haul himself up onto the roof, where he lay like a stranded whale.

He swiftly recovered and made his way along the roof ridge until he was above the lake-side entrance. He lowered himself as far as he dare over the edge to look into the boat-house, and to his relief he could just see, in the gloom, the bow of a rowing boat jutting out.

Henry decided to have a go for it and lowered himself until he was hanging at full stretch over the water. He pulled on his arms and started to swing like a pendulum until his feet came into contact with the boat. Hooking his left foot round the bow he was able to pull the boat out until there was enough showing for him to let go of the roof and drop heavily into it.

He scrambled to the back of the boat, untied the mooring rope and pushed the boat towards the entrance, feeling very pleased with himself.

He was suddenly aware of the outline of a dark figure standing knee-deep in the water at the entrance. He was reaching frantically for his gun when he heard Craig say,

"Very good effort Henry, but I thought that as my feet were already wet I'd do it the easy way." Craig lifted a wet leg into the boat as he spoke.

"Christ Almighty ... you scared the shit out of me," Henry spluttered angrily. "You might have said something before I nearly ruptured myself."

Craig, grinning in the dark, heaved himself into the boat as a ruffled Henry located the oars in the rowlocks and started to row them into the middle of the lake.

"Just as well there's no moon tonight ... we'd be sitting ducks," Craig whispered, to try to placate Henry who had remained silent since he got in the boat. Henry made no reply, mainly because he knew talk travelled well over still water. They reached the middle of the lake and Craig could make out the out-line of a large hill, to his left, topped by what appeared to be a watch-tower, but showing no sign of lights or life.

They were reaching the far end of the lake when they heard the sound of water falling and they realised straight away that they were heading for the waterfalls. Craig signalled to Henry to pull over to his left where he could see a small concrete landing area. They tied the boat up to a small wooden handrail as the first glimmer of dawn started to show in the east.

"Let's hope that watch-tower did not have night-scopes or else we are in deep trouble," Craig murmured to Henry.

"Too true," agreed Henry, then exclaimed, "look! This looks like a path." He pointed to Craig's right, at a narrow track that seemed to go towards the stream.

"Good, that's what's on the map," Craig sounded relieved. "I suppose it was added by His Lordship ... good, now we can get moving ... it's nearly five o'clock," he said as he checked the luminous dial on his watch.

They had negotiated the first two waterfalls, the pathway criss-crossing over the top of each waterfall, over small wooden bridges, when Craig suddenly pulled Henry to a stop with his hand while making smoking signs with his other.

Henry had smelt the cigarette smoke almost at the same time and they both dropped to a crouching position trying to pierce the morning mist that had arrived with the dawn light, to see who was there.

Craig tapped Henry on the shoulder, pointing to the dark shape of a man, in the middle of the bridge ahead of them, leaning on the handrail, cigarette in hand, just staring down at the plunging waters beneath him.

Henry looked at Craig and drew a finger across his throat. Craig nodded agreement as Henry slid his knife out of his leg-sheath. Craig did likewise as Henry went forward onto the end of the bridge in a semi-crouching position.

The noise of the water covered any sound that Henry was making on his approach. The man suddenly stood up and flicked the stub into the falling water, stretching his arms upward whilst yawning. As Henry increased his run, the man caught the movement out of the corner of his eye and started to swing round, bringing his arms down to reach for his rifle, which was leaning against the rail. Henry's momentum bowled the man over and the rifle clattered through the rail and into the water.

Henry landed heavily on the man, causing him to grunt as the wind was knocked out of his body and Henry smelt the tobacco breath in his face.

Henry drove his knife in under the man's right ear, pushing it upwards into his head, as hard as he could. The man gasped and slumped still and Henry lay on him for a moment, just to make sure he was dead, then he withdrew his knife with difficulty, as it was well embedded, and wiped it on the man's battle blouse.

"Good work," Craig said, joining Henry after hanging back to make sure the man had no companions waiting nearby.

Henry stood up and replaced his knife in its sheath then without a word being spoken, they picked the body up and heaved it unceremoniously over the handrail, into the waterfall and it disappeared into the spume.

They ran across the bridge into the shelter of some small trees to decide what to do next.

"I hope we're not caught now," Craig proffered the thought. "I reckon we will have to go down fighting if we are cornered."

"They might think he committed suicide," Henry suggested.

"Ho, fucking ho ... with his fucking head nearly cut off!!" Craig commented grimly, "you enjoyed doing that."

"That's what I'm paid for," agreed Henry smiling. "That's what I'm in this organisation for ... to use my skills. It beats civvy street hands down."

They said no more and continued down the path to the power house, which they reached at 05.10 hours.

"We have forty minutes to place the explosives and join the others under the road bridge ... will that be enough time for you, Henry?" Craig asked in a concerned manner.

"Sure ... I'll plant all I've got round the building ... no need to go in ... the place will go up like Pearl Harbour. They won't know what hit them," Henry assured Craig.

The next thirty minutes were very busy for Henry as he laid the explosives all round the building, keeping as low as possible, not knowing the location of the guards. Craig covered him, safety catch off his gun, ready for instant action, if required.

He could see the Mansion more clearly now, as the dawn seemed to arrive very quickly and the low mist started to disperse, revealing the tall communication mast, looking like a space-probe.

The stream left the power house, via a man-made pool, then going over a weir, snaked down to the road bridge, where they hoped to meet British and Steve, later.

They heard the birds singing their dawn chorus, in the

many trees, while over to their right, the deer who had started grazing peacefully, suddenly stopped and all lifted their heads in unison, ears quivering.

Craig, who was looking in their direction at the time, put a warning hand on Henry's back, as he set a timer. They lay low in the long grass, listening for whatever had startled the deer.

"Listen ...,"Craig murmured, "helicopter."

The deer scattered as a black helicopter swung into view, the steady whumph, whumph of its roter-blades echoing across the Park. Craig and Henry rolled over onto their backs, aiming their guns at the on-coming machine.

"Come to daddy," Henry said smiling through gritted teeth.

"Come on you buggers, we're waiting." Craig had hardly ever heard Henry swear before and saw that Henry's eyes were sparkling with anticipation of action.

The helicopter passed directly overhead towards the mansion then disappeared behind it, settling down like a big, black beetle.

"Christ! ... I thought we were fucking dead men then," Craig swore, breathing out slowly. "What do you make of that?"

"Well ... it's not Prince Charles, he's learning to fly helicopters in Yeovilton," quipped Henry. Then, with a concerned frown on his face said seriously, "I know who owns that helicopter."

"Who?"

"It's the Colonel's private helicopter, that's all." Henry put his safety catch on his gun and sat up.

"The Colonel ... are you sure?" Craig was astounded.

"Positive ... I've flown it for him enough times. What the hell do you think it's doing here, Craig?"

"The plot thickens, as they say in all the best movies," Craig said, "and I don't like it one little bit. Something has gone badly wrong somewhere along the line, but what?"

"You're telling me," agreed Henry. "So what are we going

to do now?" His voice held urgency.

Craig sat up, thoughtfully putting his safety catch back on his gun, then said, "We will carry on with the mission as instructed. The Colonel might be a prisoner, or the helicopter may have been taken without his knowledge. There's no way of knowing and I have no way of contacting the Control Room from here." He sat pondering as Henry carried on setting the last of the timers.

"Well ... what are we going do?" Henry asked as he returned to Craig's side. "All the detonators are primed and timed, now what?"

"We must carry out our last orders because, no matter what's happened, His Lordship has to be put down, one way or another ... you're sure you've set them all for 05.50?" he queried Henry.

"Yes ... I've just told you," Henry replied petulantly.

"Good, 'cos here comes the fuckin' milk-float, get down!"

They watched as the float trundled over the bridge and headed up to the Mansion. They could see two figures hanging on the back of it, one on each side, trying to keep out of the rear view mirror of the float.

"Good lads," Craig breathed to himself, "not long now."

They watched as the float trundled out of sight into the rear service area of the Mansion, and as it did so an alarm siren went off inside the power house, making Craig and Henry plunge straight into the pool. Holding their guns out of the water they started swimming side-crawl, across to the weir, both knowing without question that they had to get to the bridge, as soon as possible.

"What set that off?" spluttered Craig to Henry as they swam alongside each other.

"Not us, that's for sure ... I'm positive I didn't disturb any sort of alarm ... I simply don't know," Henry replied, spitting some chickweed out of his mouth.

They reached the weir and slid over it as four men

emerged from the Mansion, running down the road towards the power house. Three men were in combat jackets and carrying guns, while the fourth one who was wearing a white overall, tried to keep up with them. Craig and Henry watched over the lip of the weir as the men reached the power house.

"Find out what's blocking the water flow," they heard the white-coated man shout at the other three. "I'll go in and switch that damn siren off."

Craig looked at Henry. "The siren must be a warning that comes on when the water flow is restricted ... hell, that will be the body we chucked in ... we'd better get going down to the bridge ... how long until it blows up?"

"It looks like a body." They heard a coarse shout.

"About five minutes," Henry answered briskly, "then all hell will let loose."

"It's Hamish ... he's been killed." They heard an angry shout as the men discovered who it was. Henry and Craig waded down the stream and reached the bridge, as the very angry, shocked men, struggled to retrieve the body of their comrade.

The milk float drove over the bridge, the driver singing to the music on his radio, completely unaware of the drama that was unfolding around him. He was just driving through the main gates, when the power house blew up with a huge blast, killing the four men instantly.

"Christ, Henry," Craig shouted in shock, at the ferocity of the explosion, "you certainly made sure of that."

"I told you," answered a delighted Henry, face aglow with excitement, "I used every bit of explosive we were given, no point in saving any."

"Look out, Henry," Craig gasped as he saw a huge wall of water descending on them. The force of the explosion had virtually blown the pool of water they had just swum across, over the weir.

Craig grabbed a bemused Henry who had wanted to stand see the results of his handiwork and pulled him round the brick supports of the bridge. The water thundered into, and over, the little bridge that was shielding them. Bits of brick and metal also started to fall all round them and they struggled to get under the bridge for protection against the rising water level. The wall of water swept down the stream sweeping two terrified deer away with it, smashing with great force into the second bridge, before losing its momentum against the perimeter wall.

"Congratulations, Henry ... it feels like you've blown the whole fucking Park up," Craig stated, looking back at the smouldering ruin that had been the power house. He was going to say more but he was interrupted by the sound of shooting, coming from the Mansion.

CHAPTER 12
Ending the Game

British and Steve lay concealed in the bushes for almost an hour, until dawn broke, bringing a covering a mist which hung over the field, about three feet high from the ground. This made excellent cover between them and the road. The trees looked cut off at their bases.

"That's a bit of good luck," enthused British, "there must be a lot of damp ground here. We will be able to see the top half of the float so long as the mist doesn't get any worse."

They both heard the helicopter at the same time, but could not see where it was, or where it was going, then all went quiet.

"Who do you reckon that was?" Steve asked anxiously. British was silent for a moment then said, "The last time I heard a helicopter sound like that was when I was in the Colonel's helicopter with Henry ... but that doesn't make any sense ... what would he be doing here? I bet the other two are thinking the same as me."

"Do we go on with it then?" Steve asked hopefully, as the situation was far too dangerous for his liking. "Perhaps, there's been some sort of truce that we don't know about."

"They would have dropped a flare to warn us, if that was the case. No flare means we go on with the mission."

"Okay ... if you say so." Steve put a wedge of gum in his mouth and settled back to wait.

"British?" Steve asked slowly, "Why have you come all the way from Spain to do this job?"

British studied the question for a while before answering with, "Well, it's like this, Steve. I lost a very good friend on this operation, last month. He was one of the men that was killed, here, by that bastard Kai ... and I knew he would be here, so …" He shrugged his shoulders, "here I am, repaying a debt I hope." He fell silent.

"Why do you think I'm here?" Steve queried him.

"I have given that some thought myself actually," British said thoughtfully. "You are obviously not a field-trained operative and although you made it through Operation Precipice ... I really can't understand why you are here myself." He paused, thinking. "We all had a talk about it at the farm, while you were on the recce for this job and none of us can remember this situation arising before, so I really can't answer you, Steve." He sounded apologetic at his lack of assistance in this matter.

Steve lay back thinking how his life had changed so suddenly, then asked, "What date is it? I've lost track of time altogether."

Tuesday, the 10th of September ... 1974," British added with a little chuckle.

"I know it's 1974 ... but not the date, piss-taker." Steve punched British playfully on the arm.

"Not the face, not the face!" British pretended to cower away from Steve.

"Bollocks," replied Steve, and he settled back down on the grass, chewing a stalk of grass thinking how, since his brithday in June, his life had changed so radically.

He wondered what Gloria was doing now and if she was

213

missing him. Boy! He'd be in deep trouble when he eventually got home, his mother would give him hell as well, and Buster would go potty, if he lived through this.

"British?"

"What now," sighed British, who was tying to rest.

"How much money do we get for doing this ... only no one has mentioned what we get paid," complained Steve.

"We get a bonus paid into our bank accounts," British countered. "The amount varies for the different ..." he hesitated, " ... difficulties we have to face."

"Will I have been paid a bonus for Operation Precipice then?" said an excited Steve. "How much?"

"I reckon it will be about £2,000 because the risk factor was quite low and it will be put into your account from a bank in the Isle of Man," he was informed by a patient British.

"£2,000," gasped Steve, then said, "Low risk factor, low risk factor." He repeated himself in amazement. "We could have keen killed. Bloody hell, what will we get for this if that was low risk?"

British ignored him and closed his eyes for some peace.

At long last, they saw the milk float coming up the road from Ridgeborough, or at least the top half of it, swirling through the mist like a boat on a foggy river.

"Come on, let's go," British urged Steve on and they ran doubled-up across the field to the road, pausing only to put their hands up above the hanging mist to get their bearings.

They each ran behind a tree and as the float went past, they sprinted to the back and gripping the back end, jumped up and put their feet on the bumper, just above the road lights.

The driver was holding a clipboard on his steering wheel, trying to write something as he was driving along, completely unaware of his two passengers.

"Give me your hand," British said to Steve, trying to keep his voice down. He stretched one arm across the back for Steve to grab and they went along, each holding a side and pulling against each other.

The float juddered to a stop at the main gate-house, gave two blasts on the horn and the driver walked over to the control-box on the wall and pushed a button.

"Wakey! Wakey!" he shouted down the receiver. "Hands off cocks and on with socks ... it's your early morning pinta." He was chortling away to himself as he talked.

"If he's a milkman, I'll show my arse," British breathed across to Steve.

"What makes you think that?" Steve whispered back.

"He's just said a morning call we used in the Army."

"Maybe he's retired," countered Steve.

"I bloody hope so," retorted British, as he watched the man check the gate was swinging open, before returning to the float.

The driver put his foot down on the pedal and the electric motor whirred into life and off they lurched forward between the gates and on up the Mansion roadway, swaying from side to side because the road had a lot of pot-holes in it.

They had to hang on with all their strength, gritting their teeth with the effort.

"Bloody good idea of yours, Steve," British hissed across as they were nearly thrown off for the umpteenth time.

"Can't be right all the time," Steve answered back.

"I only hope the other two are in position." British echoed Steve's thoughts, as they went over the second bridge, unaware that they were being watched from afar by Henry and Craig.

The float trundled round the corner of the Mansion and entered the service yard, coming to a sudden stop outside a door, above which was a security camera.

The driver got out and picked a crate of milk off the side of his load, turned and went to the door, whistling to himself.

British looked at the camera above the door and saw it tilting to follow the driver to the door.

"Quick," he hissed, "follow me," and stepped down off the

bumper, with Steve doing likewise and they ran on their tip-toes and hid behind a huge rubbish-bin on wheels.

"My arms are dropping off," British rubbed his arms as Steve, who had also suffered with the strain of hanging on, worked his shoulders round and round, trying to get his circulation going again.

British looked at his watch and said to Steve, "It's 05.45, we've got five minutes before the balloon goes up."

They peeped round the bin and saw the driver emerge, still whistling and climb into his cab and start off back out of the service area.

British watched the security camera turn and follow the float round and knew this was the only chance they would have to get in, without being seen straight away.

He drew his gun from his holster and pulled his knife from its sheath. Steve unclipped his weapon off his belt and, not having a knife, loosened the flap on the small bag that held the extra clips of bullets.

"Good luck," they wished each other without speaking, and British ran semi-crouched to the door, with Steve hard on his heels, until they were standing with their backs to the wall, either side of the door. British reached round and banged hard on the door, with the butt of his gun.

"You'd forget your head if you had one." They heard a voice grumbling on the other side of the door, as the lock was turned. The door swung open revealing a short, rat-faced man, who gasped as he saw it was not the milkman he was looking at, but death.

British pushed forward and thrust his knife into the man's throat all in one smooth movement. The man crumpled to the floor as British withdrew his knife. He waved the bloodied knife at Steve to follow him, but Steve had frozen to the spot, having never seen a person killed before - indeed, he'd never even seen a dead body.

"Move!" British snapped and pushed Steve in front of him

and they ran up a hallway that opened out into the reception area of the Mansion, glowing eerily in the reduced night lights.

They saw a light on under a door straight across from them and they could hear voices talking on the other side.

British pointed to the huge, grand marble stairway that swept majestically up, flanked by small marble figures, set on every tenth stair.

"Up." He led Steve up the stairway, leaping up two treads at a time. They reached the top and stopped while British scanned all the doors leading off the landing.

"This way," he whispered, heading to his right to a pair of large doors with gilt ornamental handles.

He paused momentarily, to let Steve get set with his gun. Steve nodded, his heart pounding like mad, as British pushed both handles at the same time and they entered together, into a dark bedroom.

"Who's that?" they heard a man's voice gasp from somewhere in front of them, then a bedside light was switched on, revealing a bleary-eyed Lord McForson, in a huge round bed, supported by three pillows and wrapped in black satin sheets.

"Who the hell ..." he started to say when, as Steve started to aim, they were all plunged into darkness as a huge explosion rocked the building. Steve was jolted into firing and he emptied the gun in one prolonged burst in the direction of the bed.

British had turned to look down the now darkened landing as Steve fired. The next door down burst open and a man came running out, crouching down. He stopped underneath a glass canopy that gave enough of the dawn light for British to see that the man was Kai, struggling to get his gun out of his shoulder holster.

British fired straight away and Kai's face disintegrated as he was hit by four bullets. He was dead before his body landed on the floor.

"Bastard!" British spat as he pumped another bullet into the twitching body for good luck.

Steve had turned and had just joined British when another door was flung open and they heard a woman's scream. They saw in the dim light that it was Helga, standing stark naked, legs astride, pointing her arm at them.

Steve hesitated at this wonderful sight, but British responded straight away by firing at the same time as Helga did.

Steve's eyes had gone down to the magnificent bush of hair that Helga was displaying between her legs and had failed to notice that she held a small pistol in the hand that was pointing at him. It clattered from her lifeless fingers as she was thrown backwards by the force of the bullets tearing into her body. Her bullet whizzed harmlessly past the startled Steve.

They both turned and leaped down the wide stairway, three at a time. The doors were opened at the bottom of the stairs to their right, which was the room where they had heard the voices, while at the same time the main front doors were flung open letting the daylight flood into the reception hall.

They stopped halfway down and crouched down while Steve pulled the empty clip out of his gun and re-loaded.

British re-loaded at the same time as they peered round one of the ornate figures down into the reception area.

No one had dared to set foot into the reception area and so nothing was happening apart from heavy breathing from Steve and British.

"Is that you Craig?" They heard the Colonel's voice coming from the room. They didn't respond.

"Is that you, British? ... It's me, the Colonel," they heard a hard voice say.

British put his fingers to his lips to show Steve not to answer.

"Are you there, Steve?" The Colonel's voice was softer now. "You're quite safe m'boy, our plans have changed."

Steve looked at British, not knowing what to do at all.

British unclipped a stun grenade from his belt, pulled the pin and lobbed it gently over the hand rail and curled up with his hands held tightly against his ears. Steve needed no instructions for this and did the same.

A figure stepped through the front door followed by another as the grenade came to a halt, on the floor in front of them.

"Grenade!" one screamed and they were turning to leave when it went off, throwing them both violently back through the front doors.

Steve thought his head had been blown off, as the blast hit his eardrums. British grabbed him and they ran down and out into the driveway, going past the two crumpled figures by the doors.

"Steve! Stop!" They heard a shouted command behind them.

Steve stopped, surprised to hear his name being shouted and turned to see the Colonel standing in the doorway, blood was coming from his ears. He was holding a gun, which he was pointing at Steve.

Steve's adrenaline was running high and his self-preservation instinct was to fire first at the Colonel. This he did, to devastating effect and the Colonel was struck full in the chest, spinning him round like a top, sending him reeling back into the Mansion.

"Hell ... I've killed him," gasped Steve in shock.

"Come on ... let's run like buggery ... or we'll be pushing daisies up as well." British pulled Steve towards the road and they ran down to the bridge, expecting someone to start firing at them at any minute.

"Henry has really blown the power houses to bits," gasped Steve across to British as they ran towards the bridge. They could see the smoking ruin, over to their right.

"Good for him," puffed British, "timed to perfection."

They slid down the bank of the stream and arrived in a heap at the feet of Craig and Henry.

"Why is it so wet all round here?" British tried to shake the surface water off his fatigues.

"Henry created a tidal wave with that little explosion you heard." Craig answered smiling.

"Good blow, Henry ... and well timed." British congratulated a still elated Henry.

"Did you get the bastard?" Craig asked Steve.

"I emptied the full clip into his bed ... but I must admit that, because the lights went out, I didn't see if I hit him ... I can only assume I did," Steve answered truthfully.

"Couldn't miss him, in my opinion," British added, "but I can confirm that young Steve here has blown our esteemed leader away."

Steve turned crimson with embarrassment.

"We knew something was happening," agreed Craig, "but let's go. We can hold a debrief at the farmhouse."

They left the shelter of the bridge and waded down to the next bridge, without hindrance and re-grouped underneath it.

So far so good," Craig said, "only got to go under the wall now and we're in the clear."

The sound of sirens wafted over the damp morning air.

"What the hell is that?" Craig exclaimed angrily. "Go and have a look, Henry."

Henry did as he was bidden, crawling up the side of the bridge wall to look at the main gate.

He slid back down to them and reported excitedly, "it's the fire brigade, four tenders at least, and a couple of police cars and ambulances. It looks as though the whole emergency services seem to be attending."

"Who would have called them?" Steve asked.

"The milkman is my guess," British advised, "because he would just about to be going through the gates when the place blew up, and I still think that, somehow, he was not what he seemed."

They were interrupted by the sound of a helicopter and they turned to see the Colonel's helicopter, rising up above the Mansion, hovering for a moment, then swooping off heading North.

"Who's that, then, if the Colonel is dead?" Craig asked.

They all shook their heads, flummoxed at this turn of events. "Come on, the sooner we're out of this the better."

They splashed down the stream, doubled up, trying to keep a low profile.

They reached the perimeter wall in a couple of minutes and Steve ducked under the wall to follow the stream out. He returned almost immediately, cursing.

"There's an iron grille blocking our way out."

"Buggery!" exclaimed Craig angrily. "Are you sure ... is it loose, can we pull it out? ... Have another look Steve."

"Okay," Steve agreed and ducked under the wall again while they waited, keeping look-out at the activity over the park behind them.

Steve rejoined them after two minutes.

"Well?" Craig looked hopefully at him.

"There is a gap between the bottom of the grille and the bed of the stream, of about a foot ... but the bottom is soft and I reckon we can scoop enough mud away to get through," he advised them all.

"Get on with it then ... I want to get out of this stream and this park," Craig declared rubbing his hands together.

"Hold my gun, please, British." Steve passed British his gun. "I will have to submerge for a short while to dig a tunnel out for your fat arse." He laughed as British snatched his gun and threatened him with a fist, grinning.

Steve took a deep breath and gripping the grille he pushed his feet forward under the grille, digging the heels of his boots into the mud and gravel. He pushed down as hard as he could, pulling himself backward and forward as many times as he could, until he'd made a large enough groove on the bottom of the stream.

He took a deep breath and giving a tremendous pull on the grille he submerged himself totally under the water, then he was through to the other side, emerging gasping for breath, as the stream was extremely cold.

"I've done it!" he shouted back from the dark tunnel, triumphantly through the grille. Then: "Can British take the shoulder stock off my gun and pass them through the grille to me?"

Brtish heard the request and dismantled Steve's gun.

"Good man ... Henry you go next," Craig ordered, "and pass Steve his gun and stock, before you go under."

British gave Henry Steve's gun saying, "Make the channel as deep as you can matey, I've got the most muscle in this outfit." He laughed as he patted his rotund stomach affectionately, while smoothing his white beard down, thoughtfully.

Henry ducked under the wall, then passed the gun and stock through the grille to Steve. He sat down in the water, and felt his way under the grille with his feet until he was ready to go under, then pulled himself hard under the water, like Steve had done earlier. He emerged spluttering alongside Steve in the dark tunnel.

"I'll go and check the exit, Henry," Steve said. "I hope we can get out after all this effort," he added.

"So do I Steve ... I'll see these two under," Henry agreed with Steve.

Steve waded off into the dark feeling his way along the wall and was thankful to reach the exit into the field after a couple of minutes. He looked out with great care.

"I'll go next," Craig advised British, who offered no objection and took Craig's gun off him.

Craig joined Henry at the same time that Steve arrived at the stream exit. British passed Craig his gun and his own and sat down pushing his feet under the grille.

"Christ! It's tight," he complained, wriggling his bottom down onto the streambed.

"You'll be all right," Craig assured him. "Just pull yourself as hard as you can and you'll come out like a champagne cork."

"Okay ... Geronimo!" British pulled himself under, the other two waited for him to pop up beside them, but British did not re-appear.

"Give me a hand," Craig shouted to Henry. "I think he's got stuck."

They both reached under the water and found that British had indeed got wedged under the grille and his clothes seemed to be caught up in something. British was panicking and threshing around as they fought to release them.

"I'll cut him free," gasped Craig as he slid his knife into the clothing wrapped round the grille. They worked as hard as they could to free British, but he slowly stopped threshing around and went still.

"Fucking hell, Henry! Pull the bugger out ... come on we can't let him die like this." Craig exhorted Henry for an extra effort. Henry simply slashed at the clothing, like a man possessed, until, at last, they managed to free him and pull British through.

Craig held British's head, cleared the mouth and started mouth to mouth resuscitation, while Henry muttered, "come on you daft bugger, breathe."

Steve who had splashed back to them to see what the problem was, found Craig still trying to resuscitate British.

"You keep working on him," Steve said to Craig, "and we'll try to carry him out." And so it was they emerged from the tunnel into swirling mist with Craig still trying his best to coax some life into British.

They put him down on the grassy bank and worked on him for another fifteen minutes, each of them taking it in turn to keep a look-out and work on British until a weary Craig said, "Okay lads ... pack it in, he's gone."

They sat down on the grass just looking at his body, as the mist closed in, seemingly forming a protective barrier around them from all the action that was occurring not more than five hundred yards away.

"I'm getting cold now," declared Henry, flapping his arms around, making them all realise that now they had stopped their activity they were all soaking wet and sitting in a cold mist.

"What now?" he asked Craig, teeth starting to chatter.

Craig looked at his watch, "I told Santiago to pick us up here at half-past six if it was possible ... and it's almost that now, so he should be here any minute. We need to get the hell out of here before the authorities start searching the area. This mist is a godsend," he added.

"What about ...?" Steve indicated the body.

"We leave it," came the terse reply from Craig.

"Leave it ... Why?" Steve retorted angrily, upset at the thought of leaving British there, as if discarded.

"We can't take it with us ... and there is no time to bury him, so we let the authorities find him ... they will not be able to identify him ... he's not known in this country," Craig explained carefully. "We must take his watch and weapons ... that's all the material things that would be possible to trace."

"May I have his knife ... it would be a good memento of British," Steve asked, as Henry took the watch off the body and handed it to Craig. Henry undid the belt and holster from the waist. Putting it round his own, he looked up at them.

"Easier to carry," he explained. He then unfastened the knife sheath from the leg and handed it over to Steve, without saying word.

Steve strapped it onto his thigh, asking, "What will they do with his body then?"

"They'll put him in the local morgue ... but he won't be there very long," added Craig mysteriously.

"Won't be there very long!" Steve repeated puzzled.

"He'll be removed from the morgue, before any autopsy, by the 'scavengers', and taken to Wiltshire for burial in a Military Cemetery ... we'll all be able to attend ... they do it for all of us," Craig added, "with no family ties. I've also ordered the 'scavengers' to be at the farmhouse at 08.00 hours ... we'll be in London by ten o'clock."

Steve was highly relieved to hear that his friend was not being abandoned.

"Well," said Steve at length, "at least he repaid a debt to a mate of his."

"What was that?" Craig asked quietly.

"He got Kai."

"Kai's dead?"

"As a dodo," Steve replied, holding his head in his hands.

"You must have had quite a party in the Mansion," Henry remarked sullenly.

"He blew Helga away," Steve added. "She was going to shoot me, but he," he looked at British, "he got his shot off first, while I was just thinking ahout it." He omitted the fact that, being naked, she'd got the drop on him.

"Have you left anyone alive in there?" Craig was talking just to fill the time in as the shock of British's death came home to them.

"I think we got six ... how many did you?"

"Five," came the short reply.

"What did British say last?" Steve asked.

"Geronimo," answered Craig. "Why?"

Steve didn't reply, but remembered the time he'd fallen off the back of British's motor scooter in Spain, after shouting 'Geronimo' himself, and he smiled sadly at the body on the grass.

"Here comes Santiago ... right on time." Craig announced

as the sound of an engine came through the mist. A minute later the Land Rover appeared out of the mist and pulled up with wheels locked from severe braking, and Santiago leapt out and ran round the back to undo the catches.

"I on time Señor Cragg," he said as he saw them approach up the bank of the stream. "Mist veery good for us, no?" He glanced at them, then glancing round he asked, "Is Señor British having pee-pee?"

"He's dead ... let's go." Craig answered him brusquely, climbing into the passenger seat, as Santiago stood shocked at the news for a moment, then he ran round and got back in the driver's seat, grim-faced and started the engine, lurching forward as Henry and Steve just made it in time.

"Steady on," Craig warned him, "we don't want to bring attention to ourselves by driving like a Spaniard, eh?"

"Si, Señor Cragg," Santiago slowed down to a less jolting pace, much to the relief of his passengers.

They arrived back at the farmhouse in ten minutes flat, Santiago driving straight into the open barn. Henry jumped out and closed the doors.

Craig got out and clapped his hands for their attention. "Right, we don't have much time ... change out of these wet things ... Santiago you chuck 'em in the corner there." He indicated where he wanted them to go. "They'll be cleared by the 'scavengers'... then lads, we piss off at high speed ... and we'll stop at the first service station on the M 1 for breakfast ... I'm sure you'd all like a brew right now, but time is now of the essence - we need to be on our way when they arrive ... Get to it," he commanded.

Fifteen minutes later, Steve climbed into his little M.G. and started it up as Santiago climbed into the passenger seat while the others piled into the Land Rover alongside them. They backed the vehicles out and parked, engines running and waited for five minutes until a large, black furniture van

226

arrived into the yard.

Craig went across to the driver and handed him the keys to the farmhouse. They had a brief conversation, then Craig returned to the Land Rover. Steve saw a couple of faces looking at him from the cab, behind the driver. He gave them a wave of acknowledgement, which they returned.

Craig ran back to the Land Rover and drove off, waving at Steve to follow him. They bumped up the track, Steve's M.G. getting another rough ride, until they reached the wall, but this time Craig turned left and followed the car track round, following the park wall until they rejoined the road, where a sign post showed '5 miles to the M 1'.

They arrived at the Ryder Club three hours later, after having a large breakfast in the service station on the M 1.

"There is a full change of clothes for all of us in Room 36 ... I've got the key so we can walk straight through," Craig informed them all. Marmaduke had a lovely time, running between their legs, tongue hanging out as if in permanent thirst, giving them a great welcome.

"Once we've made ourselves presentable we'll meet in the lounge for a de-briefing."

They walked to the lift and held on as they hurtled upwards, all except Santiago who, not knowing the hazard of the lift, almost finished on the floor, cursing soundly in Spanish, as his companions smiled for the first time since their ordeal.

They gathered in the far recesses of the lounge after changing, with coffee and biscuits.

Craig sat back deep in his armchair until they were all settled then began the de-briefing.

"First point Steve, is the death of the Colonel ... What happened? ... In your own words," he said softly.

Steve told them how the Colonel had called his name and he'd turned to see the Colonel pointing a gun at him, so he fired in self-defence and killed the Colonel. British was his only witness to what had happened.

"I have no idea why he wanted to kill me," Steve went on, "I still can't figure it out ... Can you Craig?" he asked.

"I can throw some light on that for you Steve," Craig said reassuringly. "Since our return, I've put in a quick report of what happened to the mission and I have been contacted by our new boss already."

"That was quick," Henry interrupted him. "Who is it?"

"Can't tell you yet, it's not official until the inquest, apparently, the powers that be were expecting something like this," Craig answered back, lighting a cigar.

"Our Colonel was not who he purported to be." Craig passed cigars all round, which they all lit up straight away, then as the first large cloud of smoke rose, Craig went on. "He had, many years ago, taken the identity of a Colonel Guntripp, who died during a mission in Russia. Our Colonel was a Russian Agent called Amnat Zollerman, who underwent plastic surgery to resemble the real Colonel. When he came back to England, he said he'd lost his memory, due to getting a head injury on his mission. Our people never really trusted him fully after that."

"Why did he want to kill me?" asked a puzzled Steve. "I was no threat to him."

"Oh, but you were," Craig answered. "Do you remember two months ago doing a very obscure special trace he sent you not long after you joined us?"

Steve thought about it for a minute, then remembered the trace was for a foreign name, Petrak or something similar.

"Yes .. for a guy named Petrak ... I think."

"Well, that frightened the Colonel the way you managed to do that trace," Craig informed him.

"You mean he was worried that if I ever did a proper check on him I'd find out he was not who he said he was? So," Steve expanded, "I was going to be bumped off because I was too good at my job! What a bastard!" He slumped back in the deep red armchair, absolutely deflated.

Craig leaned forward, placing a small tape-recorder on the table, switched it on and said into it, "This is the final report on Operation Monarch at," he glanced at the Eagle clock on the wall, "eleven forty-five a.m. on Tuesday the tenth of September, nineteen seventy four. Those present are Craig Martell, Henry Aughton, Steve Manly and Santiago Mantana. We have to report that Agent Peter Steele, nickname 'British', was killed on duty this morning, at six twenty a.m." He stopped a moment then carried on. "Other people known to have died are: Colonel Harold Guntripp, Kai Svenssen, Helga Boquarn and six other personnel one of whom was called Hamish.

We believe Lord Stuart McForson has also been killed, but this cannot be confirmed. The local emergency services were called to the area and we vacated our premises to the 'scavengers' at zero eight hundred hours this morning. Damage was done only to the power house in the area. End of report timed at eleven fifty a.m." Craig leaned forward and switched off the tape machine.

"There we have it gentlemen ... I suggest we all have a bloody good lunch then go our separate ways until our new boss gives us a call ... yes?"

Santiago sat forward with a concerned look on his florid face. "Señor Cragg, what was el Colonel doing there? ... I see heez helicopter flying in ... who to see, eh?" He sat back, triumphant at having an input to the conversation.

"That's right Santiago ... good point." Craig turned to Steve. "Who was the Colonel talking to in that room, I wonder ... did you overhear any of the conversation at all?" he asked Steve.

"No ... it was just a low mumbling," Steve answered thinking hard.

"Well, it wasn't His Hordship, he was in bed, or Kai, or Helga ... So who was the old bugger talking to, and... " Craig added, "who flew the bloody helicopter away? ... Damn ... why was he there?"

"There was a man in Spain who was at the meeting in the villa," Steve said as he searched his memory trying to remember.

"Operation Precipice, you mean," Craig said. "The Colonel got that tape, but that will be in his Whitehall office and I don't have access to that ... I'm not high enough up the rankings." He gave a little laugh. "Come to the that we are all on the same rank .. I just seem to throw my weight around more." He drew hard on his cigar which acted as signal to them all to do the same and another large cloud of smoke spread through the alcove. "Think hard Steve."

"The meeting was attended by Lord McForson, his secretary Helga with Kai in the background, of course. The American financier ...er ... Martin Silverman," Steve said triumphantly.

"Not him," Craig shook his head. "He's in America."

"I didn't mean him ... There was another man there ... and I'm trying to think who he was ... Got it! His name was Gus Hall ... British said he was a weapons buyer and supplier."

"Gus Hall," Craig repeated slowly. "That old bugger ..."

"Do you know him, then?" Henry asked hopefully.

"I knew a Gus Hall, back in Aden, who was a wheeler dealer in armaments, guns and tanks. He was a tall bloke, over six foot at least and thin built," remembered Craig.

"That's him," Steve agreed, delighted he'd remembered. "I saw him at the meeting."

"I bet that was who the Colonel was talking to," Craig said.

"He wanted Lord McForson dead, or so I thought, so why did he go there?" Steve queried. "Not to kill me ... surely?"

"No, not to kill you ... he didn't know when or how we were going to operate the mission ... we had an open-ended limit on that. The bad luck for him was that we attacked, at the very time he was having a meeting. I think the fact that you were in the Mansion gave him a unexpected opportunity to kill you."

They all drew thoughtfully on their cigars.

"Heem wanna be El Kingo," Santiago offered between large puffs on his cigar.

"You are nearly right I reckon, Santiago," said Craig. "I believe now that his plan was to be accepted as the head of the two groups that are seeking to assist our country out of its economic difficulties, as their President. He needed 'King Stuart 1st' out of the frame and he still needed to deal for weapons and armour, with the likes of Gus Hall and Silverman. I think it's called 'running with the hare and hunting with the hounds'."

"What a bloody life this is," Steve declared. "We must be mad ... we never know who to trust, apart from ourselves that is," he corrected himself with a laugh.

"We reckon you've done all right, Steve and now you've done two missions, you're one of us ... despite all your bloody questions ... isn't that right?" Craig looked at the other two, who nodded their agreement, grinning at the rebuke on the questions.

"Two more questions, then," Steve grinned as they all pretended to groan. "Why did the Colonel call me to face him when he could have shot me in the back, and who shot poor Sandy?"

"The Colonel wasn't a terrorist, just a man who wanted to be the top man in the country. He still had a streak of honour in him ... but as for Sandy ... no-one knows why yet, so when you return to your office Steve ... keep alert, we'll get the bastard eventually," Craig said as he heaved himself out of the armchair. "Time for lunch gentlemen, I reckon we've earned it."

They all went down the stairs to the Eagle's Nest and sat at the same table that Steve had last sat at with the Colonel and he felt a little uncomfortable.

"This is where I first met you Steve." Craig slapped him on the back. "So let's celebrate our continuing partnership with some champagne ... David!" he called across to the barman, "The usual."

"Certainly, sir. Nice to see you again ... Will the Colonel be joining you? ... So I have the right number of glasses," David answered across the bar.

"He won't be joining us today ... just bring four glasses and a magnum of Black Label. Por favor," he added much to Santaigo's amusement.

"Señor Cragg," Santiago whispered into Craig's ear, "I have the weels still in my room ...we all sign."

"Hell ... I'd forgotten about them," Craig apologised. He turned to the other two. "Excuse us for a few minutes, I've got to deal with British's will ... better get it done now, in case we have to notify anyone for him." He left with Santiago trying to keep up with him.

"Santiago no like leeft ... come, we go stairs," Santiago led the way up the stairway and down the dimly lit corridor to his room. He went to the bedside cabinet and pulled out a pouch from the drawer.

"Here, Señor Cragg ... I take care yes?"

"Thank you Santiago, you did well ... now let's have a look."

Craig extracted the five wills and picked the one with Peter Steele scrawled across it, in bold flowing lines.

"Just shows we never know the day we're going to cough," he muttered to an attentive Santiago, who was wondering what 'cough' had to do with dying. Craig opened it and read the contents slowly before folding it up slowly, saying "Well, that seems all very straightforward."

"Si, Señor," Santiago exclaimed as if he understood Craig.

"Let's get back and show the others what British has requested to be done, I'll have to hand this to our new boss to take to the legal department of our outfit."

They made their way back to the bar and rejoined their curious colleagues. Craig produced the will and, making sure they could not be overheard, read the contents out in a whisper.

"I, Peter Steele, being of sound mind and body, hereby leave all my monies in the Banco de Bilbao, Puerto de la Cruz, Tenerife, plus monies due to me from pension or death funds, plus my personal effects, to Eileen Gardener, of the Hotel Corrida, Villajoyosa, Costa Blanca, Spain."

Craig stopped and looked round at them all. "She's a nice lady and was very good for our operations in Spain but I'd no idea British liked her so much. However it goes on ... I leave all my property and estates in Tenerife to my good friend ... are you ready for this? ... Steve Manly." He put the will down in front of a very shocked Steve, who picked it up very slowly and read for himself all the details again.

"I'm staggered, why me?" Steve sat back in his chair and passed the will over for Henry to read.

Craig answered Steve's query saying, "He left it to you because he had no other person to leave it to ... that is how our lives go in this kind of work ... we lose track of past family and can only relate to the people around us at this immediate point in time. I will take this will to our new boss in Whitehall and he will make sure it is processed correctly. We have no legal rights as such, because, as you already know, our Department does not exist, not on paper anyway."

"Your table is ready in restaurant, gentlemen," David came and advised them, forcing them to break off the animated conversations they were having reference, how the department looked after them when trouble hit.

They had a different wine with each course, finishing with the splendid Baron Otard XO cognac, then made their way to the upstairs lounge with much merriment, to relax.

"What's it going to be gentlemen, as if I didn't know?"

came a female voice from behind one of the small palm trees, and Geraldine stepped from behind, looking as gorgeous as ever.

"A magnum of the wonderful Lanson Black Label, if you'd be so kind, young lady." Craig swept an exaggerated theatrical bow in front of her, to their amusement.

"Why thank you kind sir," she replied keeping in the spirit of things and bobbing down in front of them. Her beautiful red hair swept over her sparkling green-hued eyes. "Your wish is my command, gentlemen."

She stood up, smiling, and her tasting cup settled back into the cleft of her bosom, causing Steve to catch his breath in excitement and sheer lust for her. Her eyes caught him looking down at her bosom and he blushed at being caught in such a manner.

"May I ask how many glasses today?"

She flashed a smile at the uncomfortable Steve, who croaked, "Four please."

"No Colonel today?" she remarked, starting to leave.

"No ... not today," Craig answered quickly to her retreating but sensual back. "And four La De Da's, if you please." She waved an acknowledgement and disappeared into the small bar, through the palm trees.

"La De Da's, eez Engleesh leetle joke ... yes?" Santiago said trying to work out what had been said to her.

"La de Da's ... large cigars," explained Craig, "the best Churchill cigars money can buy."

Santiago beamed back at him as Craig added, "Bigger than Canarians."

"Hang on there, matey," Henry suddenly interrupted. "With the Colonel not here ... who's paying for this bash then?"

"Our new boss is apparently," Craig answered. "I've been told to just sign the bill, and that goes for your accommodation bill as well ... so we are on a freebie."

"I'm glad to hear that," Henry said, "that cognac is around seventy pounds a bottle, that I do know."

"Bloody Nora, is it?" Steve gasped to hear such a cost was involved, he'd never heard of anyone paying that much for a drink in his short life.

"That's nothing in London, Steve," Craig added. "They'll pay two hundred pounds for some bottles of claret."

"What! ... Then piss it against the wall?" Steve was still laughing as Geraldine returned with the champagne and ice bucket.

"Cigars are coming," she said as she placed the fluted glasses round the table, her renewed perfume wafting over them all, like a gossamer blanket of sensual delight.

"Lucky cigars," murmured Henry, making her smile and say:

"Naughty, naughty, sir, we are all frisky today aren't we?"

"We've had a very hard few days," Craig said going serious, "and I might as well tell you now, Geraldine, the Colonel has had a very sudden posting abroad, so you won't see him in here again ... Well, not for a long time, anyway," he added lamely, as her smile disappeared at hearing this. She recovered almost immediately and taking the champagne out of the ice bucket opened it without it making a sound and poured a little for Craig to taste.

"That is cold enough," he indicated the glasses for her to pour and they soon had full, sparkling glasses, in front of them.

She replaced the bottle in the ice, giving it a little swirl to settle it deeper then covered it with a white cloth, before saying, "Lucky cigars, coming now," and left them, giggling to herself.

Craig stood up with his glass in his hand. "I would like to propose a toast in memory of our good friend, British."

They all stood up and lifted their glasses and said in unison, "To British." They sipped and clinked their glasses together as Geraldine returned with the humidified cigar box. She heard the toast as she approached and asked "Someone dead, then?" as she opened and presented the box.

"Yes, a good colleague of ours passed away this morning," Steve replied, selecting his tubed cigar from the box.

"What a shame ... was he very old?"

"Late thirties," Steve answered not too sure of the correct age British was.

"That's no age at all, is it sir?" She put a box of matches on the table and left them alone.

"You know," said Henry pensively. "I had no idea the Colonel was a Russian ... I mean I met him in Aden in '67, and, God help me, I saved his life on a training exercise in '71." He shook his head at the memory, then brightened up by saying, "Here ... Craig, what's happened to you since we came into the Club, then?"

"What do you mean, what's happened to me, are you pissed or what?" retorted a puzzled Craig.

"Well it's just that since we've been in the Club you've stopped swearing ... For the last few days," Henry looked round to see if anyone could hear, "you've been fuck this and fucking that, every other word you've said!"

"Stress ... dear boy ... nothing but stress, I'm a real gentleman really. Plus," he paused, "I never swear in front of women ... so fuck you." He fell about, laughing like a drain, as the alcohol started to bite.

"Santiago go bobos now," Santiago stood up and slurred this announcement to them all, turned with difficulty and with a wave of his hand, lurched off to his room.

"That's me finished as well," declared Henry rising to his feet. "I never thought Santiago would get pissed before me." He grinned, swaying in front of Craig and Steve like a seafarer who's just come ashore after a long voyage.

"He had a bottle Tequila sent to his room when we arrived and he'd finished it before lunch ... so try to do that one day,

Henry." Craig put Henry straight about Santiago's capacity for drink.

Henry waved his cigar in farewell as Craig reminded him, "Don't set fire to the bed, you drunken wassock." The response was two-fingered.

"What a day ... what a weekend," Craig sighed as he poured the last of the champagne out.

"But we are still alive Craig," Steve drew a deep suck on his caigar and exhaled it slowly, "and I only hope that I did for his Lordship ... I don't see how I could have missed anyway."

Steve stood up. "I'll call it a day, I'm knackered and I should ring mother up ... but then again, I think I'd better do that when I'm sober."

Craig stood up, offering his hand. "Good to have you on board Steve, and if by some chance you missed the bastard, you'll be the first one we'll call, okay?"

"Okay, you're on." Steve shook the proffered hand. "See you at breakfast, don't do anything I wouldn't do," he turned away laughing and promptly fell over Marmaduke, who had come to say hello and was standing right behind him.

Cat and palm tree went flying as Steve went head first over an armchair, landing in an ungainly heap on the floor.

Steve lay there gasping as Marmaduke peeped round the armchair, his tongue hanging out as if he was sticking it out at him, on purpose. Craig slowly rose to his feet and gave assistance, getting Steve upright, saying, "Does pussy always have this effect on you?" and slumped down again.

Steve felt a hand under his elbow and an arm was placed round his waist.

"Come on sir," he heard Geraldine whisper in his ear, "I'll see you to your room." She led him to his room and unlocked the door for him.

"In you go sir." She helped him through the door and handed him his room-key. He smelt her heady perfume and instinctively pulled her to him. He felt her breasts against his chest and she pushed him gently away.

"Don't be so rough, sir, you'll crease my blouse." She stepped back as he let her go, and unbuttoned her blouse slowly, her eyes burning deep into his. She slipped it off, revealing a pretty white-lace bra, which she unhooked in front of a mesmerised Steve, and released her magnificent breasts.

Her tasting cup was still resting on her cleavage and she slowly reached up and pulled the silver chain over her head, removing the cup.

She stood facing him, both breasts cupped in her hands, then slowly eased them apart and revealed, in between them, a tattoo of a Red Admiral butterfly.

He fell to his knees and, with a gutteral moan, kissed the Red Admiral.